Jes Gordon is an award-winning global event producer. She got her start at the young age of thirteen after working in her hometown flower shop. After traveling the world as a musician, and collecting inspiration, she settled into creating high-profile events for some of the world's most highly regarded celebrities and corporations. In her rare free moments, Jes loves walking everywhere and discovering new trends while also creating them. She adores dogs, music, fitness, and is a lover of life in general. Her passion for people and for making them happy through the art of celebration is her life's work, and she brings style to everything she does. Her energy is infectious, and she tends to lend it to several charitable projects and to those who need it. Jes counts herself lucky to have been able to take her creativity and turn it into a successful profession. She has also encountered the rough challenges of being a young creative person in business, thus, she couldn't wait to write an entertaining story about where some of her adventures may or may not have taken her…

For Mrs. McGlynn.

Jes Gordon

PARTY ON THE MOON

AUSTIN MACAULEY PUBLISHERS™

LONDON • CAMBRIDGE • NEW YORK • SHARJAH

Ordering Information:
Quantity sales: special discounts are available on quantity purchases by corporations, associations, and others. For details, contact the publisher at the address below.

Publisher's Cataloging-in-Publication data
Gordon, Jes
Party on the Moon

ISBN 9781645751014 (Paperback)
ISBN 9781645751021 (Hardback)
ISBN 9781645751038 (ePub e-book)

Library of Congress Control Number: 2020908346

www.austinmacauley.com/us

First Published (2020)
Austin Macauley Publishers LLC
40 Wall Street, 28th Floor
New York, NY 10005
USA

mail-usa@austinmacauley.com
+1 (646) 5125767

This book is dedicated to my magnificent parents – all of them… with a special place holder for my heart and soul; Suzy.

Much love to "Bobby from Kingston" who has always supported this crazy career of mine. Also, to the entire global event community including the flower markets that grace every city we work in. I am overly grateful to the talent bank of artists that make me look so good on every project, and to all of my associates who make up an incredibly special society of spectacular misfits. To my clients; there is no me without you. Thank you for putting so much faith in me and my team in making all of your dreams come true.

A special thank you to Luanne Rice and Karen Murray, who share the magic of words, their meanings, and how to get them down on paper.

Part One

Chapter One

"The noblest art is that of making others happy."

-P.T. Barnum

My 21-year-old intern and I had just finished off another line of coke in the back stairwell of the Plaza Hotel. This was in such bad taste. I can't even conceive of the evil that I was nurturing, yards away from the million-dollar affair going on in the adjacent ballroom. To make our behavior even more disgusting, did I mention that my intern is a male who worships me?

Not only did I *never* get a chance to fraternize with straight males in my industry, but I am usually preparing a man to march down the aisle to meet the love of the rest of his life. (Oh please, I will be doing the divorce party in three years.) It's unusual to get an opportunity to blow lines of coke and rub up against one for a quick 'getting off,' perfectly timed between the hora and the father of the bride's speech. Oh yeah, I am married, too. Fuck it. I got nothing to hide here. I don't even know where my husband is and he doesn't have a clue as to my whereabouts either. Yeah, I am a real catch. I have dabbled in marriage extensively, and it's just not for me. I am not your forever girl, but your mom would love me. I was meant to be alone. Not lonely, just alone.

So anyway, Heath's (yeah, his name is Heath) eyes were popping out of his head. He was buzzing like a fucking hummingbird and basically was useless to me now. All I could hope for is that the rest of my event production team had their shit together so that Heath and I could work off our buzz in the Honeymoon Suite before the bride and groom needed it. (Who has sex on their wedding night anyway?)

I desperately needed my assistant or shall I say my 'associate,' as the millennials preferred to be called. Did she start this fucking business in the back-room of a flower shop in Poughkeepsie, NY? No, but if she wanted to be referred to as something specific and she was willing to answer my texts before I even finished sending them, then so be it. Besides, I knew that she would have just the right something or other; in the form of a Kombucha shot or some vapor thingy to set me straight after ingesting everything horrible in the stairwell.

I decided to make my way out to the reception to find her. The room simply dazzled with all the amber up-lighting and projected monograms money could buy. I felt spectacular, my aura was glowing (or at least, I was convinced it was) and the Plaza Hotel was the perfect background to successfully harmonize with my sensational and overall glamorous persona. I gracefully tucked gift envelopes into my clammy sweaty armpits as I flowed through the crowd, just stopping long enough to ever so gently run my finger along the bottom edge of the ten-tiered, fifty-thousand-dollar wedding cake. Its icing would supply me with just the right caloric and injection of sugar to boost my existing buzz. My feet didn't even hurt, though I had been on them since four a.m., and my tummy lay flat within my DVF work-skirt (with pockets). All I needed were some fucking eye drops and some electrolytes and I would be stellar.

I spotted Suzi across the room and she looked professional yet disengaged all at once. When I first pilfered Suzi from her job as an events assistant at a nightclub, she was spelling her name with a heart over the 'i', now she was dripping in Alice et Olivia, topped off with a $200 blow-out and in possession of the most current iPhone and iWatch combo possible, complete with air pods, so she could communicate with the rest of our team without having the sounds of the band drown her out. Suzi was fucking smart and has no passion what so ever for what we do, but she shows up all of the time at any time. She is this overly functional robot with an impeccable gel manicure and no '*joie de vivre*' for anything what so ever, including her fiancé and I fucking adore her. Suzi is a Queen's girl, through and through. Her needs are simple; a lot of alcohol, a working cell phone, a membership at Dry Bar, and at least 12 hours of sleep a night. Not sure why, but millennials seem to need a lot of sleep, even though they don't exercise more than picking up their fucking phones six million times a day. Her love of family and home life is what drew me to her, since I have none of that nor do I want it I don't think. In my current state of having given everything up for my career, and on the edge of turning 'Fifty is the new Fuck You,' I have often fantasized that Suzi would be the daughter that I never thought I wanted or at least some proof of what I attempted to accomplish on this planet as a creative genius.

Suzi has easily taught me more than any of the colleges I attempted to go to or what any of my mentor associates ever could. Because of her, I am a master Tweeter, Instagram-er, Snapchat-er, Blogger, Netflix Watcher, Candy Crusher, Facebook-er, Karaoke Singer and Texter/Sexter. For these reasons, I will be forever grateful and dependent on her. Her latest trick that she taught me was how to screen shot a dick pic that someone sent me on Snapchat so I could keep it for later. She gets a bonus every time she teaches me something of 'relevance.'

Suzi is also one of the smallest people that has ever worked for me and does not look a day over twelve. Thus, sometimes, the clients try to get one over on her, which has inadvertently made her the toughest brick of a woman/child I have ever met. She protects me fiercely like a mama lioness guarding her babies, as if rich white people were looking at them while traveling on a Black-Tie Safari trip.

I have been behaving particularly rambunctious recently because of my newly found mid-life WTF, which I had always assumed was a myth until now. I also thought that menopause was bullshit too, until I woke up sweating through my sheets one night, while simultaneously having the driest vagina in the world. I have never wondered who I was, where I was going, who I was gonna be, or who would even care until recently, and though it may sound trite coming from my veneered mouth, I am quite unhinged about it. I have always been way too narcissistic to be sad or to think that anyone else was as important as I was, but now, I am as vulnerable as a girl with no money for Botox and I don't like it all. All kidding aside, I am shaken to my core, which is, of course, cool sculpted into sheer magnificence. Yet, on the inside, there is a nasty fat cell of fear. My Rock Star status has been questionable as of late, and for the first time ever, I am most definitely not the most important person in the room.

I have mixed pride when long term clients call the office to speak to Suzi rather than me or when we walk together on the street, I often see that men's sideways glances are directed only at her. I am embarrassed by my lack of confidence and the fact that my skin has thinned enough, to feel lots of stings. I needed to ease into my next chapter as I have always done in my life, but when I look into the future, it's just a dowel, with wispy cotton candy that keeps twirling and dissipating into thin air. I decided to make a conscience effort to reach back into my history and pluck the good part from it, so that I could hopefully impale them into my current existence. It was time to put my big-girl tits on and keep shit positive, but fuck I am struggling to do so. In the meantime, I will act out like a gregarious child who can afford to do drugs and thousand-dollar hair extensions.

It was an incredibly late evening for me. I am not a night person and I truly hate parties, even though I am an event producer. I adore the morning, the only time the world is mine. Everyone leaves me the fuck alone unless I want morning sex. Then I get that done and move on. I adore being alone, I am not lonely; just alone. I like to take a shit without anyone in the next room, except for my dog and the sound of my TV. I like to sleep with my electronics on the pillow next to me, including my vibrator, and I thoroughly enjoy the sound of my white-noise machine set to crickets chirping. I adore those crickets. They are on all the time in my apartment, a tiny shiny overpriced 'castle of fabulous' that looks out onto the High Line in one of the chicest neighborhoods in Manhattan. I have a garbage disposal in my sink (a rare find in a NYC apartment), a small and slow high-tech washer/dryer of my very own and a staff of doormen that will even take my dog out and pick up her poop if I want them to. I own all the best cooking gear—le Creuset, copper everything—which have never ever been used, including a slow cooker that is storing a condom and lube supply at this very moment. I have a refrigerator stocked within an inch of its life with the most expensive champagnes: Moët & Chandon Bi Century Cuvée Imperial 1943, Limited Editions of Krug and of course, a few bottles of Moët signed by Mr. Karl Lagerfeld himself. The drawers in the fridge contain peanut butter and tins of Baccarat Abysse, Sevruga Classic Gray, and Beluga Sturgeon caviars. This bitch loves her salt. My pup has her own drawer dedicated to organic air-dried chicken breast, layered within some quinoa and blueberry concoction keeping her in perfect condition. And my favorite private place in my fridge is a small crevice that cradles the finest dark chocolate treats that a girl, such as myself, enjoys on an hourly basis, several of them containing the finest hashish oil given to me by some of my more exotic clients. The freezer is a lair of Tito's Vodka *sans* gluten, some old giggle weed that I drag out whilst PMS-ing or slipping into menopause; I never seem to know now, and some heat up pre-prepared thingy in case my niece comes over. I only drink and eat out of glass that has been hand blown or crafted by someone in a faraway land whom I have never met. Suzi has also created a necessities drawer for me containing attractive water bottles that will help my hair, skin, and sleep patterns all at once and black toothpaste made up of charcoal granules that she insists will make my teeth whiter. It tastes like shit and I often use it to clean the residue in my tub left by my hemp and santal soaking balms. Suzi buys something from every pop-up ad on Facebook and then turns me onto whatever she feels is worthy of upping my credit-card usage.

I have several flat screen TVs within feet of each other, Sonos Sound systems, the Black Diamond Sonic Toothbrush (the Cadillac of toothbrushes), and a couture mouth night guard crafted by the finest dentist in NY to stop me from grinding my teeth into oblivion. The cabinets in my bathroom contain every toiletry a woman can only dream to afford that have the words "anti-aging" written somewhere on the packaging; brands such as La Mer, Chanel and Dr. Brandt face creams. I must always smell the part, so there are shelves dedicated to Guerlain, Roja Parfum (Amber Aoud only) Labo anything and of course, some Creed if I am feeling butch. My hair only gets graced by Oribe,

Acqua Di Parma and Bvlgari shampoos to keep my two-thousand-dollar keratin treatment intact. My walk-in closet is fashionably stuffed with every kind of clothing and shoes you can imagine. I tend to dress for the Crack House all the way to the White House, so shit gets real in there. I purge it monthly and I would love to give everything to Suzi, but she is simply too small. Once again, she teaches me something invaluable by introducing me to consignment opportunities such as the Real-Real, and I am tickled pink when those magic money moments hit my account without any warning like a surprise party you actually want to have happen.

Back to the Plaza: I am usually able to leave most of my events by the time the bride and groom cut the cake. Suzi and the rest of my team handle the rest, but tonight, for some reason I wasn't anxious to get out of there. My dog was with her Puerto Rican pet-sitter and was gladly nestled in with her own fat ass dogs and all of them were inhaling a consistent stream of grade A marijuana smoke, and they were probably paw deep in a bowl of rice and beans by now. I wasn't feeling confident that Heath was going to be able to perform sexually, so why hang around for that? I was kind of at a loss as to why I was even sticking around, even Suzi was giving me the 'why the fuck are you still here' look. It came down to this; I adored my clients this evening. Honestly, it had been so long since I had given a shit, such a surreal sensation guided me through this night. There was something special about these folks. I was sure that the daddy of the bride was Mafia, but he wore it so elegantly—aside from the weird bag filled with cash that he had us guard all night, and a small and fashionable handgun. His wife was so real; cancer survivor, mama to everyone. I wanted to just bury my head in her bosom and drool into safety. They were warm people, almost stupid with love for each other. The bride was spectacular. Her Vera Wang lace dress hid the scars of her skin-tightening surgeries post-gastro bypass, and her face was that of a world-class movie star. She was a real trooper and the groom was stoned out of his mind; in a great way that showed he was truly happy to be getting married. The best part about this group was that, even though they worked our asses off, they said 'thank you' every step of the way. They fed us, they laughed with us, and they didn't mind that I said 'fuck' a lot. Basically, they were a joy to work with. I had forgotten what this felt like, and my pockets were filling with that aphrodisiac; cash. Cash is better than money.

Event producers start out liking all their clients. That first call is almost date-like. Suzi asks all the right questions that I taught her to ask, delving into their innermost desires. Then she finds out that they can meet your budget minimums, so she can move onto scheduling that first in-person meeting, which is filled with such delicious anticipation, as Suzi simultaneously cyberstalks them and Google Maps their homes to see if this could be a great project for real. The scheduling task can go on for days, which is why I don't get involved until they are actually sitting at the meeting table in one of my offices.

As they enter our office, we quickly take inventory of what they are wearing; their jewelry, shoes, bags, hair roots, you name it. Personally, I love it when they walk in completely unkempt and are rich as shit. Those are probably my favorite kinds of people, but they are so hard to find, even though this type of client was all I dealt with when I first started this shit show 28 years ago. Self-confident and rich seems to be a pretty rare combination on the market these days. It's all *nouveau* rich and ass implants. I often feel sorry for Suzi not getting to experience the 'real people' I dealt with when I first started out. I told her of times when I would smoke a joint with a famous rock star, illustrate something ridiculous on a cocktail napkin, name a price, and I would walk out of there with a check for full-payment in hand. No questions asked, no micro managing, and no hassle. Those were the days… now it's all, "I want it to be exactly this," as they direct you to the same fucking Pinterest Board page the last hundred clients showed you already.

Then, of course, it's enraging when you start the meeting and we keep getting interrupted by the nanny texting our client, concerning pickup times from extra-curricular activities and which frozen yogurt place to stop off at after school with the kids that have peanut allergies. I will never fucking see a peanut again in my world, such a shame. I can tell you this though, if they were meeting with their lawyer during these interruptions, the guy would make a fortune while the money clock kept ticking. But I'm just the poor *schmuck* that's still vying for the job.

Anyway, what I do is a way of life, not a job, and I love it, blah, blah, blah…

My team seemed to have the evening covered. Everyone's breath was appropriately stale by now. The tech director was flirting like a banshee with the band leader, coming just short of gyrating on the dance floor together. Our junior assistant was in full complaint mode, and I think I overheard Suzi telling her to go the fuck home. The team was eating the sushi that had been sitting out for hours from the overly opulent cocktail hour. Shit was totally normal. It was at the point in the evening where the party was just running itself. All we had to do now was feel out the room to see if the clients wanted to go into over-time. Personally, I was silently and urgently praying to Buddha that they weren't going to go the extra mile. There is something to be said for making people leave the event wanting more. It's a fine line, so it's best to get everybody out of there on time. The photographer was already getting his paperwork ready for the father of the bride to sign off on his ridiculously inflated over-time rate. He was almost doing the 'pee-pee dance' in anticipation, and he was playing with his balls in his pockets. What a douche. Yeah, I slept with him, too.

For the first ten years of my career, I never shat where I ate, but that went out the window long ago. Now it's fuck, suck, eat, watch TV, repeat. Oh, yeah, and produce fabulous parties in between. Suzi pretty much slept with everybody, too; guys a lot older and less impressive than her for sure. The one rule was that we would never 'cross pollenate' and sleep with people that could inhibit our business or cash in any way, so we would often huddle up before one of us took the 'deep dick plunge.'

I felt like the best way to contribute to my world now-a-days was to offer up my hindsight to Suzi and to fill her in on my journey and how I got to where I was today, hoping she would someday soon be my legacy and take this shit show off my hands and do it all proud, even though the thought of my hands being empty was too hard to bear. During the lulls in the evenings or in the office while everyone else was off doing things, Suzi would come to know my world inside and out, whether she wanted to or not. This was becoming a distraction in my creative flow, wondering if it was even fair that I was putting so much stock in Suzi and pushing a future for her that was less than ideal in so many ways. One thing at a time, I suppose, which I hate, by the way.

She often asked me how I got started, since my industry didn't really exist in its current popular state when my career was first conceived. We would huddle around the fireplace at the Soho House Meatpacking District, NYC location, armed with at least four bottles of wine. Suzi doesn't drink Reds, so even during the coldest days of winter, we would have to suffer through the heavier Whites… Again, I was reminded of how proud I was of myself for accepting her for who she was. Suzi hated the winter. Her pale little body got paler and smaller, but as the flames from the fireplace danced around her and her cheeks became flushed with wine, I saw something awaken within her and she even stopped looking at her phone every seven seconds, as she listened to my Oral History.

I got into this mess by being a demented little kid. I was the worst kind because from the outside I was a pure joy, classy and well-mannered to the bone; sweet temperament and a yes girl from the minute I popped out. From what I know, I was born on a rainy Friday at 2pm in the year of 19noneofyourfuckingbusiness, (though I am sure you have already done the math) with my eyes wide open and practically laughing, as if I wanted to tell everyone how incredibly tacky the inside of my mother's stomach was. I mean, whoever created a woman's insides was clearly not proficient in Feng Shui. I was a good baby, not colicky, firm poops, the whole deal. I was potty-trained on the early side and said mama and dada at the right time. I had a small speech impediment that fucked up my R's and made me sound like someone who was raised in the less pretty parts of Boston. Luckily my parents were vain enough to get that speech thing fixed right away. My childhood was slightly uneventful, but it was no secret that I was bored with everything aside from rearranging the play area in my kindergarten classroom and rating the Christmas *décor* at the local church. I checked the church out every holiday, and even though I was Jewish, I critiqued it with such a passion that my family just basically laughed nervously and escorted me out of the church, while promising to let me re-decorate their bedroom when we got home.

The highlight of my young life was when my father would take me to the city on weekends, especially during the fall season, when New York fashion was at its finest; mixing with European trends and leather, always leather. The sidewalks would fill up with gorgeous tall models, like Giraffes running in the Serengeti. The parks would take on an overall *ombré*-flame filled hue framed by elevated Earth tones rang melodic and metallic throughout my entire being. The air took on a fresh and crisp quality, as if we were somehow biting into a honey crisp apple from the inside out.

I think my parents quickly figured out that it would be the only thing that could potentially shut me up and tire me out. As we would get closer to the city, and I started to see the variations in the building heights bordering the West Side Highway, something would happen to me. I felt an excitement stemming from deep within, my palms were sweaty and my legs would start to move, as if I was already walking quickly down Fifth Avenue. My dad did his best to keep up with my overactive need for excitement and to conquer everything the city had to offer. If that level of entertainment wasn't enough, he would take me to see a Broadway show. Let's just say shit got very real for me once I was exposed to this genre. In fact, it was so addictive and influential to my well-being that I would often suffer 'post theater depression,' when we came back from the city and I had to go to school again. Coincidentally, I would get sick every Monday and stay home from school to simply fantasize about what I had seen onstage for a full day, before being able to return to real life.

It wasn't as if I was even interested in the acting or musical part of these shows, I found myself constantly looking behind the curtain and wondering how they physically pulled things off. How did a daytime scene turn into nighttime within seconds? How did one actress change into five costumes within a single act? How did the floor move to reveal an entirely different set in a blink of an eye, and how could we hear an actor loud and clear even though he was whispering on stage, and where the fuck was the music coming from? My head would spin so much so that I even recall throwing up after a performance from the sheer angst of trying to figure it all out. Then, of course, I could never sleep after these types of outings, so Dad would have to continue to entice me with everything the city had to offer. We ate in amazing restaurants and I experienced types of cuisine I certainly wouldn't be exposed to at home. Then we would most definitely shop in the trendy department stores. So basically, I was becoming a cosmopolitan little princess, and nothing would ever match this way of living for me in the future. The bar was set high for me early on and I will always be thankful to my dad for exposing me to all of it. But, at the same time, I was somewhat angry at the world that it just wasn't up to snuff most of the time outside of these weekend excursions.

Later, as I attempted public high school, I was a bored and mediocre student, completely let down by the public-school ambiance. The linoleum flooring, which worked its way up to hundreds of putty colored lockers that simply made a long hallway reminiscent of a 'dead man walking' pathway, and the mismatched window shades, desks and even the radiator covers brought my mood so far down, my production level simply plummeted into nothing-ness.

Thankfully, I was half privileged, meaning that my daddy had means. I quickly transferred to a gorgeous prep school that had man-made lakes and overly green trees and lots of woods to fuck boys and smoke pot in. The female student population all had the right sized diamond studs in their ears and hair that tucked smoothly behind one ear, while the other side cascaded perfectly down the opposite side of their angled faces. The boys were all just goofy enough to be charming and even though their pants would hang off their flat asses, their long limbs would be finished off with a perfect vintage Rolex that would simply just save the day and make us girls want to fantasize about which venue we would be married in someday.

I did not fully come from this type of background, but I, somehow, harmonized perfectly within this setting, working the crowd like an invisible man, popping in and out of conversation like a perfectly timed *soufflé*. I had an authority about me, a saucy arrogance that gave me the power to tell people what to do, what to wear and how to think without them even questioning it. Their eyes big and unblinking, zombie-like, they followed me into a luxurious abyss without question. I wouldn't say I was an imposter but more of someone who was playing a role that people readily latched onto. On the inside, I was aware of this role, and I suppose I lost myself long ago, if there ever was, in fact, a 'myself' to begin with.

Since I was kind of a rotten student and there was no hiding that and I couldn't seem to hypnotize my professors otherwise, my mother thought it best to make sure that I had some sort of trade to fall back on. In her mind, I needed to do something that I could take with me wherever I went and be able to support myself in a way that would gain respect from the kinds of circles I was running in. This was a tough puzzle to solve; how does someone, who pretends to be privileged and smart, keep up the charade? I'll tell you how. You become someone creative or an artiste of sorts. No one can fight with that and you become a novelty that everyone wants around for a change of pace and some interesting conversation.

Suzi was able to attend a school specifically geared towards this industry and able to get an actual degree in it. She went to school, blew a ton of coke, fucked a lot of boys and came out as an expert in what I do in just a mere four years. The blank commitment she has for all of it, just makes me feel sorry for her since, if she is anything like me, she will most likely never take more than a three-day vacation, have a child that she will know very well or make enough money to ever come close to compensating her for the amount of shit she will have to put up with if she chooses to stick with it all. Hopefully, in this new world of ours, she can come up with a hybrid of me, of sorts, to use as a benchmark for her career, so could potentially have it all. It was hard for me to visualize that there being such a thing, but I suppose anything is possible. As I continue to tell her the tales of my life, the look on her face takes on its very own emoji presence that is just too hard to describe. The biggest difference between Suzi and I is that I am a creative and she is a logistics person. We are a true Ying and Yang, but in order for her to handle my shit, she needed to get creative with a lot of things on the fly.

I try to support everything I tell her with visual aids such as photographs, but we didn't have digital or clouds back then, so I frantically try to scan proofs of my existence from frayed newspaper clippings and yellowing polaroid photos to show her some sort of evidence of my evolution, all the while knowing that her attention span probably wouldn't go the distance. Don't get me wrong, even though Suzi couldn't sit through an extended conversation, it didn't mean she wasn't getting shit done. On the average, when Suzi sat in a chair or at a table, she was shopping online, answering about fifty emails from clients, batting away her mother's requests on how to hail an Uber while inconspicuously picking out which men I should or should not make eye contact within our general vicinity. She is a constant churning of wispy knowledge and I hang on her every word and notion. It has come to the point where I don't even cross the street until she motions with one of her pointer fingers for me to do so when we are walking together. This 25-year-old woman/child fucking owns me.

When I was thirteen, my mother, somehow, convinced her dear friend, Belinda Katz, to let me observe her high-end retail floral and event business during school breaks and summer time. Apparently child labor laws were not of a concern. I kept up a fancy life every other school break by accompanying one of my school 'besties' on their family vacation to the Maldives or somewhere else perfect. Most of the time, their families didn't even realize they were paying for me, and I was always a welcome neutral addition on their dysfunctional travel escapades.

Belinda was kind of her own encapsulated heart-break. I have come to learn that everyone in the event business or connected with it is broken, in some intriguing way, much like how light reflects beautifully off broken glass or how garbage can somehow look captivating if piled up in a certain formation. We have these synapses that don't connect like everyone else's, and we are phenomenally schooled in swallowing bile, while turning it into champagne by the time it hits our stomachs. Belinda had a shitty marriage, shitty kids from what I could gather, and her only refuge and happiness was this fucking flower shop that would never really pay her back in the way she deserved. And if it did pay her back, she probably wouldn't want it. This perversity was infectious, and I wanted to be just like her but richer, and a lot more glamorous. This was something I was sure of at a very young age.

While working in the shop, I basically swept the floor and had some pretty deep grown-up conversations with folks three times my age. The floral designers that inhabited the back room were probably the most fucked up and magnificent people I have ever met. These people did more drugs than my entire boarding school. Unbeknownst to Belinda, during the holidays, we would quietly make several nice hot steaming mugs of hot coffee, laced with some Bailey's Irish Cream, accompanied by large bowls of Spaghetti-O's, topped with gratuitous piles of psychedelic mushrooms. I can still remember how slimy and delicious the meal got, as we anxiously awaited the beginning of our dream-like state. When the 'shrooms didn't take fast enough, we would smoke joints ambitiously in the flower cooler, just to rush the high. Meanwhile, some middle-aged pudgy broad took people's flower orders just a few feet away, only to hand them back to us, where we would create the magic that would soon land on their dining room tables for all to admire. It's great how you only love your mother one day of the year, eh? Mother's Day was our biggest drug day out of the year, along with Easter.

Anyway, this was the foundation of my career, and perversely enough, I will always be grateful to these misfits of society, who were painfully talented

21

and bitter all at once. Every floral designer is just a frustrated masterpiece of a super-star waiting to happen. It's a whole existence of, "I think I should go back to school and figure out another career choice," as the years just keep flying past you within a decoupage of floral fantasy, filthy finger nails, multi-lacerated hands, swollen feet, and crushed vertebrae. I was fucking hooked. The rhythm, the filth, was all just foreplay that led to that one minute of blissful 'oohs' and 'ahhs' from a client fawning over your work. Then, you move on to the next event, and you never ever go back to school or explore a second career choice, you are simply too exhausted to do so.

All of this, somehow, built the foundation of the business that I own today, which represents as an international event production and planning phenomenon. If a client drops an exaggerated 'Wow' response over an event I have executed, it's enough to get me on to the next one and the hundreds after that. Even if the work orgasm only lasts a few short moments, the best ones always do, and this has, somehow, held me over for thirty years now.

Currently, however, the instant gratification has become a bit delayed and perhaps, not event present at all. I have been panicking lately, having seemingly lost the one thing that turns me on, aside from an edible and a large throbbing boy part. It never occurred to me that I could potentially fall out of love with the most consistent love child of my life, so I never arranged for any extra-curricular plan. Sure, I could travel the world which I have already done, and I will again, but my fear was that I wouldn't have anything I wanted to come home to aside from Suzi and I was aware of what a burden that could potentially be to her.

Meanwhile, Suzi ensures that my social media presence is that of a pop-star, and every young thing with a vagina or a cock that prefers men wants to be me. I never post a thing until I see Suzi's visual reaction to what I am suggesting. I carefully watch to see if her pupils dilate a bit more from one image to another and this observation gives me the right answer every fucking time. We take bets every night on how many followers I will gain with each scrumptious choice of photo we pull from my now, extensive content choices. The great thing about being in business for a lifetime is that I have a stellar library of mind blowing and beautiful things to show. Some of my work could even seem dated at times, but never fear, that shit always comes back around and back into style, you just gotta sit tight and ride that shit like a ski-lift, glide down the mountain, and go back up again and again.

When the day resembles being finished and Suzi goes off to her Queen's world while continuing to answer emails until she passes out, I often sit at restaurants alone, drinking my dinner as young girls slip me their resumes and requests of wanting me to mold them to be exactly like me. All the while the chefs from these restaurants send out special dishes, they have prepared for me, along with their favorite pairings of wines, bourbons, and ports, in hopes that I will stick around for closing, which, most likely, I will. Nothing like fucking a real man in an apron and clogs, who is most likely married with a gazillion kids. The gushing girls continue to tell me how incredible the parties they threw for their sororities were; ones that made event history in their schools, providing them with the perfect spring-board to take over the event industry in the real world. While they were throwing college parties with 'instagrammable' moments, at their age, I was doing parties in Dubai and signing NDA's, so no pictures were ever allowed because my clients were so chic and fabulous. I am thrilled that Suzi isn't with me, she hates these girls and refers to them as 'Schlampe,' the German word meaning slut, drab, bitch, and floozie. We quietly label most young girls on the street and a lot of our bridal clients with this affectionate yet degrading term. I even came up with a gay boy version 'Das Sphincta' and we get a giggle out of it every time.

Whenever I try to fully recount what I have done in my career, I often feel like a little boy crying wolf, but I am so thankful there was no social media back then to record all of the stupid shit I have done.

I try my best not to text Suzi or anyone else on the team after midnight, but as I become super sloshed, it's Suzi that usually calls the Uber that will get me safely back to my sparkly nest high in the sky.

Not only is she making sure that I don't get jailed for the evening, she is most likely dealing with 'issues' from the business. One night, I got a call from the hospital saying that Suzi had been bitten by a Racoon. I assumed someone was fucking with me and I was rather high as well. Turns out that we had been in the middle of producing a million-dollar re-launch for Hostess Cakes and we were storing thousands of their signature snacks in our warehouse space, which grabbed the attention of a large family of Raccoons, who didn't waste any time of making them the ultimate feast. Suzi had simply stopped in on her way home to make sure our production guys locked the gate properly, only to be met violently by the mama beast that was on the lookout for meal interrupters. So, now, Suzi's list of fears had expanded into the category of small mammals and currently, we do not store client product any more in our warehouse.

I openly admit to Suzi that things were confusing for me when I was just starting out. My friends were not becoming florists or 'party people.' They were choosing which legacy college they were going to attend, and taking the summer off to travel, going to concerts, and avoiding their parents as much as possible. I would dabble in hanging out with them, but as Belinda allowed me to do more and more in the shop, I was a girl divided. One unsuspecting day sealed my career fate for years to come. I had no idea it was happening. Turns out that three of the floral designers called in sick on the same day. This is something that floral people never ever do, knowing that the world will collapse for the business owner and their clients, so it's considered a real 'fuck you' and you'd better have a plan B in terms of a job waiting for you. I was too young and stupid to really know what was going on at the time, but it had something to do with Belinda owing everyone a lot of back pay. I suppose they decided to go on their own version of a strike. This was one hell of a happy accident for me, since Belinda had no choice but to let me try my hand at designing and not just sweeping. Long story short, I rocked as a floral designer. Who knew? Strangely enough, I remember this day very well. I had a sense of accomplishment tinged with a surge of dread knowing that I was going to become a floral designer and not some famous pedestrian something or other like my friends. A seed of loneliness mixed with elation enveloped me all at once, and I really needed to smoke some pot. I took a stroll in the alley behind the shop to take a toke off my one hitter. There was a cool homeless guy who hung out there every day. He would take the flowers we threw away and sell them on the streets in the business district to guys that fucked around on their wives during lunchtime. We locked eyes for a moment. Little did he know how much we really had in common, and that I was strangely attracted to him.

When I got back, I heard Belinda call my mother and inform her that she could stop paying my salary for her, and that I was her new golden goose of a designer. We were back in business and all Belinda needed was lil' ole me.

I can brag about my talents in this area, because I had none for anything else, aside from wanting to make people happy and having fun. I was creating masterpieces in constant motion; a thrill to watch, my arms moving gracefully and my clippers creating a soundtrack of hummingbirds, kissing flowers to an occasional hip-hop backbeat. The town was aflutter with my talents, thrilled that this small place had given birth to a new da Vinci. I was going to take them places and folks would flock in from cosmopolitan snobby cities just to get a taste of me. I was thrilled with where I was landing at that moment. I had lost interest in everything else, possessed with my new-found career and my new-found wisdom. For a girl who couldn't pass a foreign language class, I was suddenly fluent in Latin flower names, spewing them out when walking in the woods with friends, while jovially complaining about how we would need to drop acid earlier in the evenings from now on due to my early wake up times to drop off wedding designs. I was in this awesome little niche of my own that my friends envied and regarded as strange enough to leave them devoid of any opinions on the subject. I mean, I wasn't hurting anyone. I was just doing something extremely out of the norm.

My mama always said, "Special people lead difficult lives." Somehow, that made me feel better, even during the most alienating moments.

There were times though, as I settled into my golden veneer, that I felt out of place and left out that I hadn't approached the college thing along with everybody else. Was I ready to make this kind of commitment and give up on the college dream? Nope. I wanted to stay with the beautiful, rich blonde people a little longer.

I decided to apply to college. After all, who goes to prep school and doesn't go to college, unless you get expelled for some horrid reason and don't have a last name resembling 'Kennedy' to fall back on? My mother went to Skidmore, where she excelled with her left and right brain skills. I did not possess the same abilities, so we weren't shocked when I received a 'skinny' envelope from her alma mater. My father felt that since he had paid a hefty amount in tuition to my prep school, they should find us a school that would take on a special category such as myself. Since I had filled in the bubbles on my SAT score sheet in a flower pattern, I was going to need to get into college on my charisma and winning personality. There were schools out there that could always use a cute Jewish girl who played the WASP role successfully. Not to mention one whose father could afford full tuition and a possible donation at the end of my hopefully, successful time there. The fact that I was a successful working woman certainly helped. I ended up being accepted by Bennington College.

While I was relieved to be on a 'normal' path, I found that the environment and overall practices of college resembled the prep school experience too much. The drugs flowed freely, and the boys could 'go all night,' which was a plus, but again, I was bored everywhere and anywhere. I needed to get back to work full time. My parents weren't overly thrilled with this decision, and they would eventually convince me to try Vassar College, which was close to home, but that didn't take either. The only thing I took away from Vassar was an expanding waist line and a few friends that were just passing through like I was. Coincidentally enough, the school was short on housing and they put me up in a small house just outside of campus, along with the other two people that I was apparently destined to meet. We became instant friends. We all had the same birthday, and on our first night of getting insanely high together, we found ourselves getting what was supposed to be matching Scorpio tattoos, but each separately resembling a lobster, a strange rabbit-like creature and a demented frog; mine was the lobster, thank God. My friends, both, grew up to be extremely successful; the boy was a world-renowned fashion stylist, who was also married to a diplomat, so he and his husband lived all over the world in fabulous apartments paid for by the government. I often went to wherever they would be living, in order to detox and re-asses my life, but I often came back 're-tox'ed' with suitcases filled with ridiculous amounts of fashion that I would never wear or be able to give away. The other friend became a mom of three and had the most successful marriage I had ever seen. She was the only one out of us that got arrested basically every time we went out drinking, just for taking her shirt off in the wrong places, so I truly admired her for turning her life around and making it stick. Now, her kids write to me in secret, asking if I would take them for their first tattoos and such; my, how shit never changes.

I could see how disappointed my parents were with my dwindling education, so I decided to compromise and try to work and go to college at the same time, which, in hindsight, was one of the dumbest things I have ever attempted, which is saying a lot. By this time, my parents consisted of an entire group. My mother was on her third marriage and my OG father was on his fifth. I loved everyone they married and I feel like the task of figuring me out had become a collective effort that really drew everyone together. My step brothers and sisters just stayed out of all of it. I didn't even know half of them, and they were all supposedly 'normal.'

I landed at Bard College, which was the most digestible of the schools I attended. The main reason was because Steely Dan was formed there, which was my favorite band of all time and who was responsible for the soundtrack of my life. They were also my ideal 'get stoned and drive to my job' type of music. I distinctly remember a time when I could not even attempt to get into my black Volkswagen Jetta with the Harley Davidson sticker on the back window, unless I was stoned out of my mind, even if the drive was just around the corner to the store.

It's tough to explain to Suzi about my college career, simply because I didn't remember a lot of it, and I wanted her to latch onto the parts of my life that were more 'me'; the ones that I felt would make her proud to know me. Suzi is aware of the 'soft boiled' parts of who I am; she is probably the only one. Therefore, she is the most powerful person in my life. I wanted her to know the areas of my existence that were calloused and the others that were silky. I was a bowl of Sweet and Sour soup that I wanted her to ingest all at once, so she could get the Good, the Bad, and the Ugly bits of my life all in one bite.

After a short time of working and going to school, I began to be bored with the flower shop environment, even though I was still only a part timer there. That creeping desire to move on was starting to nudge at my soul. I always dreaded this feeling. Much like holding in a fart in a public place, I would start to panic internally and look for higher ground for safety.

Being bored has been and always will be the reason for me wanting to do anything worthwhile.

Chapter Two

"A wedding without cake is just a meeting."

-Julia Child

For some strange reason, my parents openly accepted every dip and turn I took throughout my life, and they let me take the wheel over and over again, though I often ended up at a dead end or stuck in a traffic circle that had no exit choices. My mom wasn't the least bit surprised when I told her I wanted out of the flower shop and into my own business. I saw a flash of panic cross her beautiful face, mainly because she knew there was going to be start-up money involved, also that I wasn't going to be leaving town anytime soon, which, let's face it, would've been a nice reprieve for her, since my step-father was constantly negotiating my speeding and parking tickets with the local cops at the 7-eleven before the sun even came up. We both knew it was time to surround myself with rich, blonde people again, so we decided it best to join a club that I could suckle the teat off of; it was time to learn how to golf, play tennis, and join the fucking country club.

When I spoke about this, Suzi spit her heavy White Wine into the fire and the flames burst and leapt up in laughter with us, so after a quick bathroom break and a session at the in-house photo booth, I continued with my oral history. She was finally seeing how perverse my path was and was less terrified by it; after all, I lived to tell her about it, right?

Once again, within the Country Club environment, I was floating amongst a gorgeous clan of butterflies, moving slowly above the masses and only dipping down to smell or drink something containing alcohol or to land upon something shiny and bright. I traveled within a circle of men and women that were bored out of their fucking minds and thankfully trying to 'one up' each other in absolutely everything, especially entertaining. And since I still had the stink of fabulousness on me from the flower shop, I found myself being fought over for every celebratory date on the calendar. I would overhear ladies in the locker room trading dates for me and almost auctioning me off between each other. Some even tried to piggy back their parties from one another, so they could kill two birds with one stone by hiring me for a very long fucking day that had lots of parties in it.

The club, itself, is never ever something you would want to see from the inside out, much like every other famous or supposed high-end venue I ended up working in. From the outside, the club was so green it was almost as if you were wearing tinted glasses or you were really stoned. It just looked so pristine and sharp you felt that you were in that west coast frame of mind, where every day is perfect. Even when the weather wasn't cooperating, the inside of the club was flawlessly staged with a raging working fire-place and a huge bar that was stocked with only premium choices, along with being consistently supplied by an exclusive wine cellar that lived beneath the main club-house. Members also kept their 'private stashes' of their poisons of choice in a private room that only a few of us had the key to. Thank God surveillance wasn't a big thing back then, or I would have been responsible for many divorces.

The insides or what we call the 'back of house' of the club were that of a colonoscopy. You don't want to see the behind the scenes of any institution if you can avoid it. It's kind of like meeting a celebrity you have always worshipped on screen or on stage, and then, in real life, they are just extremely small and mean. Venues and restaurants didn't have the cleanliness alphabet grading system back then either, so you can only imagine what they were able to get away with. It was common practice to grease the health inspector's palm when he did a surprise drop-by. One cool Benjamin would do the trick just fine. It wasn't an odd experience to feel a rat scamper across your feet on his or her way to some leftover French fries that had made a home in the corner of a back stairwell. There, the rats would battle a small army of cockroaches to lick the plate clean. It resembled a West Side Story type of choreography/mirage, if one was stoned or open-minded enough while observing them, then it was quite entertaining.

The average sex of a wait staff member in any service venue was predominately male, middle aged, angry, pudgy, and most likely over-sexed yet impotent. They also often drank away their paychecks and somehow, had an average of 2.5 wives and at least six children that they were responsible for somehow, somewhere. I fucking loved these guys.

I was growing into a sexy device of a woman. I was independent and completely different from anyone at the time, so I was either deemed as fiercely attractive and desirable, or for some, a walking plague. In hindsight, my most powerful feature was that I was young. This power was not something I understood until I later watched how people reacted to the young girls that worked for me and what they were able to accomplish just by being young and beautiful. I wasn't savvy enough to use this magical power, but I was stellar at letting married men flirt with me and then later, they somehow allowed their wives to spend a ridiculous amount of money on my services to rid any residue of guilt. To me, this is exactly what algebra really was, not the stuff they tried to teach me in school.

Suzi was in a different position. She was growing up roaming within packs of girls; all also independent, maybe not as much as her, but career driven, tough on men their age folding their penises into precise millennial shaped origami boxes, ready to be crushed or set on fire at a moment's notice. These girls ruled their guys by making more money than them or training them to be the bread winners, while they maintained beauty, babies, and blogs, as the young men evolved into products of early onset baldness and 'dad bods.' We watched them walk down the aisle every week end as the last piece of marriage advice to the groom escapes, as a whisper under my breath; a bi-monthly 'blowie' will be the highlight of your first year of marriage, then it gets worse from there, hang tough.

Suzi's kind did not sit by the phone waiting on a man's attention; they went out and posted as many photos of them having as much fun as possible on Instagram, recruiting unsuspecting male hopefuls to pose with them to perform a passive aggressive jealousy inducing charade. Then, if that didn't work, they would simply delete, block, and ghost the shit out of these guys, until they would evaporate like a vampire that had been exposed to the sun. During all of this, not one tear sheds or a heart string broken.

They get up, curl their hair, apply that shimmer powder on their cheeks, wax their vaginas, get art that takes five hours applied to their nails, and apply fake lashes that will last at least a month. Now, that's a fucking super hero, if you ask me.

My first commission from the club was a lovely lady whose hubby owned oil delivery companies throughout the entire tri-state area. They provided the oil for every home that was built before the 1970s and even afterwards, and it was a fucking gold-mine. These were not particularly well-educated people, which was perfect for me, and they didn't really have good taste either, which, again, was the perfect scenario for the likes of me. They most definitely required my services. I remember showing up at one of their homes, which was situated in the rolling hills of upstate New York and where the wife lived, while hubby stayed 'in town' at an apartment because of his work schedule. I also learned that it was best not to discuss these arrangements or even ask about them, and that women had an incredible way of turning off their systems to this type of information, and that their best revenge for any adversity was to spend money. Yay! I was learning so much.

Turns out, my client didn't even really know what she wanted from me. There was no party planned and simply no reason for me to be there really. She kind of just wanted someone to talk to that wasn't in her regular circles and I figured since I was there, we would talk, drink champagne, and perhaps, look around the house and re-design some shit. There was an intense amount of burgundy in the house. Burgundy used to be the color of wealthy people, according to some, but when used incorrectly and in too large a quantity, it was a sure giveaway that people didn't know what the fuck they were doing design-wise. Just from looking at the amount of burgundy or scrolled wrought iron mixed with glass in someone's home, I could quickly surmise how insecure they were and how I could possibly wiggle into their trust circle, while simultaneously make a living from working with them. Hey, doctors and lawyers do it. Why shouldn't I? Also, I was always on the look-out for tassels of any kind. Tassels that tied back curtains or hung off a window treatment were a sure giveaway that I was in the home of the *nouveau riche*, and that only I could save these people from themselves. We got to know each other, and it turns out I truly enjoyed my time with her. It was strange, coming from my perspective and how young I was, to discover that insecurity and vulnerability knew no age limits. Everybody needs somebody to lift them up, and I was ready to lift.

We decided to create an installation in her foyer—a Wow! Factor or Focal Point that would cause people to swoon as soon as they entered her house and create enough stir that people would talk about it for months to come. I learned this important short-cut early on in life; that if you create something so spectacular in one area, the other areas simply don't matter as much. Thus, you can, in fact, put a lot of your eggs in one basket design-wise and let the rest just harmonize with this one magnificent thing; the focal point. She would be the belle of the ball. We would debut the piece at a house-warming party and perhaps, rekindle the fire of her life and re-raise her status in society. It's amazing how much confidence it gives people to have something they want to show off. By the time I was finished with this lady, she would have a twenty-inch cock and triple D tits and possibly, a husband, who would come home once in a while or better yet, a new lover all together.

The biggest obstacle is to be able to get people to trust you and listen to you enough to let the lion out of the cage and create. It takes some balls to let someone else turn your house upside down and then open it up to the world for all to see. Don't get me wrong, this type of practice takes an enormous amount of time and it's not something you can ever put a money value on, so that's why it's so very important to charge a lot when you finally can. Looking back on it all, my first gig probably took me about three months, twenty hours and fifteen minutes to accomplish. If I could have billed by the hour, I would have been rich after this project, but it just doesn't work that way in my world. All these years later, it still doesn't.

I hung out with her pretty much every afternoon after school. I gave her my mother's number, which we made sound like a business number, so she could call any time and leave a message for me. My mom answered a couple of times by mistake, but quickly rectified herself into a proper sounding professional on my behalf. I think she even used an English accent a couple of times.

I spent countless afternoons touring my client around the local flower and accessory markets. In return, she would take me with her to shop at the markets in Paris, London, and Italy to look for trinkets I would include in my design. We flew private, stayed in the best hotels, and ate and drank like we were going to the chair. This was before being a lesbian was fashionable, so I think people thought we were a mother-daughter combo, which really messed with my boy-time. When she would retire early for the evening, I would sneak out, get loaded, and end up in some non-descript alleyway for some much-needed bump and grind with some hotel worker dude in London with bad teeth and smoky breath or in Paris, it was always with a street *Crêpe* maker guy, then I would fit in a quick disco nap before shopping our asses off. This was an incredible experience for me and I owe her a lot for it. As we shopped, I learned several languages, learned about foreign currency, saw things that I never would have seen at home and became an expert in all things design, not just flowers. At the same time, I got major respect by association, just from traveling alongside of her. The vendors and shopkeepers automatically gave me buying power, thinking I was traveling on the same level as my client. I was guilty as charged and thankfully so. For years afterward, I would show up at these markets and everything would roll out for me gracefully and I would be welcomed with open arms, as I brought more open wallets to the game.

I would enjoy seeing the wonderment on Suzi's face, as I would pass the golden baton of respect to her from time to time when we shopped. I would hand her the Black Card and she would pass it discretely to whomever, as I saw the little hairs on her arm stand up. We would pick up exotic items she could bring home to her parents in Queens that they would display proudly on their mantle or talk about at church. They were a little scared of their daughter who was becoming fancy and more bougie by the moment and she was bleeding out of the lines of their comfort zone of knowledge and worldliness. Suzi was very good at being a Queens girl, but I often caught glimpses of her getting silently annoyed when a waiter would pour wrong or pronounce a region incorrectly, while describing a fine wine and it made me proud. She had one foot on the curb with fading yellow paint and the other on a street paved with Gold and the straddle wasn't easy. One of the more important things I tried to teach Suzi was patience with people. She grew up speaking to people through a device and not in real life; it's easy to underestimate the potential emotional clues that can seep off of them like little golden nuggets into their inner thoughts. Once you collect these clues, you can use them to your best advantage; Suzi had no patience for that whatsoever. I often saw her out of the corner of my eye, as I told people what they wanted to hear before they even knew about it and it piqued her interest for sure, but I think she was exhausted by the idea of attempting it herself. Some of our older clients would become enraged if Suzi referred them to a link or a website by ways of communication, thinking that we weren't providing enough of a comprehensive service to them; this baffled her. I explained that with the charges we demanded, a client expects us to explain to them in words or even in person how to do anything; including the simplest of tasks, like swallowing or smiling. Once someone pays you, they own you for the term of their contract; plain and simple. There were passive aggressive ways to create boundaries, of course, but they still have you by the nipples, regardless.

Soon, it was time for me to deliver creatively to my first client and really show my stuff. Upon our return, I felt that the most influential part of this trip was watching the glass-blowers in Venice. These guys were bat-shit crazy and brave. My lady had an inside hook-up that allowed us to go to one of the original glass-blowing factories on the island of Murano to see how the old timers blew hot, molten glass. It was terrifying, mystifying, and it blew my fucking mind. I spoke in broken Italian, asking an ancient man to replicate the look and feel of Niagara Falls (which, coincidentally, was where she and the hubby had honeymooned), to be installed in the forty-foot high corner of my client's foyer. I would, then, backlight it with a slow-moving effect, while creating an organic base of elements, such as moss, rocks and of course, something blooming and burgundy. Then we would, somehow, have to have this piece or pieces shipped to the States, along with a small Italian army to install it and touch up whatever broke during the trip. Truthfully, this is the most stressful part of being a designer. The logistics of it all can really fuck up your creative dream within seconds. I noticed how my client watched me express and sketch out how I wanted to create this real-life fantasy in her foyer, and I saw the pride in her eyes as she looked at me, much like a parent looks at their kid after scoring a goal, and I instantly fell in love with being accepted on such a respectful level. I loved my job that day and I even liked myself, too. Today, I love when a client hands Suzi a fat envelope, thanking her after an event. I know she feels what I was feeling that day and I am sure she would agree that it's the highest of highs.

I would have to find the people that would light the masterpiece artistically and in ways that didn't blow the whole vibe. I was young and I didn't have a rolodex of design partners to grab from yet, so I expressed this to the glass guys, who just happened to have cousins in the lighting field. The Italians always have a cousin who can 'help out.'

You gotta love the Italians.

When it was time to install this masterpiece, my client's hubby still had no clue as to what was about to take place in one of his homes. I hadn't even billed them yet, not really knowing how, so he had no understanding of the financial tsunami that was about to hit. Rule number one; always take a fucking deposit, along with a signed promissory note, and get paid in full before installing the job. If there is an issue, you can always fight it out after the money hits the bank. Rule number two; never, ever work for free. A more ethereal rule to live by is to realize that no one can ever disrespect you, except for you. Think about it.

I could easily attribute this very first client experience as the defining moment of when I started to understand the kind of employees I would need someday, but I just didn't know it.

A gazillion years later, Suzi acts as my 'Bad Cop' and she makes my concepts come true logistically. Every creative type should have someone else to talk about the money and the behind the scenes stuff, even if they are child-like in appearance. Suzi has a way of just saying what needs to be said, with no emotion or regret. She sets the rules and collects millions of dollars from our clients, even if they laugh at or bully her at first. She makes it very clear that the shit doesn't leave the truck if the money hasn't left their bank account beforehand.

When the client's hubby, whom I hadn't met yet, finally came home, the place was crawling with Italians. There were grubby men everywhere, sitting against the walls, eating, using the bathrooms, napping on the huge central stairwell, and even flirting heavily with the Mrs. in her huge kitchen. Frankly, this activity alone made the place come alive. It makes one wonder; if a house is filled with love and activity, does it really need to be designed at all? Fuck, yeah, it does! I saw his car coming up the drive (a custom Rolls Royce, duh) and I remember being nervous. I don't know if it was because he was the one that I was going to need to collect payment from or if it was because I was part of this big secret his wife was keeping. He was a big man, pretty schlumpy overall, but he had a nice face and his sideburns were beautifully manicured and he carried a Wall Street Journal tucked under his arm that looked as if it was part of his superbly tailored suit. He flashed a smile at his driver, and I saw him take a moment, before opening the door, to his original life. I think I learned at that exact moment that the human body has a magnificent knack for going numb at certain points to protect itself from harm or just simply to deal. He stood rock still and took it all in. I could see the engines turning in his head and his face turn different shades of color. But pleasantly enough, I also saw the biggest smile spread across his huge face, while it shone upon the entire room. He laughed and said, "When the fuck does the parade start?"

I took that as my cue and walked up to him; arm outstretched for a handshake, and introduced myself as the one that was responsible for this mess. He grabbed me and hugged me, and the last words I ever heard from him, after he slapped my ass, were, "Now, where the fuck is my soon-to-be ex-wife?"

The design, itself, went off without a hitch. It graced the cover of Architectural Digest and was featured in every design magazine, including the ones across Europe. I was given no credit for the design and I was never paid a dime for it. I was eighteen years old. This enraged Suzi I could tell. There was a little tear swaddled in the corner of her left eye. She would have never let this happen, and it was so crazy to me that she cared so much about something that she had no control over and that doubled as what proved to be a valuable lesson. I tried to alleviate her stress by informing her that no mistake was technically irreversible and or you just shouldn't try to make the same one twice.

Needless to say, my mom hired an accountant to set me up for real in business, along with paying a small retainer for a lawyer who would be my bull-dog, in case of future occurrences like this one. We held our heads high at the club and gracefully declined any advances from the bad people, who acted as if nothing, whatsoever, had happened. In fact, they recommended me to several other clients and acted as if they had launched my career, which, I suppose, in a way, they did. I decided to view this as a good experience and chalk it up to a lesson learned. At least, I didn't sleep with any of them. To me, when you get something wrong in life, you need to see it simply as another chance to get it right the next time and move forward.

I was in, fact, weaving school into the equation, still half-assed about attending classes, but attending them, nonetheless. Suzi always found this very intriguing and just the most rebellious thing ever. I think it even made her a little nervous knowing that my mind could even entertain the thought of not finishing school. In her world, this was just not an option, ever. Even before she was born, her working-class parents put money away for her college education, her wedding, and of course, for their future grand-children. If she had strayed from that life plan, they had mapped out for her; along with being

Catholic, I think she feared that she would combust and disappear into thin air one day while riding the subway into Manhattan. I was living proof that one could survive even after falling off of the straight and narrow pathway.

I rented a small house adjacent to campus, which had a cool shed in the back where I could design all my flower stuff and bide my time in between classes. The house had a lovely porch, from which, I could sell cash and carry bouquets during graduation time for an inflated profit. It was May and everything was just buzzing along with me; bugs that are unsightly in the winter, became iridescent and spectacular in the spring. The flowers, well, the flowers…were just Biblical; being re-born into their most beautiful formations. As the years go by, spring, now, brings us the hybrid blooms, whose beauty has been manipulated through the soil they grew up in. As their floral faces greet the sun for the first time, there is an audible gasp from everyone marveling at their eccentric color and pattern formations. The Matisse Rose is one of my personal favorites. Just picture a normal rose with inlaid paint splatters all over it, in the deepest tones of Fuchsia. We will later see Black Dyed Phalaenopsis Orchids, resembling an ink pen etched road map, when their biggest variance used to be either a cream or violet colored center. As the tools to change our physical appearances emerged such as Botox, so did the tricks for manipulating nature's palettes. I definitely found this depressing and exciting, all at once. On one hand, I could match a floral landscape exactly to one's dining room wallpaper, on the other, was the ability to match itself, and creatively speaking, feeling it was more of a curse than a blessing.

My accountant had given me the magic flower formula; just take your costs including tools, a portion of my rent and the rental fee on my floral cooler, and multiply those costs by three. It was impossible to factor in the time spent on setting everything up, but this came much later in my career, when I was old enough to insist upon this cost and actually profit off of it. As I sold hundreds of bouquets off of my porch during graduation time, little did the proud parents of the soon-to-be graduates know that I was still up from the night before, after having dropped ecstasy, and that there were twenty people I didn't know sleeping on the floor of my house right on the other side of the porch wall. I was always in motion. When my friends were sleeping off their drug and alcohol-fueled evenings, I was hitting the local flower markets, conditioning flowers or fantasizing about a design I wanted to produce. I was restless, but I felt like it was productive restlessness overall. ADHD wasn't invented yet, so I settled for restless, bored, and just searching for something fabulous all the time.

There always comes a time in a girl's life when a boy makes her travel off course and fucks with her life-plan a little bit. It makes sense that I would have a boyfriend at some point; though it was never something I pined for or envisioned. I saw Hugo one day at a local pub, while he was out with his then-girlfriend of two years, who ceased to exist as soon as I walked into the place. He was also with his best guy-friend, who was a complete doofus and was pre-jealous of me, even though he didn't know me yet. He attended Bard and was a year or two younger than me. Since I was a visual person, I first noticed that his overall aesthetic was perfect. He looked like a modern-day god, which is strange, because I tended to be attracted to less perfect types. Sex appeal is everything to me and far more valuable than flat abs and a nice smile. A consistently ambitious cock is a must, also that 'size doesn't matter' shit is not for me. He looked up at me as if he recognized me. Maybe he did, but it must have happened while I was under the influence at a party on campus or something. He motioned for me to join them. Fate sealed, heart aflutter, I walked over to part of my future. My hand was intertwined with his under the table within the first ten minutes of sitting down, while his girlfriend sat on the other side of him, oblivious to it all. Poor thing...

It was a fast and furious coupling. We had an incredible attraction to one another, and he seemed to embrace my eclectic lifestyle. Hugo looked like one of the blonde people I grew up with; yet, he was brutally poor and came from a highly intellectual background. He didn't own any of the social graces I had nor did he understand the concept of money, whatsoever. I think he rather enjoyed being surrounded by wealthy people and had no problem letting them pay for him either. In fact, I often found money missing and my drug supply would dwindle daily from the secret hiding place in my house that only he and I knew about. I don't believe he was malicious, but he was quite aloof when it came to the giving and receiving thing. Frankly, I was so in love with him and his gorgeous cock, I just didn't care.

I was not one of those girls who stopped being productive once she got a fella in her life. In fact, I became even more focused, since it seemed that I would be carrying him financially.

I was still attending school, though it was coming time to take all those classes I had put off, because I knew I wouldn't be able to pass them. This was a horrible strategy that I knew would backfire on me at some point. The 'point' was here.

I will never forget the fateful day that my multi-part college career came to an end. It was raining. I hated the walk to campus in the rain. My culturally unkempt hair got exasperated, and I just didn't feel cool, confident, and attractive that day, but in hindsight, this day was long overdue.

The professor for the dreaded music theory course I needed to take was pompous and guarded, which, frankly, surprised me, because Bard didn't have much patience for that shit. She must have been a visiting professor or something. She honed-in on me as soon as I walked into the room. It was as if she knew I was dumb in certain ways, as if she could smell it on me. She called on me with a three-part question before the rest of the class was even seated. I couldn't even listen to it in its entirety, it was so long and dull. My eyes were glazing over, and she was licking her lips in delicious anticipation of flustering me. I was suddenly in a dark hole, hardly able to hear the sounds around me, and I was spiraling, as every eye in the classroom was shooting lasers into my well-being. Oddly enough, I was embarrassed. It was a sensation I hadn't felt before, and I certainly didn't like it. Any educator that takes the opportunity to bully someone into revealing their stupidity in public should be shot in a town square for all to see. To me, the best educators don't point out how smart a person is, but rather, how they are smart. I use this tactic on my staff today and it seems to work quite exquisitely. One of my main production guys, who is tall and skinnier than a new-born cat, seemed a bit dim-witted when he first started working for me. As I watched him work one day in the studio, I saw that he was overly passionate and phenomenal at getting used wax out of our votive candle holders. Now, this may sound ridiculous, but this is an item that we use over and over again in our business, and we make a healthy profit off of doing so. I swear I saw a ray of light on him, as he smiled a gold-toothed grin after successfully restoring three-thousand votives to their original state. To me, he resembled Thor, while holding his little, scoop handled pocket-knife in place of a Golden Axe.

Back to that fateful classroom, I took a moment and breathed in long and hard, then I smiled, stood up, and blew a kiss to the pompous professor. I could envision the kiss floating down the levels of stadium seating of the classroom and up onto to the stage where that bitch stood. The kiss itself had wings on it, and I could feel myself floating out of the room like a proud bird that had just realized after being stuck in an airport for a long time that there was some obvious exit it hadn't noticed right away.

Once outside, the crisp air and the trees overwhelmed me. It was fall, my favorite time of the year. The beauty of the campus sparkled; even the student center glittered, as if I was looking at it through a kaleidoscope. I suppose I had always seen Bard this way, and beautiful things always made me happy, yet there was a huge lump in my throat, ready to regurgitate the truth I had been hiding from everyone and myself for so very long. I was about to drop out of college for the very last time with only a few classes to go. I found a pay phone and with the only dime I had in my pocket, I called my mom. She picked up before the first ring even went through fully, as if she knew her daughter was fucking up again. There was silence on the phone, but the lump in my throat was making its own sounds to communicate to my mother, once again, that I was dropping out of school and this time, it was final. All I heard from my mother's side of the conversation was, "Babe, run, don't walk, get the fuck outta there and go make some money." And now, you know for sure, where I get my colorful language skills from.

I could see in Suzi's eyes that she was still stuck on the fact that I used a payphone and a dime, I saw her subconsciously reach inside of her bag for her hand sanitizer, wanting to stop the germ-covered pay phone from touching her; it was official that she was drunk. She just couldn't wrap her head around it and I saw that her wheels had stopped turning. I also saw a small vial filled with gorgeous white powder slide from within the contents of her bag, which she quickly pushed back in, and now, I was wondering who was corrupting whom.

There you have it. I attended Bennington, Vassar, and Bard Colleges, and didn't graduate from any of them. But I am a visiting professor at all of them, and I have art centers named after me on every campus—including my old prep school.

Coming back to life, Suzi exhaled a boozy breath, I could tell she was realizing that she didn't know me as well as she thought she did, and an element of caution was mixing within her blood-stream, along with her eighth glass of wine. I needed to re-capture her sense of pride in me and start to recite some more of the 'up' moments of my career development. It was funny how I continuously wanted to impress Suzi and I wondered if this is what parenting was like; always wanting to be the hero to someone who had no fucking clue that you are trying to do so. I could see that it was freezing outside, and even though my apartment was ten blocks away, I knew that we weren't leaving this fireplace or the bottles of wine any time soon. In a way, I had successfully held Suzi captive of her own free manipulated will.

After my last curtain call on college, I was re-born with a renewed ambition, ready to attack my business from all angles, because basically, I was left with one choice for the fork in the road. I had abolished all other options for myself, and I suppose, I knew I was doing it all along, but now the shit was real. I was stuck in a lease for the little house just outside the main campus, and since my tuition wasn't refundable, I decided to hit the college up for some business. I quickly learned that academic budgets weren't for me. All they ever wanted to do was drink cheap wine, meander within each other's living rooms, and eat pre-cubed cheese, and speak intellectually, while keeping the music at a painfully low and depressing level. There were only so many fake oriental rugs, creaky hardwood floors, and out-of-tune pianos I could take.

Part of my talent was that I was capable of quickly assessing whether something was worth my time or not, much like a bear chancing upon an uneventful dumpster filled with inedible items, such as cheap furniture and clothing. It was possible that I was, in fact, in a dry county, party-wise. I didn't want to earn a reputation for being the person who hung around the local country clubs trolling for business. And all the rich people lived deep in the woods, so they were hard to bump into, naturally in town.

One night, while racking my brain about my next move would be, I befriended a 'gay' while drinking at a local pub. It was as if we were long-lost misfits who were both purposely told to be at the wrong place at the same time. Put it this way; we were both drinking champagne in a beer joint. He was one of the first gay people I had met, believe it or not, or shall I say, he was the first who openly admitted his gayness. While I was traveling in Europe with the oil lady, I am sure I came across a lot of gay people, but in Europe, they led adaptable lives that blended so smoothly into every environment. One minute they were family men, adorning their wives with baubles and playing ball with their kids while they wore sexy tight turtlenecks and a cigarette hung fashionably out of their mouths. The next minute, they would be sucking cock in a gorgeous cobblestone alleyway or sticking their dicks into a glory hole to get sucked off by an anxious tourist. These were my kind of people; folks who faced adversity, loneliness, and pain, but made it look so attractive all at once. He and I became extremely fast friends. He was my mentor, my reality, my fantasy, and most importantly, one of the most incredible fashion designers of all time who happened to own one of the mysterious and untouchable houses in the woods outside of town. His clientele was basically a wallpaper pattern of what I wanted mine to be; extremely wealthy, bored, insecure, yet secure enough to want to try to be fabulous and consistently open to discovering the new hot thing that no one else had. They also had to be willing to share with close friends, so that they could discuss us and have something to talk about.

When I really look back on this time of my life with him, I felt kind of like a baby girl Tarzan left in the jungle, who finds herself pleasantly surprised by the coddling of animalistic gay strangers. My friend taught me how to listen visually and turn off the volume of everything else that didn't matter. I would meet with his hordes of women clients, and they would talk and talk, while I carefully took visual inventory of their homes, cars, wedding rings, nail colors, choice of shoe, and belt colors and if they coordinated at the same price level, lipstick shades with or without a glossy top coat and anything you can possibly see on or around a person. I was learning how to listen visually, it was priceless. He taught me how to pick out key words, such as homes rather than home (plural was essential here), divorce, alimony, pre-nup, depression, elective surgery, and so on. As for their homes, the tell-tale signs were that if they were in a country home, they had to have a mud room that would almost deliciously dampen the expectation of what you would actually see in the house until you ventured further through a kitchen with two stoves (never one), a brick pizza oven that got used once a decade and an island that could seat twenty guests for dinner, and off to the side, there should be a small bedroom where a private chef could nap or make notes for next week's menu. If the client never made mention of a great room or at least one bonus room, get the fuck out of there fast. If you could look out the windows of the great room and see a horse or two or perhaps, a small collection of vintage cars, even better. This type of research can all be done by using Google within minutes now, but what's the fun in that?

My friend taught me the art of having a Jewish clientele, which, to this day, tickles me pink. Having gone to Catholic grammar school and then on to prep school, my actual exposure to a Jewish population was a bit diluted, beyond my own people and the ones that changed their names to get into the country club I belonged to. My own family was a mish-mash of a species that often forgot extremely important Jewish holidays or were too tired to do them up right. I think I even recall seeing a PB&J section on a Seder plate one year. The fact is, is I just fucking loved the art of understanding people. I didn't really care what religion they practiced, I just wanted to know what I could do for them and for how much.

Suzi was not 'Jewish savvy' when I met her. Even though she graduated top of her class from Johnson and Wales with her Event Planning Degree, she had no idea what a *Chuppah* was or how to say it, often referring to it as a 'hoop-er.' It took several months before she got enough mucus in the back of her throat and enough nerve to really throw the word around. Now, she can *Kiddush, Yarmulke, and Meshuggah* with the best of them. Suzi had friends that were Bi, Poly, and every other letter in the alphabet, but none like my original 'daddy' types that made my world a better place to live in. I tried to introduce her to some of my original pack-mates, but they never remembered her name and that pissed her off to a point of a complete shut-down around them.

Hearing how I first got my start interacting with clients made Suzi come alive again; this kind of stuff was something she could relate to, because though it was many years later, people just stayed the same and so did the rules of how to get the most out of them. My main purpose of exposing Suzi to my past world was so she could make some sense out of my madness and to adore and worship me for it. It was never something that I thought much about, but she had something in her that inexplicably seemed to have come from me even before we met. She was the only millennial I knew that suffered from shingles, which was such an old school ailment, it made me think that we had been connected in a past life. There was an ageless kinship between us that hit me in my inner most nostalgic core, which was strange, because I could've sworn I had no core anymore. I knew that at some point, by us knowing and working with each other, she would feel that she had more in common with me than anyone else in the world, including her Irish Catholic clan. She was wasted, slurring her speech in the most adorable way. I had a room at the Soho House available to me at all times, so I put some cozy pajamas on my tab and sent her into dreamland. We had meetings scheduled there in the morning, so we would meet, mimosa, and then continue.

After an intense three-hour workout with my trainer and several cinnamon buns later for Suzi, we were ready to start the day and carry on with my colorful tale.

The event industry had its lulls and seasonal dips for sure. I was always busy doing something, but there were distinct times when the party world lights went a bit dim, and all of a sudden, an entire society of workaholics was left holding an empty bag. One of the biggest challenges for anyone in the biz was to stay consistently inspired during these times, enough to kick-start back into action when the time came. Also, when Holidays roll around and we finally get some down-time, as does the rest of the world and all they wish to do is talk about their up-coming events, so no matter what, our phones are ringing and our emails are dinging. Long ago, I started to dread these times, since I didn't have much of a purpose outside of my industry and I knew it was time to become internationally known, not only for parties but simply for being fantastic me, so I had a consistent reason for staying alive. Suzi would go to her family and they kept her intensely busy with family duties, such as calling trappers to take care of the squirrel posse that was taking over her parent's two-family home in Queens or taking her one-hundred-year-old grandmother to the doctor. The rest of my crew would head to every corner of the planet to visit their families, since none of them truly came from New York. Though large amounts of invites would grace my kitchen counter every year, I often found myself alone on New Year's Eve, wondering what the next year would bring for me. How could I be better, do better, just everything was a gaping, open-ended question, it was exhausting, daunting and yeah, pretty fucking depressing. If I was without a husband during these times, I would even attempt to fall in love knowing full well that this charade would end in an exasperated sigh and the desire for him to get out of my house. I would fill my place with groceries that would rot in my refrigerator or die of freezer burn after several months. I was constantly trying to fit in and enjoy mundane things, as the rest of the world did, such as the ball dropping or opening presents, but in reality, I was driving in my own lane that nobody else was allowed in and even worse, I was on auto-pilot. Relaying my past to Suzi was the sport of the moment and it seemed to be doing the trick for both of us at the time.

My first major party client from my new gay bestie's stable was a truly dazzling lady. She was funny, creative, smart, gorgeous, and just a delight, for the most part. Her hubby was a criminal lawyer, and she used to joke that if they ever moved, the new owners of their house would have to build a new foundation since the existing one was built on cash. In those days, it was easy to get paid in cash, you never got audited and it wasn't a strange occurrence to make very large purchases with cash. Cash just put everyone in a happy place and no one thought anything of it.

She hired me to produce and design her first-born son's *bar mitzvah*. We were to produce one party in Manhattan for the 'A-listers,' one in Israel for the family, including step-parents and siblings, and one in the country for the 'C' guest list and camp friends. I made sure to have her sign a retainer and she gave me a hefty deposit to get me started, which, of course, went right underneath my mattress.

While my career was gearing up for greatness, the boyfriend was a distraction. He started making noises about wanting to travel after he graduated. I was hoping that because he was poor, he wouldn't really be able to, but suddenly, he was trading in his motorcycle for a van-type thingy that we could sleep in during the long trip to wherever the fuck we were going. He had always wanted to live in a quaint ski town, which I found barbaric and just 'bleh,' but with me being a Scorpio woman and all, my vagina made the decision to go with him. I could easily call this one of the biggest mistakes of my life, but one can't ever know that, and I hate that 'woulda, coulda, shoulda' type of existence.

The deal was that I would work with this lady on the easy Manhattan part of her son's *bar mitzvah*, and then she would be on her own for the other two. I would bid goodbye to my time in the woods and follow my huge cock of a boyfriend to a ski town somewhere. You must remember that I was still such a young person, and the thought of never living anywhere else was simply not an option for me. The more I got caught up in the web of my career, the farther away I got from having any kind of life plan that my peers, including my boyfriend, could relate to.

The client and I spent four days looking at venues in Manhattan. It was a blast because we would stay in her pied-à-terre, go to lunch, shop, and flirt with men at bars in between our appointments. In the meantime, her husband was freeing criminals and getting them back onto the streets for an exorbitant amount of money, which we were spending as fast he made it. It was one hell of a glorious and vicious cycle. We would use these visits partly as excuses to do the business at hand, such as getting loaded on champagne, then spending an hour in the Hall of Ocean Life at the Museum of Natural History, pondering whether we should hold the party under the big blue whale. Then we realized that since there were displays of sperm whales in some of the dioramas, we probably shouldn't... A lot of how we thought things through simply didn't make sense, and when you really peer into what I do, much of the way I need to go about things makes absolutely no sense at all. There is basically an excuse to do what you want or not do what you should do at any given time, meaning all right or wrong flies out the window. If my daily occurrences were to be presented in front of a board of elected officials or representatives from third-world countries, there would be an overwhelming reaction of ambiguity to whom or what I represented in the world. I lived an odd secret life of sorts, and after many years, I stopped trying to explain what I did for a living at cocktail parties. The industry began to grow popular and even now, no one truly will ever understand what I do. All of my competitors and my employees hold onto this special mystery as well. We all belong to a witch-like covenant that is celebrated rather than feared, and even though it doesn't feel that great all of the time, we wouldn't trade it for anything in the world.

My client's family belonged to all the great temples in town, but we settled on the Park Avenue Synagogue, which would host the religious portion of the event, and would be the reason for the first of many outfit changes. We would do a trial photo shoot about a month before the ceremony, so we could use some of the photos of her son blown up *huge* as *décor* at his party, which would then be a total waste, since he would grow a foot and sprout facial hair before we could even get them developed. When the date of the event rolled around and after her son spent countless hours with his *mitzvah* tutor, we would have the ceremony in the main temple, then a Kiddush luncheon would be held in the newly renovated basement, complete with a shit ton of schmears on bagels, whitefish, and the best Jewish food money could buy. Then everyone would take a nap, re-shower, redo make-up and hair, change the outfits, take another set of photos, and finally, attend the huge reception bash later that evening. Her son would be subject to getting his braces on and off twice, before the big event for photos, and trying on a lot of suits, only to have to have one custom-made because he would grow an abnormal amount before the big day rolled around. It was all worth the three hundred or so cash envelopes he would receive at his party, which he wouldn't even know existed until they at least quadrupled in worth after his father invested them in the correct money market funds.

We hadn't chosen the venue for the big bash yet and time was running out, especially for the custom invites we wanted to design (and hand deliver, of course), which we needed at least six weeks lead time for. The client wanted a venue that was iconic NY and artsy, too, yet traditional enough to be digestible for the older and more conservative guests. The museums and landmarked properties weren't really 'mitzvah-friendly,' since kids had a way of fucking up trillion-dollar marble floors within moments of arriving at these types of parties.

Just the anticipation of an enormous amount of candy and entertainment to come was, perhaps, simply too much for the average youngster, and they liked to wreck shit, and it has always blown my mind that parents would spend millions of dollars for me to create an incredible one of a kind explosive environment for their kid's event, only to watch their kid's friends come in and fuck it up immediately upon their arrival. Glass vases get pitched across the room, ceiling installations that took fourteen hours to install get ripped down within seconds, kids swinging from them howling at the top of their lungs, while parents look on with complete joy and pride; clapping with the urgency for them to continue with this incredibly massively destructive behavior. I suppose they feel it's better for them to let it out at the party than at their home(s).

Long story short, we settled on a very famous restaurant known as the Jewel of Central Park as the venue for the big party portion of her son's *bar mitzvah*. I was only familiar with the place because I had often dropped acid with my prep-school friends in Central Park, and it was the only place that had a bathroom we could use without leaving the park. I fondly recalled strolling in barefoot, completely mesmerized by my surroundings, catching my reflection in the huge hall of mirrors, while trying to decipher the thousands of patterns and textures that graced every inch of the building. The owner of the venue was quite the visionary and way before his time or anybody's time for that matter. The place was gaudy, magical, pretentious yet family-friendly, all at once. You could often find Barbara Streisand amongst many of New York's rich and famous, eating lunch in the main dining room, admiring the plantings or the gigantic Christmas tree that would go up the day after Thanksgiving each year like clock-work. You also saw gangs of tourists who traveled to the city in hopes of getting a reservation there, and even if they couldn't get into the main dining room, they were happy with just having their pictures taken amongst the life-sized wild-life topiaries that were one of the spectacles that made the place so very famous. There was work; being done on the front entrance, so I remember having to walk through the kitchen to get to the event space. This was not a pretty site, though the client didn't mind nor did she hear

45

the men referring to us as '*chuleta de porco*,' basically calling us pieces of meat. Who knows, maybe she was flattered by it all. Anyway, it was exciting going into a major New York City venue with such high prestige, knowing that her son's mitzvah was the first of the season and that no one else in her circle could claim to have an event there before her. When we walked in, we saw someone she knew across the room, and I felt the world go flat. I knew what we had to do. One of my step-parents once told me that if you could throw money at something, it's not considered a problem, and she was right. We bought that bitch out, along with the ambitious sales-person who could potentially afford to quit after receiving the bribe we gave her.

It was thrilling to play those power money games, even though it wasn't my money. It was fun to be able to look someone in the eye and tell them that you are right and they are wrong, no matter what the price. I felt myself getting power hungry and addicted to the rush that it brought to my little world, which made the thought of leaving town all the harder to imagine. I was still a good person then, so I knew that I would follow through on my promise to Hugo and flee town, but deep down in my mind, I knew it wouldn't be for long.

I remember when I gave Suzi her own corporate credit card and the look of terror and excitement that came across her face. It was like I handed her an invaluable collector's edition of a Playboy Magazine that held promise on the outside and an air of a dirty secret on the inside.

The event was a huge hit. We, somehow, landed on a Broadway theme/concept, and yes, the little boy, who is now a man, is gay and uber-fabulous. Coincidentally, we ran into each other in a unisex bathroom in some club many years later, and even shared some laughs and drugs together.

The party was off the hook. Tommy Tune showed up to sing to the family and dance a little dance, which is basically the equivalent of Lin Manuel popping by for a quick performance in today's world. The party room was a sparkling carousel of magnificence, which I was thankful for, because the buy-out for the space and to close the restaurant to the public on a Saturday night was so shockingly expensive that if it turned out to suck, I would be ruined forever, no matter how far I moved away. I quickly came to realize that there is no dress rehearsal to what we do in this biz. You can't re-do a million-dollar party, you can simply just have another one so fabulous that you will undoubtedly forget that the original fuck-up ever happened, but it's rare that your client will ever trust you again.

As I collected my enormous cash tip from her husband at the end of the evening, I was filled with sadness. I watched the horse-drawn carriages approach the circular driveway outside the venue to collect the guests for a 'private/illegal' fireworks show in the park, and as I heard the horse hooves tap on the pavement much like Broadway performers, Hugo pulled up in our van, huge paper map open on the dashboard and our cat glaring out the back window. I locked eyes with one of the horses and with a look of understanding and pity from him, I climbed into the seat beside Hugo, kicked off my shoes, and we started to head out west.

This part of my history was particularly puzzling to Suzi, I could tell. She still lived with her parents after she graduated college, so she could save money for her future, so the idea of me being okay with leaving my parents and the rest of my life to head over three thousand miles away with a dude just seemed reckless and dishonorable; and in hindsight, she was right. In those days, we just did the same stupid shit our parents did; humans hadn't been fine-tuned yet through synthetic drugs, gluten-free breads and technological advances. We were now able to use filters on our photos at the touch of a button to hide our imperfections, which translated into a squeaky-clean image to the rest of the world, even if our insides were rotting out; an exquisite scam that was impenetrable. I was also incredibly thankful that there were no social media devices back then that could record all of the stupid shit I had done.

I needed to get food into her little body, but it looked as if Suzi was eating bitterness and resentment shoved into some sort of quinoa concoction for lunch. I didn't feel the need to explain myself too much though, because times were simply different back then. The definition of sexual harassment, though never acceptable in any form, that causes discomfort for someone was very different back in my day, too. The call-outs on the street or when I walked through the kitchen at work was received in a friendly manner and I never felt the need to put a hashtag on it. These hashtags are today's superheroes that bring the crimes to the surface for all to see and prosecute.

Suzi had also been mortified to learn that I had been sent away to sleep-away camp at the age of nine. To her, this was almost criminal, sending a child out into the woods with bugs and mold. I think that's what bothered her the most; the dirtiness and sloppiness of it all, not the pot smoking, pre-mature make out sessions, or the act of hot wiring the camp director's golf cart in order to go for a joy ride. Suzi was contained, I was not.

Chapter Three

"If life gives you lemons, make some kind of fruity drink."

-Conan O'Brien

Turns out that after leaving my life and sitting in an unstylish car for hours on end was not my cup of tea. I made Hugo change our course constantly, in search of something pretty to look at on the drive. Going through Texas was devastating. The flat bland landscape put me into a depression, but one day, late in the afternoon, we, somehow, found ourselves in New Mexico. As we rounded a huge incline and hit the top of it, my breath caught in my throat and surprisingly, I cried at the site of the Rio Grande. The altitude alone made me feel so high, I mean I was high, but now more so consciously, hyper aware of the beauty I was witnessing for the very first time. The textures and dimensions were out of this world. I had never witnessed anything like it. It was like a monochromatic masterpiece that informed me of a color palette that I would have never considered otherwise.

As we drove up the mountain, it was warm and sunny, and green in parts, but then, like changing the channel on a television, it instantly turned into a winter wonderland, surrounding us with the purest gradients of white snow and clouds. Hugo was happier than a pig in shit; he couldn't wait to hit the slopes, as I was wondering what the fuck I was going to do there in all this pretty nature crap.

We found a cool apartment in an adobe type of situation. I decided to open a flower shop/art gallery in the front of it while we lived tightly in the back, while Hugo worked on the mountain making snow for adventurous tourists, who would brave the dangerous slopes for people willing to meet their maker every season. None of this made sense to me, so I passed my days by working out, making pretty flower arrangements, and trying to sell pop art to conservative Texans, who were mainly there to buy a piece to go over their sofas or an extravagant bronze sculpture of a group of horses. I wasn't very successful and I was starting to hate the fucking place. I figured it was time to branch out. I heard that fabulous people did, in fact, live in Taos, but it was so spread out it was hard to find them, and their 'earth ship' way of life didn't really present the opportunity to walk up to one's doorstep and say hi. It was rumored that some fabulous celebs were pioneers who had turned Taos into a great place to be. I spied Julia Roberts a few times in the town square, but other than that, it was a world divided between the natives and the gringos like us, trying to come in and gentrify the place. I felt like I was living in the wild, wild west, and I was starting to blame Hugo for taking me out of my bedazzled life back in New York.

It wasn't as if Taos had nothing to offer, it really did in visual ways specifically.

You had to drive everywhere, kind of like L.A., but when you drove, you saw the most magnificent landscape, no matter where you ventured to turn. You could often find yourself on the most terrifying roads that were so vertical and narrow your nose would start to bleed and God forbid, you looked out at the view and lost a millisecond of concentration, your car would go tumbling down into oblivion. Thankfully, texting wasn't available back then. I can only imagine how many lives the Rio Grande would eat up on a daily basis.

I took up mountain biking since one of the painters I represented in my store/gallery thingy was an avid rider, who had an ass like an award-winning stallion. He would teach me how to hold the bike steady with my thighs, while painfully scaling down a rocky mountain-side that even a goat would shudder to think about attempting. I was embracing being physical and staying in top condition. The natural hot springs that we would go to after a tough ride were one of nature's little gems. I absolutely adored them, until I found out that they were a breeding ground for bacteria. They were condemned shortly after my departure from New Mexico. Looking out at the landscape while soaking naked in the springs and smoking a joint with a gang of men whom I didn't know and who were thankfully so stoned they didn't even consider raping me, I found myself, once again, wondering what the fuck I was doing with my life and why I was in New Mexico.

A rabid animal may be bat-shit crazy but at least it's productive, always looking for food to kill or someone to bite. I was becoming a bit rabid myself and it had only been a few months, so giving up now would have not only been embarrassing but unacceptable. I hated the thought of failing after, uprooting my semi-successful existence back home, so I thought it best to look for the pretty people and get some business, even if it was different from what I was used to. I strategically scoped out the higher priced art galleries that held openings that served the more expensive wine and got myself on the invite list. While Hugo was with his snow people, I dressed carefully to achieve the perfect mix of artistic black and large turquoise jewelry that was the quintessential accessory for being accepted in Taos. I think I even went as far as wearing feather earrings. I was that desperate. I noticed that a lot of the cars parked near the gallery had Santa Fe plates, which was a plus since that's pretty much where the rich people lived. With a high-altitude pre-buzz, I walked into the gallery. The place was hopping, and all the women were dressed like me and the men were weathered, masculine, and rich. In fact, it was so crowded you couldn't even see the art. That's when you know it's more about the scene than the art, thus confirming I was in the right place.

The first people I noticed were two women standing together, both with very up-to-date haircuts. I figured they flew somewhere to have them touched up every couple of months. They both had great jewelry and stylish shoes that you wouldn't find in any of the shops on the mountain, so I figured they had other homes elsewhere and that this was a 'jackpot' type of scenario for me. I got myself a round of sage martinis at the bar and introduced myself to them. Turns out they were a couple, my first introduction to a power lesbian couple, and we hit it off immediately. Not only was I a possible 'third' for them, but they were New Yorkers as well. They had moved far west to feel free about living as an open and out lesbian couple. As liberal as New York was, it wasn't overly lesbian friendly yet, so these two needed to be able to express themselves elsewhere. The prettier and less butch of the two was pre-menopausal and already retired from being one of the most kick-ass women on Wall Street. Frankly, once I knew that, I didn't really care what her partner did. It was best to hone-in on the one that pays the bills while placating the other one with flattering conversation, kind of like stroking a man's balls while you are sucking him off. One needs to be very coordinated to master this type of art. Luckily, I was ambidextrous.

We took a quick spin around the gallery before they invited me back to their Earth Ship mansion that they had custom built in the past year. My timing, for once, was impeccable. The place was fucking gorgeous, which surprised me a bit because it was rare to see rich people have their own good taste. The home was warm and embracing, and every tchotchke had a purpose and was placed strategically. But the fucking home was underground, and even though it was environmentally fabulous and energy efficient, I will never understand the Earth Ship way of living. The absence of light worried me about everyone's welfare that lived this way. The house was built with materials I never knew about such as rubber, clay, recycled glass, and types of plaster treatments I had never seen before. Everything was huge and purposeful. The furniture and seating areas were built into the house itself, massive banquettes that ran the entire perimeter of the five thousand square foot living room complete with custom made ethnic-looking cushions, which joined harmoniously with a massive dining and kitchen area all melding into one big play pen for adult entertaining. All their electronics were classically hidden; televisions built into hidden walls that opened to other secret items, such as sound systems, light dimming systems, and even air purifying machines that gracefully circulated the underground air into a pleasant oxygenated cocktail. It was an elegant mix of modern technology and design, which I truly respected and wanted to learn more about.

The three of us became inseparable, Hugo didn't even exist, mainly because he worked most overnight shifts on the mountain and skied during the day, and because they had no use for men, unless they were gay or their family members, and even then, it was questionable.

These ladies represented as a self-sufficient, smart, and always ready to take everything to the next level duo. They had wines delivered weekly from all over the world that they couldn't get locally. Their home was filled with anything and everything all of us wanted but never took the time or money to obtain, such as exotic soaps that had refills always ready in storage, like a bunker filled with much needed ingredients in case a war or a toiletry meltdown occurred. They had friends that sent them the finest hashish from Morocco in the form of mailed letters. They rolled the hash perfectly flat, like a piece of paper or a slice of Prosciutto that was almost transparent, yet so flavorful. They were excellent entertainers. They were so well-oiled, the way they moved around their guests in tandem, topping off wine glasses, washing dishes as they became dirty, adjusting the volume of the music, and even providing back up clothing for us, in case one of us accidentally vomited or perhaps, peed their pants during some of our more adventurous evenings. I didn't know this at the time, but I was witnessing the art of hosting and entertaining in its most perfect state, and I was ingesting the rhythm of what it took to put together a perfect evening in a fine home.

They were phenomenal at putting the right crowd together as well. They would weave an intricate social web almost every Friday night at their place, filled with the most eclectic yet harmonious crowd; costume designers, painters, architects, writers, even a handful of impressive locals, including an amazing and discreet drug dealer, of course. God knows how they found these fucking people on the mountain, but they were all quite impressive and I was thrilled to be among them. Even though I was the youngest one, most of the time, the people I was surrounded by were all ageless and somehow timeless. They were all so successful, which made them seem almost over relaxed to me, and I suppose that's why they all flocked to this mysterious mountain town in the middle of nowhere. They reminded me of Santa's elves that only worked a few months out of the year as seasonal geniuses.

Every one of them, at one time or another, admitted to me that they had scoped out my little gallery and that they were intrigued about what was really going on inside the head of its owner. They were pleasantly surprised to find that it was my head they were wondering about. As I eased them into more of what I did for a living in my New York life, we started to slowly open the door to how we could all work together. They understood that I not only needed work for income but also to feed my creative soul, which I feared was drying up, along with the desert surroundings. But first, we needed to experience a sweat lodge together.

If you have never experienced a true Native American sweat lodge before, let me save you the trouble. Just don't fucking do it, especially if you are a Catholic girl trapped in a Jewish girl's existence. There is already enough guilt and demons in there to blow up a fucking airport. The initial sweating, chanting, drumming, and such was lovely, but it was the herbs and tea that really took me down the dark and windy road. The yurt structure, filled with people who don't look good naked, gets hotter than the most potent parts of the equator, even years later, after I had survived the sweat, I randomly caught a whiff of something close to death on an city street, and it would conjure up the nest of devastation that these people took me to, as if it had just happened. I still have no idea what I drank or smoked, but it will always be a poison that lives inside of my psyche and body that reappears during the darkest moments of my life. I suppose it was meant for me to sweat out the bad, but I felt I inhaled a world of evil that day. We didn't do that ever again. I'll take a kick-ass Upper East Side psychoanalyst who can at least prescribe me the good shit that will numb me to my inner evils over a sweat lodge any day.

Suzi looked like she wanted to vomit. This was a person that wouldn't ride the subway if it was above 65 degrees on the platform and if she wasn't armed with a vat of hand sanitizer. She was terribly claustrophobic for a young person, too. We often took the stairs on site visits, winding around the back of house in order for her to bypass an old and crowded New York elevator. Some of our meetings took place in the tallest buildings in the world and I would hold her cold and sweaty, tiny hand in mine in the back corner of the elevator, as we floated into executive offices, which usually hung out amongst the clouds. Suzi would sit half-perched on the corporate sofa taking notes and holding her breath as her cheeks slowly turned red, as the rest of her existence went pale. She disappeared into the ethereal layer of the outside view mixing with her reflection in the huge floor to ceiling windows of the office. We would review her notes after the meetings and they would be gorgeously efficient as usual, but with the addition of the word 'Help' written vertically along a far side of the paper.

After a few weeks of socializing with my new best girlfriends in New Mexico, I learned another valuable lesson about these ladies. I had judged it all wrong. I discovered that the less glamorous of the two had more money and connections than her partner, as she revealed to me that she was one of the most powerful Hollywood producers known to man or woman. The reason they were initially interested in my work, aside from wondering if I was hot, was because they thought I would make an amazing film set designer, go figure. She was about to start a huge project in New Orleans and she thought I should go with her and get the lay of the land on a real movie set. New Orleans was a playground for low-taxed film productions that had yet to be discovered; it was a real find that Hollywood was devouring by block and beignet per second. Famous actors were thrilled to be stationed there, getting all the alcohol and pussy a man army could take, and it truly was a magical place to partake of, much like getting one of those codes via scavenger hunt that gets you into a magical party or club that no one else knows about.

We secretly spoke about all this *sans* Hugo. And after a long night sitting around their eighteen-foot-long, custom-made, antler dining table, drinking wine and intermittently going to take pisses in their compost style toilet, we came to a decision. I would be moving on to New Orleans. But they both made it clear that they wanted to get to know me a bit better before they invested in my trip.

Kissing these women was doable. They were both clean, well-perfumed, and I was so incredibly high and drunk that I kind of felt like I was just riding downhill on a fast bike, lifting my hands in the air without a care in the world, as to where I would land. Too bad Hugo was working on the mountain that night, because I think he would have truly enjoyed watching me bumble my way around my first major pussy experience. I had never gone past first base with a woman before and here were two very hungry lionesses that I needed to impress. I also had never felt up fake boobs, which both of my girls were in possession of, and frankly, that didn't matter to me much. I decided to go to a place in my mind where I was most familiar, and they both became flowers. I was back in that flower shop, where I would manipulate a stubborn rose that I needed to open by party time. By blowing hot air onto it, you can open the outer petals and expose the stamen, so the flower can get oxygen and nutrients that it needed to bloom into its magnificent potential. My technique was something I became quite proud of, and truthfully, it thrilled me that I was taking the women to the brink and back for what seemed like forever.

I will say this with the upmost conviction though; this girl prefers cock.

Suzi just shrugged at this, I mean there was really nothing to say. However, I do feel she made herself forget this nugget of information immediately. She was really good at that. Her mind was that of a Snapchat moment, one that could be so incredibly vivid one moment and then just gone forever like it never happened.

I was starting to see a pattern in my behavior. Apparently, I wasn't ever going to stay in one place or with one person for very long. In hindsight, I was always disappointed by this and always wondering what was wrong with me, while my friends were settling down and cementing themselves into concrete lifestyles. I was also leaving a path of cadavers, the people who had had the misfortune of falling in love with me.

Hugo came off the mountain at dawn, and by lunchtime, he was single. I don't think he ever forgave me, but I knew he would find a mediocre girl, settle down, reproduce, and be happy. Thus, I felt better about moving on without feeling guilty.

I didn't even bother to clean up the mess I had created up on that mountain; the back rent we owed, the unfulfilled lease, and a pile of bills that I never even opened. One simply cannot move forward with a barrier of money problems in the way, so best to deny it all and keep going. All I cared about was keeping the cat. I was ready to move to New Orleans and embark on this new part of my career/life.

Even though she was a young person, Suzi would never consider leaving something in mid-air like that for fear of getting in trouble or simply not being able to sleep at night. She was so fucking responsible, yet she would pee her pants after drinking too much, without a single drop of humility or apology. What I was coming to realize is that since the young ones could potentially manage their entire lives on their phone, there truly was no excuse for letting shit go undone. Even the stress that these loose ends would sometimes cause was part of the adventure. It would create a churning and a clenching that would propel me into my next level, whether it be lower or higher. Nowadays, you took one toke off of a CBD pen and your worries evaporated into a magnificent eucalyptus seeped sauna that soothed the brain into nothing-ness. I still wanted the journey to something wickedly ambiguous, along with a view of it chasing me in my rear-view mirror at all times so I could never fully rest.

Chapter Four

"You cannot find peace by avoiding life."

-Virginia Woolf

The ladies bought Hugo out of his portion of the van we owned together, so I could drive there and get set up in the Garden District apartment they had scoped out for me beforehand. They also gave me a small stipend for start-up costs that would be taken out of my first paycheck from working on the movie set.

New Orleans is still something I am not sure I can ever fully describe correctly because, along with the amount of bodily fluids you lose just by living and sweating there, and with the amount of alcohol you ingest daily, your chemical and emotional landscape changes hourly. Once you finish feeling one sensation, it's already morphed into something else by the time you recognize it. It's a confusing place, but at the same time, it's fucking great.

The drive there was scary, to be honest. There were no GPS contraptions or apps back then, and I was using a paper map, which for someone like me who couldn't even navigate through a diner menu, posed quite a challenge. I was kind of winging it, and now that I was traveling to a lower altitude, I was smoking pot, talking to the cat, and singing at the top of my lungs to the same Steely Dan album repeatedly the entire way there. Upon arriving, I felt an instant transformation. It was humid and wet and coming from the arid desert, my body went into an instant shock that was enticing and so strange. It was spring time when I first arrived, and the heat had already begun to cause folks to get their porches ready and their ice makers in check, so they could drink away the impending heat and humidity. In hindsight, I also noticed that parked cars were running on the street with no one in them. In such an old city, there was such a thing as people turning on their cars and air conditioning by remote, which I thought was incredibly high tech. One could literally fry their ass if they didn't let their car cool down to a human level before entering.

If I had to really nail down what New Orleans did for me, it would be that it successfully awakened all my five senses at once for the very first time. Though it was considered a somewhat sleepy town overall, I have never been so attacked with such stimulus that engulfed my senses of smell, taste, touch, sight, and sound with such rigor. Everything I experienced there created an everlasting memory that somehow permeated those senses long after I moved away to different cities. Once you live in New Orleans, it lives within you forever, if you live to tell about it.

Suzi has never gotten her license, having grown up in Queens with every type of public transportation imaginable and not a lot of parking. The thought of it completely shut her down. I tried to explain to her that driving was a freedom of exploration that you simply couldn't get by playing Pokémon Go or from a setting to a foreign place on the treadmill. Still, she had no interest, but when I really look back on my life, it was the experiences of getting lost which made me feel mostly found. The jolt of pride I would feel when I would finally land in the right place was exhilarating, and then, shortly after, anti-climactic, of course, but there was always a new place to find. These never ran out like a monthly pill prescription did.

I found the way to my apartment on Prytania Street, which was accented with foliage that smelled like it was bottled in heaven. The magnolia trees that graced the adjacent St. Charles Avenue felt embracing. They were so eerily beautiful that I was hypnotized by them, and it was as if they directed me to exactly where I needed to be. Unlike Taos, I was excited to be there. It felt like I had landed in a big, soggy, magnificent spot that would slowly but pleasantly drown me, and it would be difficult to climb out of there of any time soon.

The apartment itself was lovely. I knew the girls wouldn't move me into a shit-hole. There were high ceilings with decorative and original crown molding in every room, floor to ceiling windows, a formal dining room, and a horrible kitchen, which they knew I wouldn't need anyway. The floors were slightly warped but with all the humidity down there, it was hard for that not to happen. Along with lovely interiors, there were armies of cockroaches everywhere. They would scatter like spilled rice every time you would enter a room or turn on a light. It was more unnerving than my bank account at the time, which was always a source of stress. I was thankful that I had the cat, and crazily enough, I got really used to having bugs around. I was often drunk enough to not really notice them after a while, and in rare times of sobriety, they were almost comforting, acting as friends that were just there and not really taking anything from me.

My first mode of business in New Orleans was to align myself with a wonderful and traditional florist who would have a lot of expertise in the New Orleans genre of design, since it would be featured in many of the scenes of the movie we were working on. The movie, itself, was based on a best-selling novel about glamorous vampires who lived a decadent and sexy life in the

French Quarter. The movie would feature the most up and coming and irresistible to look at actors of the time, and the author of the book was a true New Orleans native, who, I quickly found, outlived a mere few blocks away from me in the Garden District in a huge plantation-style home filled with her creative family members.

The shop I found to align myself with was situated on St. Charles Avenue, also close to my place, and was owned by a colorful lady who was 'no doubt in my mind' a lesbian and a charming, raging alcoholic, like most of the local population. I had driven by the shop several times and, after catching a glimpse of it through trolley car traffic, I thought it was perfect for our needs.

You can tell a lot about a retail floral shop by looking at its window displays, which are mostly horrendous. The windows are often an expression of its most frustrated and undiscovered, back-room floral designers, just dying for a chance to break out of their daily clipper routine and into the wide world of window displays for a larger audience to see and hopefully, elevate them to a higher status. The shame of it all is that this chance is one that is taken on way too ambitiously and is over-thought and usually brutally over-designed. The designer excitedly braves some long-forgotten storage space, looking for the perfect items to create a window environment that will somehow catapult his or her career into long-awaited super-stardom, only to simply regurgitate a design that is so distracting and over saturated and stinking of the invasive moth ball smell from the storage unit. A truly great designer of any kind always takes a 'less is more' approach, even if it's an opulent canvas overall. The art of leaving the eye wanting more, rather than suffocating it, is a huge feat to attempt and few succeed at it. There's the fact, too, that most of these designers don't get out into the 'real world' in order to seek inspiration or design ideas. It's a vicious cycle; how do you find new ideas when you are forced to stand in one place day after day and asked to design the same things minute by minute? I admit to Suzi that this has been my largest responsibility in my career; the search for inspiration and applying it to my craft in order to make folks go gaga over it.

I often drag Suzi along to design shows in NY, Paris, London, and Japan, so she can see all of the new products available to the design world. After she sucks down her sugar-free Red Bull and only an hour into exploring the show, her hair is plastered to her little face and her eyes are glassy. She is basically a small child that is over stimulated with shit she doesn't want to see and is way over due for a nap. Meanwhile, I come alive scouring the aisles for new items, talking to the people in the booths who stand there for eighteen hours a day explaining to us how great their products are, while they scan our badges and pray for us to make a large order that will win them a trip to somewhere mediocre with sunshine. Most of these people are from the mid-west or somewhere else pale and white, and they simply cannot wait until they can get off of the floor and meet at the hotel bar and get sloshed. These trips to the cities and the endless hours within their ten by ten booths are easily the highlights of their careers.

As I've mentioned, Suzi knew nothing of flowers when I hired her. She shamelessly pronounced flower names incorrectly and her tastes were not overly refined but let's just say she was a very willing candidate to better herself in that arena. One of the first things Suzi said to me was that she didn't have a creative bone in her little body. This statement always makes me cringe, simply because there is creativity in all that we do, including taking a garbage pail out to a street curb and lining it up perfectly, so it's primed for pick up. Consistently, I would manipulate scenarios where Suzi would have to meet me on the NYC Flower Market, so we could glide down the sidewalks filled with blooms that I would recite the names of in their proper Latin origins. I would hear her either whisper the names back to me or she would bury herself in her phone when the name just didn't seem pronounceable or if she thought the flower was ugly. Either way; this knowledge soaked through several layers of her intelligentsia, making her an official expert in this unique nook of information.

On Charles Street, the outside of the flower shop looked like a beautiful, traditional New Orleans-style home, complete with a huge wraparound porch, accessorized with oversized rocking chairs, couches, settees, and even a large *armoire* filled with the makings of a spur of the moment cocktail hour at any given moment of the day. The floor-to-ceiling windows were, in fact, designed, but in such an organic and harmonious way that it seemed almost as if the designs themselves could have easily opened the door, walked down the steps, and existed amongst the real outdoor landscape. The interior tree designs created out of faux latex climbed the window panes and proceeded to travel into the rest of the parlor of the shop, encasing the display coolers and checkout station in a lush nest of Spanish moss and branches, so the customers felt as if they were lolling around in the intricate yet inviting womb of the oldest and most revered tree in the city. I respected the atmosphere of the entire place and thought we would work well together. I met with the owner, who instantly marveled at my New York chic-ness and young nubile physique. She was in love with me from the second I walked in, but if her designers could have spit fire from across the room and hit me, they would have.

They were all 'existers,' meaning that the owner's daddy owned the shop before her, and his daddy owned the shop before him and so on for several decades, centuries even. The designers that worked there were also, somehow, connected to the family or felt indebted to them in some way, having moved to the sexy city from lesser cities, in hopes of becoming sexier themselves if possible, and truly believing that by designing for the shop, it would help them achieve the status they truly strived for.

The common lineup of a back-room of designers, no matter what the city, includes one overweight gay man who could possibly be handsome if he lost weight and dressed better. He often has a pinky ring or some sort of jewelry on his person that he inherited from a straight relative, who would roll in his grave if he knew that a gay man was wearing it now. He usually dresses quite preppy and clean, though he is the first one to wear a leather mask at a gay club later that night. He would be the rock star of the entire group of designers, the leader, and the one that rich women would come to for design advice for everything and anything in this very small part of the world, making him feel important. At night, when he would go home, he would wish for a bigger world to admire him, thus, making him an angry old man, no matter what his real age truly was. Next, an overweight younger and less-talented girl, who idolizes the gay guy and fantasizes about talking him out of his gayness and marrying him one day and having his children, whom they would take to Church every Sunday where they would pretend to be other people than themselves. Then, there is usually an older woman who is a work-horse, who, if you saw pictures of her as a younger pretty woman, you would be shocked, because she is now skinny with rotting teeth, thick glasses, and smokes like a chimney, but gets more done in a day than everyone else. She is usually married to the rugged old delivery guy who everyone forgets about, until he comes back from a run and uses the bathroom and eats a sandwich. In this scenario, they would all wreak of liquor constantly, especially the owner. The owner was often a non-definable type of person with no real distinct personality traits, who usually became an owner against their will, meaning that their original life-dreams had been shattered, and even though they may not have had any, they are still pissed they didn't have the option to have them. Overall, you were always dealing with miserable and extremely dissatisfied people who genuinely wanted better lives but wouldn't go out and get it. At the same time, they had one thing in common; they wanted to make other people happy.

New Orleans was one place in the world aside from an actual liquor store where alcohol was present, no matter where you were. You could have a twenty-ounce daquiri, along with your jumbo popcorn and Twizzlers, while watching a movie in a theater. In fact, I would personally recommend using a Twizzler as a straw for the twenty-ounce daquiri. It's totally possible to get loaded and fall asleep before the movie even begins, so you would have to repeat the routine all over again to see the movie. You can go through a drive-through and get a fifth of bourbon on your way to go home or to the office or both. And during the summer months, why not get a frozen mudslide drink at a to-go window off Royal Street, just for shits and giggles? You can drive drunk out of your fucking mind and not get a ticket. Sure, it's okay, the cop is drunk, too. Then, you can go to a dinner party, eat like a pig and drink an enormous amount of wine, and then continue on to blow coke at some after-hours joint located in a swampy area somewhere, while collecting several dangerous and scarred men to sleep with. This was my kind of fucking town. I even thought I could call this place home for a while, but there was a slowness to it that often made me anxious. People took longer to articulate their sentences, and there were times when fast food would easily take an hour, when I wanted it within ten minutes. I was worried that if I slowed myself to their pace, I would get lost in the thickness of the environment and that I would, in fact, drown in the moist center of this city forever.

I could, now, pretty much confirm that Suzi was no stranger to cocaine and hooking up with unfavorable men, too, which was yet another reason I adored her. Young people these days were so asexual, and way too absorbed with how many Instagram followers a guy has rather than accounting for his swarthy sexuality. I could picture her at one of her local Queen's bars, hooking up with guys much older and dirtier than her. She looked so young these men were bordering on pedophilia, but she didn't shy away from going to the dark side and losing herself in a spiral of what could potentially be dangerous in order to get a thrill that would carry her through to what she ultimately wanted. She had no fear, but more rules than me, which made her the grown up of the two.

I decided I would immerse myself into the work, which I was still trying to define at this point. The girls had still not arrived from Taos, and I was starting to wonder if they were going to come at all. I had met with the director several times and I always left the meeting more confused than before I got there. He was a pompous jackass of a man with a hot temper, bad breath, and he couldn't communicate his vision for the film in a language any of us had ever heard before. I couldn't even sleep my way into understanding this form of animal, so I retreated.

I decided it was best to observe the movie set and try to map out whether there was any rhyme or reason to how it all worked. Turns out, there wasn't. I just needed to fit myself in somehow. One day in my neighborhood, I saw the author of the book the movie was based upon. I decided I would approach her and get her take on things, which was scary for me, but I pushed forward. She seemed super imposed onto the scenery of the town like she was a recessive gene that was holding her own amongst the masses. She looked lonely to me, which made me like her instantly. I told her I had read the book, which more than held my interest, so that's a plus. She wrote with such an incredible amount of description that I could visualize, smell, taste, touch, and hear every scene and chapter. It all started to miraculously meld together and make sense to me, and she urged me to express myself and ignore all other distractions including the director, since I seemed to be on the right track according to her. My reaction to her novel was what she wanted everyone to feel, so I felt confident to plow over everything else and see where things fell. I might have even dreamed that I ran into her that day, simply because I needed to.

Another problem that I run into, even, now, is how to dazzle upon request. Suzi has seen me struggle in meetings by responding to hopeful clients with a lower level of magnificence. They come to meet us as if they are going to the world's most revered astrologer, waiting for me to wrap up their entire lives in the most intricate and gorgeously tied bow, while encasing them in glamour and beauty within the allotted hour. Sometimes, I just go blank and I have nothing beautiful to offer. I make a joke of it and tell them I need to go drink some wine and get back to them, which I always do, but the initial struggle is happening more often and lasting a bit longer and I can tell that this scares Suzi. I can imagine that for her, it's like watching a lion-tamer lose his pretty red jacket and whip.

I watched the set builders, the flooring guys, the wallpaper people, the lighting and electrical teams, the furniture makers, and an entire posse of accessory set dressing people. In this instance, the most fascinating people were the costume designers. I think I grabbed most of my inspiration from this element, because the costumes were inspired by the wealthy and upper-class social chapter from centuries ago, which I have always found to be so saturated with rich textures and an 'I don't give a fuck, my girl will make me another if I shit in it' kind of attitude. They were clothes made for royalty, and I knew that every element of this set needed to match that level of superiority. It was my job to have every aesthetic element of this movie land onto the same page and form a cohesive design palette, which went way beyond my current professional capabilities. I felt like I was being thrown into an ocean to learn how to swim for the very first time. I quickly learned that when you don't know what to do, sometimes, it's best to do nothing at all. The answer will come to you at some point—hopefully, before it's too late. I kept my eyes and ears open to everything like a cat watching a fly buzzing around a windowsill, ready to pounce if the fucker ever slowed down, this was a good exercise for me; a real practice in impaled patience.

In the meantime, I explored the city's night life, which often extended into minutes before I would need to report to the set. I would usually go and sit at the bar of a nice restaurant, and eat a proper meal, and drink, of course, while chatting up gaggles of men that came to New Orleans for many reasons, including going home with the clap and a potential love child that they never know of. Though I was living in a city that was filled with so many incredible food choices, I would often have a hard time even thinking about food until it was dark and the heat of the sun was gone. The thought of food while sweat was creating, slow moving creeks along my body, was just incomprehensible. Once my hunger hit though, I needed to satiate myself immediately. I am still this way, going for hours without eating but then when the time came, anything not nailed down better watch out!

After dining, I would find myself at my favorite dance venue, which was situated off the French Quarter and specialized in Brazilian cocktails and Salsa dancing, which was quite exotic, even for the eclectic neighborhood it was located in. People just danced their fucking asses off in this place; clothes came off as sweat poured off people's bodies, landing on a slick and sex-filled dance floor. The cleaning process for this place must have been beyond painful, so I had a feeling that they just never really cleaned it and prayed for the sun to go down in time for opening, so no one could see how truly gross it was in there.

Again, the city was showing me how incredibly alive it was through all the five senses. Music poured out of every opening it could, food and drink flowed 24/7, the smells of the city were a mix of sweet flowers, sweat, and garbage, and it was intoxicating. The textures were heavy like velvet saturated with debauchery and sex; the colors of the houses in the French Quarter were celebratory and elegant in a quirky way, mixing brightly colored window shutters amongst stately colored backgrounds. I was falling in love with the city, and it was gently guiding me towards how to do my job as the designer for this film, without me even knowing it. I was coming alive as a person and the arid desert of New Mexico was a vague memory to me now.

I started to organize inspirational field trips with the rest of the designers working on the film for them to experience what I was experiencing and to get them to come alive enough, so they could meet me in a similar dimension that would make this film look and feel spectacular. During certain days, we would get on our bikes, get stoned out of our minds and ride through Audubon Park, where we would study the local bird population, huge dripping trees, and the park's lagoons to get a feel for the organic textures that could somehow inspire us design-wise. By nightfall, we went crazy, tasting exotic foods like alligator meat *du jour* and drinking, dancing, and sexing ourselves silly, much like the vampires that were in the film we were working on.

My team was beginning to feel like a real crew, and along with this, came a kind of pride of belonging to the coolest club in town, we were exclusive, our very own VIP. Everything was a third; the price of anything we had ever bought anywhere else in the world, which simply made us grab anything we could find, whether we used it or not. At the same time, we were also genuinely producing fantastic work; hand-made flocked wallpapers, using materials such as magnolia leaves and Spanish moss we would steal off the huge trees when the parks would close; lush and huge furniture pieces that we built to mirror the luxurious looks of items that could never be found in today's modern world; food styling that would make your mouth water, and the flowers…oh the flowers…. I could even walk into the flower shop I had forcibly aligned myself with and get greeted with open arms, cheers, and smiles.

I had become a leader.

Suzi currently gets a little jealous when I bond with our production crew. We speak a language that comes to us in a private and raw way that others just don't understand. It's an innate and inquisitive love for beautiful things and for making things beautiful. It was an exclusive hunting trip that not a lot people wanted to go on, but our mouths watered at the thought of getting away to do so. Large dumpsters, dilapidated homes, and strange looking people were just a few items found in our encyclopedia of inspiration. The art of 'people watching' was probably one of the most important practices of what we do, even though I want nothing to really do with them aside from observing them. This is why I have always needed to be located in cities, big or small. I need to be able to perch somewhere; watch humans and formulate how to make them better and prettier.

When I got back to my apartment, which I hadn't been in for weeks, luckily, the cat was still alive, feasting upon a cockroach family, and he seemed just as happy as I was. On my fold-out dining table was a huge basket of fruit, chocolates, and some very high-price champagne. It was from the director of the film and my lady friends from Taos, congratulating me on a job well done.

This was the first time that I really noticed that a magic would happen when I made others proud of what I had done for them. I just simply wanted to feel that way all the time. It was an elevated surge of power and pleasure and I suppose that being a people pleaser and understanding the art of not giving up before you make everyone happy is a mixed blessing. The desire for everyone to not only like me but to also respect me, for what I did, became the reason I would wake up each morning. This has waned a bit, as I have gotten older, but back then, it was my 'crack' and my reason for existing.

Strangely enough, I never saw my buddies from Taos ever again, but my romance with the director was just getting started. Somehow, after the film was a huge success, his foggy breath seemed to disappear overnight, and he became an incredibly sexy man to me. I was attracted to my first powerful man; it's a disease I don't wish upon anybody.

We waited until the film was a wrap before going public, and there was the small matter of his wife and three small children to consider as well. The powerful men I have been with, have gained their power not only because they are intelligent and talented, but also because they don't consistently give a fuck about anybody else, so they are free to soar to the top, without any emotional cargo to weigh the trip down. Don't get me wrong, there are scenarios of these men smiling, while their children are born or as they stand flipping a fifty-dollar steak at a barbeque, but they are able to turn that smile off before it warms anyone else around them and fucks with their own self-preservation. I suppose some of this behavior has seeped into my ways of conducting myself but I am not proud of it nor has it brought me any kind of happiness.

I blamed our love affair on the city, you simply need to be in love in New Orleans, or at least, have consistent sweaty change-your-sheets-every-ten-minutes kind of sex. The way I saw it was that being in love there put you into a constant honeymoon. It just wasn't reality and let's face it that was my favorite place to exist. We were drunk all the time, surrounded by other drunk people, and we were all traveling within a cloud of a Xanadu type of existence. We knew everyone in town, the best chefs, bartenders, and even the strippers and hookers, who turned out to be some of my favorite people. We knew the high rolling lawyers, judges, cops, and politicians, too, we were huge fish in a tiny pond of corruption, and it felt fucking great. We found fabulous people that were living under the radar, there such as famous rock stars, authors, movie stars, you name it. What I truly loved about the town was that it attracted real artists, not just rich people that liked to have houses in towns like L.A. or Miami. These were all people that felt a kinship with the city, as it fed their creative souls. It was the real deal.

One of my major goals, though the thought of it was exhausting, was that I wanted Suzi to travel and see the rest of the world outside of Queens, Manhattan, and the Hampton's. Her world was so small that it almost made me panic and feel sad for her, even though she was perfectly happy not going anywhere. My personal travel experience came about in such an organic way; the work opportunities came to me and then I went to them. Currently, there was always so much minutia to deal with locally, it was hard to perceive that I could take her out on the road as much as I would like to. I had anxiety about the fact that she would marry a Queen's boy one day, probably a school teacher or something like that and she would never see the world, except, perhaps, on her honeymoon. I almost envisioned her as half a person and not a finished product because of this. She could easily experience the world through virtual reality and not even have to change out of her pajamas. The world was filled with youthful kinetic brains trapped within sloth-like bodies. When I did take her on the road, her world was filled with hotel business centers and luxurious beds that she didn't get the chance to sleep in, only on top of. It was a constant flurry of flight changes, lost luggage, and botched plans, while I flew private with the clients. Someone's gotta handle it all and she did.

One early morning, the director and I were drinking ourselves silly (shocker!), and we found ourselves in some crazy hole in the wall bar that had been open for 48 hours straight. In fact, the businessmen were just now coming in to collect their Bloody Marys in to-go cups for the rides into their offices. The bar was also a music venue, almost everywhere in New Orleans was, it's a city that was built on music, so every bar, no matter how small, had a designated area where one could dance the night away. We had just been hanging out and we heard someone throwing down incredible electric guitar runs in the adjacent room. I didn't think anything of it until I got up to pee and walked past the tiny dilapidated stage where the one and only BB King just happened to be playing by himself, eyes closed, with urine stained pants, stuck in a trance of musical magnificence. It was one of those private special moments that I had while living there that was so dream-like, I almost had to second guess myself as to whether it really happened or not. I came back to my bar stool and kept that one to myself, until now.

I wasn't used to not working, and after the film wrapped, I was getting more and more restless and bored by the minute. Doing nothing but fucking the director just wasn't cutting it; I had stayed in touch with my floral people at the St. Charles Avenue shop, and after the owner had begged me to stay on and work there permanently several times, I finally said yes, but it would be under my terms. I would be a specialty or guest designer there, heading up only their most expensive and exclusive projects, which, instantly, made me a target of hate for the rest of the crew. The chubby gay man couldn't even look at me without his blood pressure going so high you could see it creeping it into his fat face, and his short love affair with me during the movie had been lost forever. If he could wish me dead, he most certainly would have, *but* I was smart and manipulative. I would bring him in and ask for his design expertise or his opinion, even though I never ever needed it. It was just the right passive-aggressive thing for me to do to stop him from spitting in my coffee.

Suzi was often faced with dealing with the 'snippy gays' that worked as part of our design crew. She quickly learned that the 'snippier' they acted, the more miserable they probably were outside of our studio; most of them dealing with lover, money, family, and sore body issues like everybody else in the world. It also meant that they adored her, though she never felt that was possible. It was just their way of being affectionate. If they didn't like her, they wouldn't have expended the energy to be bitchy to her; it was a perverse compliment. A normal person probably would have backed off from their actions, but Suzi would purposefully act hardened to this kind of behavior and she often went head-to-head with the misery clan until she was the last one standing. Thus, she became one of the most highly respected millennial women I have ever had the pleasure of meeting. Personally, I was still scared shitless of the crew and had no problem letting her be the 'bad cop' on a consistent basis. Overall, it was hard for me to need people. I was the dream weaver, the conceptualizer, and art director of what we did, but it took a village to accomplish and that was something I needed to watch my back on for sure. These people owned me more than I wanted them to. I needed to delicately juggle their egos in a way that I was simultaneously always making it about me, without them knowing it.

There is a society of the super-rich in New Orleans that consists of old money, parents of celebrities, plantation peeps, the folks from Tulane University, and an insanely elegant and surprisingly large fabulous Jewish community. Southern Jews just have a certain charm about them. They are the perfect mix of 'Waspiness' and 'Jewish-ness' that makes them desirable to be around and they were able to fit in anywhere, even in the country clubs.

I spent most of my time making wealthy people's homes magnificent for the holidays, including Mardi Gras; when I would, somehow, make the color combination of green, purple, and gold look acceptable and glamorous. Even the local churches and cathedrals were vying for my design attention, and it was impressive how much money these institutions spent on Christmas and Easter. I guess those little donation baskets they passed around on Sunday mornings really did the trick.

The average height of a Christmas tree in a New Orleans church was about thirty feet, and everything had to have a touch of gold in it, no matter what. There was never just one of anything, there needed to be multiple Christmas trees in the Church, and they would all be huge. I would create winter wonderlands in the lobby of all the hotels in the French Quarter, and even though it would be quite warm outside, the interiors of these places would look like a frozen winter wonderland. I worked a lot faster than anyone down South, so I became a fast-moving train of a marvel to them. As I walked onto my design projects, I had a Technicolor Dream Coat vibe to me as I became a Goddess of the community.

I was continually entertained and inspired not only by the beauty of the city but more so by its inhabitants. Everyone had charisma, and not only because they were drunk most of the time but a lot of them were so politically incorrect, you couldn't imagine liking them but somehow, you just did. Everyone was special in their own way and they copped to it even if they were corrupt. In fact, my house was robbed several times, and little did I know that I should not have invited the local police inside because it was common that while you turned your back, they would potentially steal the rest from you or even try to kiss you when you faced forward again. I was lucky in so many ways because the city was also incredibly dangerous. When you have that many drunk people existing in one area, it's certainly not always peaceful. I look back and breathe a sigh of relief, knowing that I could have potentially turned the corner toward danger many times while I lived there, but my turns always turned into pirouettes, somehow.

I was very happy and feeling 99.9 percent satisfied with my life for once. I was having a great dysfunctional relationship, and my work world was keeping me at a glamorous level. One night, I was on a high, having had a couple of drinks on the way home, and as I neared my street, I spotted my van moving slowly down the street as if it was floating. It was so very strange. As I got closer, I noticed it was floating downstream in water, and next to it was a collection of dead bodies that had been freed from the above sea level graveyard nearby. The city was flooding. It wasn't the first time this would happen, and it certainly wouldn't be the last.

There is a real unhinging effect that occurs when someone, who lives their life in a shiny narcissistic bubble, finds themselves involuntarily in the middle of something horrible, without having any warning of its impending arrival and its lingering after-birth. My pretty world filled with lush environments and gorgeous things suddenly became smelly, soggy, moldy, and dark, and I was not one to embrace the situation and have a 'kumbaya' moment. I wanted to get the fuck out of there. I didn't want to deliver casseroles to the people cleaning up the city or help drain the water out of the flower shop floor or even call my parents to let them know I was okay. I just didn't want to deal with this ugly shit that imposed itself on my life and that was really fucking up my good time.

The director, however, did have a 'kumbaya' moment and he left immediately to try to get back into the good graces of his abandoned wife and children, after he scrawled a note with permanent marker on one of my apartment walls telling me to never ever try to find him or contact him again. I was tiring of him, anyway, but even so, I would have preferred to have been the one doing the dumping. The powerful man won out as he usually does.

The thing was that the people and the city had truly gotten under my skin, and for once, I didn't just get up and leave. I stayed and waited for the city to get pretty again, so I could re-emerge back into a consistent state of splendor. Also, I didn't have a car anymore.

I returned to the flower shop. The calls weren't coming in as urgently, requesting me to swoop in and transform people's lives, but it was a place to go where my status wasn't interrupted by the flood, and I needed the money. I was really eating humble pie those days. I even tried to waitress at a local steakhouse, which was a fucking disaster, yet I used my passive-aggressive skills by pre-warning my tables that I was a horrible waitress and not to expect good service. Then, in turn, they would laugh, feel badly for me, and tip the shit out of me. It worked for about a week, until I was let go with a giggle and a door hitting me in the ass. I also tried bartending, which I was particularly good at. I found that mixing drinks was much like solidifying a flower recipe for a potent outcome. The issue there, or issues, I should say, was that the bars never close and my hours would be continuous, eating up days into nights. I also found myself sleeping with a lot of my customers in the bathroom, which didn't go over so great with the female crowd. Southern chicks are seriously competitive. This was not my beautiful life, and I was starting to panic.

One day, I was working in the shop just before closing, nursing a glass of bourbon and subconsciously taking extra care by cleaning out my design area, knowing before I had admitted it to myself that I needed to move on from that place. I heard the door open at the front of the shop. Everyone had gone home and the place was dark, aside from the illumination coming in from St. Charles Avenue and the interior lights from the display coolers. In walked a short man with a silhouette that was somewhat theatrical and round. I could tell that he had an ascot on, even in the scorching weather, and for a moment, I was slightly afraid because he seemed to be a mystical character from a different land or at least a different city. He walked in with purpose and as he got closer, I saw that along with the ascot, he sported a beautifully tailored wine-colored velvet jacket, mastic grey, pinstriped trousers held up high on his expansive belly by leather and silk suspenders, which lay perfectly over a custom-made paisley shirt. He wore thick framed glasses and his shoes were almost clown-like, large and detailed in what looked like a perfect hybrid of a wing tip and a loafer. He walked straight up to me. He reeked of luxury and arrogance, and I adored him instantaneously. He was also quite sexless to me, I couldn't tell what his story was until he told me what he wanted. He spoke steadily and softly, and I was slightly lulled into a hypnotic state, as he informed me that he had just made the acquaintance of the most stunning woman he had ever met at a gentlemen's club in the Quarter. He wished for me to send Miss Allison Pussycat three thousand Red Roses by the time her shift finished in two hours.

This girl loves a challenge. My fingers get tingly, I often have to take a shit due to an excitable metabolism, and I just get a rush of joy at the thought of doing something that is next to impossible and having others marvel at me just for accomplishing the task at hand, but this was going to be beyond challenging. First, I had no roses in the shop, secondly, the only place I could potentially get them was in Baton Rouge, which was a 45-minute car ride away, and I didn't have a car. Also, my wholesale place usually closed by noon, since they opened at 3 o'clock every morning to receive and unpack the flowers coming in from all over the world. I had a sneaking suspicion that if I could pull this off, something great would come of it, so I simply had to make it happen. I turned to him and assured him that I would do it, but I added that I would need to be paid in cash and that this arrangement would forever stay just between the two of us. He readily agreed, and I ushered him out of the shop, so I could figure out what the fuck to do.

One of the guys, who ran the wholesale place in Baton Rouge, was this crazy Dutch dude who, somehow, landed smack dab in the middle of the deep-south selling flowers. He was a good-looking guy, and he and I had a very flirtatious yet respectful relationship. I, most likely, spent more money on flowers than any of his other clients, but I kept him at arms-length sexually because at this point, in my career, I didn't shit where I ate, yet. I called his house number several times; it was the only Van Vliet in the entire southern telephone book I can assure you. There was no answer, but I also got his home address and I knew this was my only shot. When I look back on what I did to make this task happen, I am overly thankful that I even lived to tell the tale of how I got shit done.

With no wheels, I first tried to borrow a car, but at that late hour, everyone I knew was already drunk and not answering their phones. I turned the shop upside down and was lucky enough to find the keys to the owner's excruciatingly old and beat up Bronco truck. Cars rusted very easily in the moist climate, and I specifically remember being able to see the highway move beneath me through a rusted-out hole in the floor of the truck. I made it about fifteen miles outside of town when it just stopped. I wasn't going to let this mess up my plan, so I simply stuck out my thumb. This was an incredibly stupid thing to do, but again, I lived to tell you about it so fuck it.

Suzi looked at me in absolute horror after ingesting this information; she was, in fact, listening to me quite closely. Not only was she even more embarrassed that she didn't know how to drive, but she couldn't seem to metabolize this level of stupidity. I reminded her that we didn't fucking have Uber back then. I also reminded her that I was privy to the knowledge that she needed to sleep with a rubber sheet on her bed and keep an extra set of jeans in her bag, since she always peed herself when she got drunk. I loved having that knowledge about her, and I brought it back around often. Even so, I could tell my story was making her 'hangry,' so I ordered her a glutinous snack and continued on.

I was picked up immediately by an El Camino, which was driven by a huge and handsome black man. He had a gorgeous blonde girl sitting next to him and there was room for me squeeze in right beside them, so I did just that. I told them about my situation, and they seemed extremely thrilled that I was including them in my challenge, as if they were driving around with nothing to do and looking for some excitement for the evening. The clock was ticking, and we needed to get going. We got to the Dutch guy's house and it was completely dark, which didn't surprise me. I figured he was sleeping or just not home. I went up to the porch and creeped around the perimeter of his house. Most of the houses down south were railroad style, long and skinny with rooms that occurred in succession of each other; living room, then onto the dining area, kitchen, bathrooms, and then bedrooms in the back. There was simply no one home. I jiggled all the windows, and nothing budged, and I wasn't even sure why I wanted to get inside, but perhaps, there was some sort of magic clue in there that could help me unravel my situation.

The El Camino was humming in the driveway like a purring panther, and as a silly last-ditch effort to get in, I tried the front door and surprisingly it was unlocked.

I called out Van Vliet's name several times with no response, but I saw a sliver of light coming from beneath one of the bedroom doors. I knocked lightly a few times before trying the door, which was locked and incredibly confusing at the time. I guess he allowed himself only one safe place at a time. I thought I heard some noise coming from behind the door, but I got one of those bodily shivers that told me not to investigate further; to protect myself from a vision that I could potentially never recover from.

I continued to look around the house and came upon several match-books that had the name of a local bar on them. I figured that he was probably there, so I quickly exited the house, and was happy to see that my new road buddies were patiently waiting to take me to my next location. They had also smoked a huge monster of a joint while I was inside judging by its remnants in the ash tray, so things were officially heating up and about to get weirder.

We found our way to the bar, and there is no other way to say it, but judging by the demographic in there, the big black man that was driving me around was certainly not welcome inside, so the girl and I took a gander on our own. We found my Dutch friend completely passed out on top of one of the billiard tables, pockets turned inside out, while his head rested comfortably on a semi-dried pile of his own vomit. He was of no use to me and though I was feeling very sober and focused, it didn't stop the girl and I from downing a few shots of bourbon, which would give us the energy to get to the next level of solving my problem. I was feeling a bit down about the whole thing, but I simply could not fail. The plus side was that I had an impromptu team with me in the form of these two misfits, who just wanted to be a part of it all for no apparent reason. We parked by the river and talked about next steps which included breaking into the wholesale place, but I knew for a fact that the place was heavily guarded by dogs and there was no human security guard whom I could bribe to let me inside. I didn't want to mess up my relationship with the wholesaler, knowing that I would need them for other projects, so I was kind of at a dead-end with what to do next. The dude driving the El Camino (I never did get his name) said that some his 'people' owned a funeral home in the area, and perhaps we could go there, since there were always flowers lying around. We needed to make a stop first to his cousin's house, which was close by, so that we could collect the keys. I felt elated that we were making some progress, but the clock just kept ticking quicker than usual it seemed.

We arrived at his cousin's house, which was populated by an enormous amount of people, either dancing, smoking, drinking, laughing, or play fighting. It was like a joyous prison yard. The girl and I were suddenly very white, but that wasn't what scared us. It was the fact that there were guns, just lying all around the place; on the coffee table, in between the couch cushions, and even on the kitchen table next to a hearty spread of fried chicken, collard greens, and several bottles of bourbon. I wouldn't have been surprised if there was a gun in the soap dish in the shower. There were babies crawling all over the place amongst the guns, too. I had arrived at a kind of environment I had never been in before. The other white girl seemed to be having a blast. I figured out later that she was Swedish and the Swedes are up for anything. It made me feel better that she was calm about everything, even though she shouldn't have been. Things got a bit blurry after that. I found myself sitting on a large lap of someone in a rocking chair on the porch, smoking a blunt I needed to use two hands for, and I had certainly kicked back some of that bourbon as well. It truly was the best way to deal with the situation I was in.

Suzi looked at me as if I was dirty. I was scared of letting her into some of my past, simply because she was so incredibly sheltered, I didn't want her to become wary of me. It's hard to not hold a memory grudge at times. I get it. She was conjuring up her own gritty image of what was happening, and I knew she just wanted to douse herself in hand-sanitizer and get a blow-out with two shampoos immediately. She needed to know these things, simply because it would be the evidence, in order to solve the mystery of who I truly was. She already knew the shiny candy external shell of me, but the only place to go now was to the gooey chocolate center of it all.

The next thing I remember was feeling the warm and heavy breeze on my face (I had switched to sitting in the back open part of the El Camino), and the stars were egging me on to get these flowers to this fucking stripper on time. We arrived at the funeral home, which was obviously quiet but not in the creepy way I had expected. The juxtaposition of how clean it was compared to where we just came from was oddly cleansing for my soul and I became clear and focused again. We visited each room that branched off from the massive entryway vestibule. The entire business ran out of a gorgeous and huge Victorian-style house, where you could feel literally right at home while visiting your dead loved ones. It was well done and sadly flowerless. We even went out to the dumpster and still there were no flowers to be found. Apparently, they had already been donated to the local church or retirement homes. I was feeling depleted and simultaneously asking myself why I even cared about getting this shit done for this sexless stranger, who had walked into my world and fucked it up. The problem was that I did care, and I truly felt there was going to be a worthy prize waiting for me if I achieved the goal. This stubborn gene that wanted to see only certain things through was what would make me incredibly successful in one way only, but I suppose that's better than no way at all.

The man and the girl hung their heads low, sad they had disappointed me, and they suggested we go back to the city and get me even more loaded and show me a great time for the rest of the night. I figured what the hell; at least, I made some new friends. I was frustrated, and I just couldn't let go, but I got back into the car with them, hoping that something genius would pop into my brain on the ride home. We still had about forty minutes to either go big or go bust at this point.

We were riding down the highway, and I noticed that on the median walking, in the pitch dark, were small ethnic men carrying buckets of red roses to sell to men on dates with women they wanted to impress. I had seen these men before, usually waiting outside expensive restaurants. As a couple would exit the place and experience that awkward "Am I going to go home with you?" kind of a moment, *BAM*! This little man would give the rich guy the power with one simple rose to convince his lady friend to let him do her doggy style that night. We had found the mother land of red roses, praise GOD!

The car came to a skid and a halt, and with one glance at my new huge black man friend behind the wheel, the little ethnic men started sprinting down the highway, scared out of their minds. My friend tried to placate them, but they all just dropped their buckets and got the fuck out of Dodge, leaving a magnificent red velvety path down the highway for us to collect. It must have been quite a sight—the three of us running all over the highway, ducking in and out of drunkenly driven cars to collect every one of those roses. There weren't three-thousand roses, but I knew I could make it work by using smoke and mirrors in the form of some cut Magnolia that was available to me pretty much everywhere. I would grab an almost-too-small vase from the shop to enhance the bouquet and make it look huge. I would design it in a pave style, which meant that the flowers would be designed bunched together tightly and there would be no way to count them without taking them all out and ruining the bouquet. I windsurfed in the back of the El Camino, standing tall, and creating bunches of the roses in my hands, held together by mine and the other white girl's hair ties, so that I could literally slam them into the vase, pre-arranged and perfect. I did just that, and we got to the strip club just in the nick of time. The stranger hadn't provided me with his name nor a gift card to put with the roses, so I just ran into the parking lot of the club and started yelling out for Allison Pussycat. After what seemed like an eternity, an extremely high-heeled shoe peeked out of the back door to the club, connected to an impossibly long leg, connected to tight hips, a teeny tiny waist, huge tits, a long and graceful neck, a gorgeous face, and a silky mane of hair that even a horse would be jealous of. Allison Pussycat was a vision alright, and whether she was actually male or female, just didn't matter here. I completely understood why the quirky stranger needed to get those roses to her tonight, because I was sure that she would be receiving thousands more before the sun came up. She flashed me a huge smile, and I fell in love, not only with her but with the whole idea of falling in love. The urgency and bold declaration of it all was just thrilling to me. Even my partners in crime for the evening got teary-eyed when I finally handed off that bouquet. I would hand off thousands of bouquets to beautiful brides in years to come, but Allison Pussycat was the OG of them all.

I was on a bit of a high for a few days after my floral adventure, feeling like a botanical Indiana Jones of sorts, and I was equally thrilled with the wad of cash I had hidden underneath my mattress, which was stolen out of my house several days later, without me even knowing it, most likely by some guy I had brought home one night after partying.

What really blew Suzi's mind about this particular tale of mine was the physicality of it all. Young people are just simply stagnant these days. They will conjure up the energy to take a spin class but after that, it's all sitting on their asses or at the most. walking over to an Uber, and if it doesn't stop exactly in front of them, they will give the driver a shitty rating. There are times when Suzi and I will be sitting in our office working and a light-bulb will go out and I see her looking on her phone to see if there is an app that could change it for us, rather than considering climbing on a ladder to fix the problem, almost as if the act of unscrewing and screwing is just too fucking much. Don't get me wrong, Suzi is not a lazy person by any means whatsoever. Simply put, her generation can make the world spin with the push of a button and without having to leave the house for days at a time. As for me, I can't even consider a task without it having a physical element to it. My whole body needs to be in motion in order for my brain to work, much like a windmill needing wind in order to operate effectively. The adrenaline and endorphins that my body creates is a gooey, milky-way type of magic potion that spills into my universe and makes my world go 'round, thus creating a gravity that pulls other planets into my hemisphere. Suzi gets inspired by my energy, but it would never be something she would want for herself, and she is most certainly exhausted after every day she spends with me. My clients enjoy the same sensation, our meetings mirroring a marathon sex session, leaving them deliciously depleted and most definitely coming back for more.

I had resumed my normalcy and was working with one of my clients on re-doing their entire home, all just for a two-hour cocktail party. I loved these ridiculous projects that were brainstormed in order simply to kill time and money. I was outside of their home when I noticed a stretch limousine following me, creeping along Royal Street. It was a cool car. It looked a little gangster-like, with its bright gold rims and deep burgundy fins that gave it a dramatic effect, kind of like the car had put on a smoking jacket. It wasn't ominous really, just noticeable, even though it was trying not to be. The car finally came right up next to me. The day-time hookers were all craning their necks out of their voyeur windows to get a peek at who this money man could possibly be. At first, I thought it was a pimp of sorts. I have always respected pimps, with their ease, in which, they expressed their original and splashy sense of style and their raw business instincts and all, but I must admit I was slightly put off and feeling claustrophobic as this car infringed further into my personal space. A tinted window cracked open in the back and I saw a man's well-manicured hand, complete with a large pinky ring, and a long brown cigarette in a gold custom holder resting between his thumb and forefinger. The pinky ring had a cool opalescent peacock emblem on it, and I remember really wanting it for my own. I looked past the hand and saw a woman's long silky legs and bare feet sitting across the back seat. I couldn't see her face, but I instantly recognized that it was Miss Allison Pussycat, so I could readily assume that the man with her was the quirky stranger who sent me on my floral adventure. His smiling face suddenly filled the window like a weird child looking out of a huge building. He said he just wanted to thank me in person for finishing the arduous task he had sent me out to do, and to ask me if I would

74

be interested in becoming the next events director for his well-known property in New York, otherwise known as the Jewel of Central Park.

I was going back home.

It didn't take me long to quit my 'kinda sorta' job and pack up my shit from the apartment, the missing cash didn't even faze me. I was moving onward and upward! I still didn't have a car, but it didn't matter because we were flying private. The entire process took six hours. I hadn't even called my parents to let them know I would be arriving, and I had nowhere to stay, but I was fucking thrilled at the thought of being catapulted back into glamour. The man said that he would put me up at a hotel close to the venue while I got situated, and later that day, Miss Allison Pussycat would take me shopping to ensure that I had sexy yet professional attire in time to start my new job, complete with a grown-up haircut, polished nails, and a proper overall grooming session.

I was finding that I was a chameleon of sorts, slipping in and out of scenarios and personality changes with the ease of a well-oiled bicycle chain. I could leave places, friends, personal belongings behind, and go become a new person every few hours. I was like the girl who fell to earth. Within 48 hours, I was living in a five-story walk up in Brooklyn Heights, a total of 250 square feet that had a little bachelor kitchen, which I never ever used and a working fire-place, along with a futon thingy that acted as a bed and a couch. I was about to lead a life filled with 'fabulous.'

Having never been out of Queens for more than a week at a time and only for our jobs away or for an occasional Bachelorette party, I could see that my constant, erratic, and nomadic way of life made Suzi nervous. She was a mix of "in awe" with me and "wary of me," all at once, much like how one regards a cancer survivor. She was also intrigued by how little my parents knew about what I was doing in my life, especially since she spoke to her mom several times a day and was raised in a home where there was always a room waiting for an elderly relative welcome to stay in, when they could no longer take care of themselves. This was simply not done in my world, where as folks grew older, they just kept marrying new people that would take care of them or they would just slowly evaporate on their own, within the comfort of their own homes and then we would either go to the funeral or not if our schedules didn't allow. Don't get me wrong, I come from an incredibly loving tribe, just different and deliciously narcissistic.

Suzi and I were about to travel for one of my speaking engagements and she made sure that everything was in pristine condition, even though travel made her nervous. I think she kept herself ridiculously busy in order to fight the anxiety monster and it greatly benefitted me. The luggage she choreographed for me was more intricate than a CAD, but I respected the energy it took to do so.

The dog-sitter had been arranged, along with several state-of-the-art cameras I could watch my pup on at any time of the day from any angle of my apartment. Suzi had also made sure that these cameras were artfully camouflaged. I could only imagine the look on the guy's face, who installed them, when she insisted on providing him with specific paint colors, so they would blend into my custom painted walls.

My schedule was tattooed into every database on all of my devices, so I could see it every minute from everywhere and she set the alarm notifications, so that they would go 'dim' during most of my desired nap times. My dietary requirements were pre-known pretty much in every deli from the moment we left my apartment, onboard the flight, the car from the airport, and of course, in the restaurants, hotels, or private apartments we were staying at. I had every form of CBD known to the pharmaceutical industry, all lined up in my pill box, which was arranged not only by day but by the hour. She created several different mood music playlists for me as well, in case I needed calming on the plane or an adrenaline rush for the gym, if I chose to workout upon landing. I had an amazing selection of movies and 'binge worthy' shows all downloaded and ready to play, and she even created a watch-list of documentaries, in case I was feeling grown up. I had enough books on tape and podcasts to last me a lifetime and many of which, I would probably never listen to, but Suzi was smart; she wanted to be sure that I never had to ask for anything. She would much rather be armed with an abundance of filled requests, rather than fall short and none of this was even in her job description. This was her brilliance really, and this aspect of her personality would be the key to her success in my industry and in sustaining her place by my side. She was basically an entire Downton Abbey staff existing within one tiny being.

She made hundreds of reservations in restaurants, not only in town but in the outer lying areas as well, just in case I was feeling in need of an adventure or was bored with the scenery. The work part of the trip was always flawless as well. Truthfully, Suzi was an incredible producer during her most fear-provoking times. She went into this hypnotic rhythm that never broke and stayed consistent our entire time away. My presentations were rehearsed, re-written, and audience tested. In fact, she screened the audience as well. Not just anyone could buy a thousand-dollar ticket to listen to the inside scoop on how to become the world's next party guru. Suzi made sure the huge group had several categories; young girls, of course, young gay guys, duh, media, 'fashion forwards' or influencers, spiritual types, chefs, rock stars, and even some neutral political types, in case I wanted to run for office someday or at least, host a talk show. The final and smallest group was made up of men/boys I would potentially want to sleep with. Suzi was particularly good at making these choices, which caused me to revere her quite highly. She offered up a broad range of fellas, some bordering on the cusp of inappropriate, but this was her expression of 'letting loose' while still getting the job done. Brava!

I was always warmed by finding her little pale face in the audience, beaming with pride at her boss up on stage entertaining an adoring audience. I could see the slight wrinkle in her brow, as she would remember all the shit that she still had to do before I got off stage. The trips were such a mixed bag for her, and I realized that as soon as we landed somewhere, she would have to start planning the journey back. We could have easily taken our exploits from the road and turned them into a show, 'The Millennial and the Menopausal.' I can see the first episode now. Today, on The Millennial and the Menopausal, Millennial asks what it means to be served with papers, while Menopausal still struggles to use the search feature on her email inbox. Stay tuned...

Chapter Five

"Don't you worry your pretty little mind; people throw rocks at things that shine."

-Taylor Swift

My first day of work back in New York was surreal. It was also winter, so I was having major withdrawal from the southern climate and the lack of light was bringing me down. I tried to concentrate on the electric excitement of the city, while not giving in to sudden mover's remorse.

I walked in the back entrance that I had gone through with my last client before leaving town, and nothing had changed a bit. The men still leered at me, whispering bad Spanish sayings under their breath as I walked past them, but something was happening to me. I felt invincible, like an awesome destiny awaited me, and it could not be denied. This feeling lasted for a cool ten minutes until I walked into my office. The space was an eight-foot box of a room, including a rusted-out flower cooler that inhabited the corner of the space, much like the focal point of a depressing murder scene. I also noticed that I would be sharing the room with an assistant whom I had not yet met, but who I knew already hated me, simply because they had worked there for the past seventeen years and had clearly not been offered the position that I was waltzing in and taking from them. I could see his small and feeble setup on the linoleum counter that graced the entire perimeter of the room for us to create floral masterpieces on day after day. I once calculated that we would produce over eighteen parties a week out of that shit-hole.

A nervous energy walked into the room in the shape of a young man, and the misery just wafted around him like a polluted halo. He looked at me sideways and boy, oh, boy could I feel him gritting his teeth with hate and contempt for me, so I walked up to him and hugged him, fuck it. He was shocked at my display of affection for him and he froze for a moment and then after what seemed like forever, his little sausage fingers gripped the curves of my back and he started to weep. Poor kid was actually a lot older than me.

The day was filled with men in bad suits stopping by to visit the little room and introduce themselves to me and to give me the lay of the land. These guys were practically dancing a celebratory jig at the notion of having a female in the trenches with them in this insanely claustrophobic den of misfits. Then came the introductions throughout the entire venue; the general manager, the lead captain, the wait staff, the hosts, the rest of the sales team, the controllers (money guys), the cleaning crews, the maintenance people, the groundskeepers, the valet parkers and most importantly, the pastry chef, who was, lo and behold, a woman! She was like a breath of fresh air. Her pastry kitchen was situated at the highest point in the building, and the sun shone through some skylights that were like a gift from the heavens in such a place. I would take three steps at a time to go and visit with her every afternoon, just to sit and talk with her. while we sipped Baileys and coffee and she made me taste every treat she would concoct to keep the bosses in a constant state of mouth-watering orgasmic anticipation. She wasn't as pretty as I was, but she had the men in that place under her spell like a vampire temptress, because of her treats and all of the deliciousness they had to offer. She was Midwestern, which is always a good thing. Midwestern people will do whatever the fuck you want them to, yet they are not stupid, whatsoever. They just like to keep the peace and you can respect them at the same time. To me, they are the perfect kind of friend. We became close and allied with each other, a sisterhood of sorts, which I never really had in my life before meeting her.

I marvel at Suzi's gaggle of girlfriends. There is always catty displays of jealousy or overall moodiness, along with passive-aggressive posts on Instagram for some ridiculous reason or another, but nothing is never bad enough that a glass of *rosé* couldn't fix it all back to love, bubbles, and rainbow emojis within moments. If a guy ever fucked any of them over, the 'girl posse' would cash in their air miles, or beg, borrow, and steal to be by their friend's side, who probably was already going on a new date plucked from Tinder and had gotten over the heart-break by the time they got there. Then they would just make the best of it, blow some coke, order an outfit online, and get a blow out before hitting the night.

My relationships with women on the whole aren't many, and they are more one-on-one in practice. I always hated the way some women would look me up and down, before they went in for a hug or reciprocated a heart-felt smile. We girls are placed in precarious positions; having to fight for what's our right when we come out into the world as babies. I remember my mother being angry yet proud of the day traffic started stopping for me and not for her as much. I learned early on that I would do everything humanly, surgically, and medicinally possible to look gorgeous but that I needed to offer something besides all of that to sustain people's interest in me and stay relevant in this crazy world by mainly being the best at what I do. Young women, today, seem to be a bit more empowered. In fact, Suzi and I, both, encounter lots of young brides that by 'Kardashian standards' aren't that gorgeous, but they come in to see us with incredibly handsome and successful men, absolutely blinded by them in terms of beauty and overall awe and respect and it's pretty inspiring. These young women are smart, fearless, and imbued with the self-knowledge that no matter what, they are fucking right about everything. This makes them difficult clients for sure, but inside of me, I am saying a quiet 'Amen, sister.'

The GM at my new job was a total prick, and I later came to discover that any GM, anywhere, is a prick. I think it's a job requirement of sorts. He walked around like he was next in line for the crown and as if something very unpleasant was stuck inside the seat of his high seamed pinstriped suit. His jaw was set tight like a perfect preppy *wasp* of a man who most likely had a gold chain on, underneath his wife-beater tank-top, which, undoubtedly, had yellow stains in the armpits. These guys all had veneers of complete power and grace, but if you caught them off guard, you would see a rusted out El Camino of a man who quickly morphed into a withering little boy, who was always scared shitless of losing his job and getting dealt out of the game.

Suzi became very good at manipulating this type of animal and she was extremely proud of herself when she got a smile and a 'Thank You' out of these guys after initially being met with an extremely cold and gruff response. I didn't want to break her spirit by letting her know that they were just living out their sexual fantasies by being nice to her and thinking about what she could potentially reward them with. It got them through their days; a smile from pretty young girl.

My job was going fine. There were many obligations that were not disclosed to me during the hiring process, such as making sure that the entire restaurant had fresh flowers every day before opening, which meant that we would need to be in at 4 a.m. in order to receive the flowers and cut and design them in time for a 7 a.m. roll call for the wait staff, which was really fucking annoying, particularly because I often wouldn't get home until a few hours before having to go back in again, and the job was simply too big to pawn off onto my assistant for him to do solo. Then, there were the holidays, which were bigger than the parting of the Red Sea in this fucking place, so on top of all the parties we were producing, we would also have to deck the fucking halls to the nth degree with layers and layers of decor that people would come from all over the world to see, as we cursed and spat on it as we installed it.

There were fun perks to being there, too, such as walking into the main dining area during a busy lunch time and seeing all my favorite movie stars and musicians. The place was most certainly a go-to joint and somewhere that people wanted to be seen at, so there was a certain NY fun drama to it that I had missed during my time out West and in the South. One time, my assistant and I went out to the dining room to check on the planters that graced the entire perimeter of the room to make sure they were all alive and without ugly leaves etc., and a very small woman came up to me. She was extremely petite and was dressed head to toe in winter gear, including a hat and sunglasses, so I simply had no idea who she was. I noticed that my assistant was doing his nervous jig and sweating profusely, so I was aware that we were conversing with someone very important, but I just couldn't place the voice. I answered her questions about the plants with authority and kindness, and she rewarded me with two tickets to see her live at her concert later that week, which she had hand-delivered to my shitty little office. She was a pop-star goddess dressed in normal garb, who knew? During that era, it was normal to float amongst great celebrities. There wasn't this blockage of sorts like there is now. You could speak with them and advise them within your field of expertise, without having to wait for hours to see if you were popular enough on social media to be let into their world. It was much more organic back then.

I became the darling of the venue for sure. I had graced my ways with everyone that worked the 'innards' of the property, all the way to outer guests, who were our regulars and needy for my attention. I had a part-time boyfriend who I met in some random bar that was populated by normal people my age. He was proud enough of me to bring his parents by to see me in my glory, every time they were in town. He was also angry enough to break up with me again and again, simply because I was never around or available to hang out with him, and when I did, I usually just wanted to fuck, eat, sleep, smoke pot, and watch TV. I was like this bright and shiny novelty that people were eager to show off to the outside world, but when they got me home for an extended time, they would have just as well pitched me into the refuse out of boredom and disappointment.

My existence, as an outsider, grew even more pronounced amongst my peers, but I was also morphing into a different society that was so exclusive they had no choice but to respect it. Either way, it was still proving to be a lonely place for me. I also saw the graveyard effect it had on the people that worked in places like this for too long. They got stuck in the eye of a storm or a type of quicksand, filled with days that blended into each other, along with the addition of an enormous amount of alcohol and other stuff intake, and just an overall feeling of regret about everything for no given reason. Even a simple task, such as picking up dry cleaning in the daylight made me feel so strange, as if I were trespassing on a sidewalk that belonged to everybody else but me. I was feeling segregated in such a severe way that I was finding the simple public tasks impossible to achieve, like going to the post office or the supermarket. I was becoming agoraphobic, yet I could obtain an incredibly gregarious level of engagement at my job. I had become an official extroverted-introvert; I was doing my best making peace with it. Perversely enough, I was really beginning to relate to those vampire characters from the movie I worked on in New Orleans. I was joining an underground species of sorts, and once again, I was starting to get antsy and a thirst for new blood for fear that I would be cemented in this world forever. I absolutely couldn't quit my job just yet. My mother would most likely never speak to me again, and I instinctively knew that I had to have some sort of a plan in place before doing so. Instead, I did what I was supposed to do when I didn't know what to do; nothing.

I was naturally forming some incredible relationships through work, mainly with the flower market vendors, since I was ordering over a million bucks worth of stems a week during the busy seasons. I would often accompany the Dutch flower guys to the strip clubs after their shifts were over. This was in the middle of the day, since they started their shifts at 3 a.m. after the flowers arrived from the local airports. They would get good and toasty by 4 p.m., home by 5 p.m., then on to a very fast sex session with whomever they were living (or themselves). Then it was off to bed for those few precious hours of sleep, before having to do it all over again. I got to know the other event vendors that we sub-contracted work out to, such as specialty lighting, staging, and sound dudes, tent contractors, specialty dance flooring, fancy table linens, extra lounge furniture, and of course, the huge entertainment groups; bands, DJs, dancers, you name it. These people opened my world a bit, but we were all part of the same underground clan. Everyone was so miserable and jaded. It would have affected me if I hadn't been as young as I was. I, somehow, held myself in a much higher regard than most and considered myself the golden child of the misfits, who would, somehow, separate herself from the rest and fly well above their stormy clouds one day very soon. I was collecting a lot of information, without even knowing it. I had a rolodex filled with vendors and clients, and I could even get you a sex worker of your desired flavor at any time of any day. Little did I know that I was, in fact, building the foundation of my next career.

That old feeling was starting to kick up in the pit of my stomach; resembling a restless-ness and desire to move onward and upward again and it just wasn't going away. Some would label this characteristic as someone who is successful, but when you are living it, you feel like a hammock with no trees to tie onto. Having never taken a vacation ever, I decided to go ahead and take advantage of my work contract and get the fuck out of Dodge for a few days to contemplate my next move while getting a tan. I hadn't been on a non-work trip since prep school, and I had never gone away on my own dime. So, frankly, I didn't know where to go that I could afford and not feel terribly disappointed, because of my past lavish and luxurious experiences while traveling with rich clients. I, somehow, landed on Mexico after speaking to some of the guys in the kitchen about it. They basically said that if I stayed away from Mexico City, I should be fine. I had also read about where my famous pop-star client had gone on her honeymoon, and I found lodging there, very different from hers, of course, on La Isla De Mujeres. It was such a spectacular place I believe she even wrote a number one hit about it. Vacation was, and turns out, would always be, quite boring for me, uneventful aside from fucking strange guys, drinking a lot, and getting really tan. I mean, I could do that at home. After just a few days, as the weather was taking a turn for the worse, I was thankful to get a work emergency call. The details could not be disclosed over the phone, which meant it was a mega-event, and there was nothing more exciting than that according to me.

I boarded the plane and I instantly had a bad feeling that I just couldn't put my finger on. I took my seat next to a clean and classy middle-aged couple who seemed mellow and nice. The rock on her finger was bigger than my carry-on bag, so I felt that my seat was situated perfectly for the trip. I was anxious to get back and start work on the supposed mega-party. Perhaps, it was just what the doctor ordered to keep me enthralled with my job.

Suddenly, the plane plummeted at least ten thousand feet in a downward spiral. It was fucking terrifying, and frankly, I had never experienced such a tragic sensation. A feeling of doom came over me, and at first, I thought that I was being punished just for being me. I felt the lady next to me grab my hand as I slipped my way into darkness… I passed out through three hours of altitude struggle, falling items everywhere, the dropping of the oxygen masks into the cabin, screaming passengers, and finally, a brutal emergency landing somewhere in Florida. I awoke to find I had peed my pants and developed a severe fear of flying. (It would later be cured by some savant hypnotherapist I went to for several sessions at a thousand bucks a pop, but it was well worth it since I wasn't flying only private just yet.) Some people would say that they found a new lease on life after an experience like that, but I kind of went to numb to everything around me. Frankly, all I cared about was the big event I was going to produce, which was pretty telling about where my focus would forever be in my life. I knew then that I would never have the attention span to have children or a needy husband. I had figured out that my capacity could only handle a huge career and maybe, a puppy or two.

For the most part, every client that threw an event at the Jewel of Central Park had to use me to produce their event, except for a select few that would provide a buy-out fee, so they could bring in other vendors, such as designers or celebrity chefs. This way, the restaurant still made money off you, whether or not we actually did the work. You can imagine my devastation to arrive home after the horrific plane ride to find out that the event I came back for belonged to someone else, and I just needed to be there to watch another person create the magic that should have belonged to me. I was to act as a liaison of sorts and take care of his needs. What a blow.

I will never forget how it felt to loan the space out to another event professional, who was producing one of the largest non-profit galas known to mankind. Non-profits were incredibly interesting because their sole purpose was to earn money for a cause of some sort, such as cancer research or animals that got left in dumpsters. Therefore, the people that sat on their boards were mainly wealthy housewives who had stopped their careers to have children and then woke up really bored one day after the kids had a gazillion activities to go to and no longer required any attention from anyone aside from their nanny and a driver to get them to and from all those activities. The mommies would, then, hope to become part of something wonderful, so they could both feel great about themselves, less ridiculously rich, while passing enough hours in the day, so they could take their minds off starving themselves to look gorgeous and searching for hubby number two or three. It was a win-win situation. I had had to pitch to these types of committees before on smaller non-profit projects, and it was tough as hell. Every rich mommy had something to say and their opinions clashed, no matter what, as if it was some fun sport they got addicted to and could only play the game one way. They also demanded the type of attention that went way beyond a creative service, which resembled a live-in servant's job. I would present ideas to them, only to have to do it all over again with their best 'artistic' friend in tow, then he/she would piss all over my concepts to secure the veil of expertise they had placed over their rich friend, and continue the reign of power over her long enough to get into her will as a beneficiary of some sort. This was always a lose-lose situation for me. The only saving grace was that we would usually take up so much time going back and forth that we would simply have to go with my initial ideas, because we had, in fact, run out of time. My career, when it came to these types of events, resembled hitting a *piñata* a gazillion times without ever making it to the candy part, but I suppose that's what kept me engaged. It never lacked the excitement of a challenge, even if it was brutally annoying overall.

This was Suzi's least favorite type of client. Not only did she want to protect me from these 'she-wolves,' she just didn't understand what, why, and where these events came from. They just didn't compute in her brain and it was hard for her to sit with that and be productive, so I often gave her a 'time-out' during these types of projects and brought along another team member to endure all the torture and who I knew would quit shortly after the process had begun. The other members of our team who added up to fifty people at least, were ghosts to Suzi. Even though they answered mainly to her before they got to me, she barely knew their names and she kept them at a very low level of importance, just to keep them treading in a shallow pool. I was often surprised at how territorial she was of me and I felt guilty about taking up so much of her brain space at times. I knew there would come a day when she would put her energies into a man and potentially a child or at least a puppy, but it just felt like that scenario existed on another planet for now or at least, it felt that way.

I had heard of this outsider guy who was producing the event on my turf around town, and to me, he was an intruder who would be spear heading what should have been my event. Seeing him for the first time will forever be remembered as a major transitional moment for me, and I'll tell you why.

The event itself was only A-listers, raising money for God knows what, I never even knew, but this was the event of all events in NY at the time. They even had to build an extra space using a large tent that was adjacent to the exterior garden, since the guest list was busting at the seams. Moving the massive animal topiaries was as devastating as a poaching expedition. They were stashed in their own custom-built storage cage, creating their own Central Park Zoo of sorts, but it was just so very sacrilegious to move them, and I am sure they paid the owner an insane fee to do so. One thing I knew was that I was sure as fuck not going to be held responsible for putting them back into their 'wild' post-event. The pre-work was the usual buzz amongst the property; drilling noises, a huge population of men, which me and the pastry chef had no issue with, as we watched butt-crack after butt-crack, while she lured them in with sweet treats she would concoct daily just for their pleasure. Strangely enough, it turned out to be almost a relief to watch a huge event getting set up and having no responsibility for it, aside from marveling at the sheer production value of it and seeing what levels could be reached within my industry. The pre-production went on for about a week, and then it came time to make the place look pretty and cover all the mechanics. I remember hearing a loud car arrive at the service entrance, which often resembled a third world country fresh off a war, and in came a shiny, dark muscle car, super-imposing itself on its normally drab existence. The car was so powerful and mean-looking and uber-sexy as well. The windows were tinted, and the rims were so shiny that every ray of the sun was captured in their reflective surfaces. The car drove right up to the loading dock, where there was usually a waiting time of an hour per truck to make deliveries to the restaurant, but this vehicle just took its place front and center. The car idled for a moment, resembling a purring tiger. I could hear loud disco music from its interior, and I could have sworn I saw smoke seeping out from every orifice of the car, even though the windows were closed, making the car look like one giant and magnificent bong or in current times, a vape.

Slowly, the driver's side door opened, and a foot was visible encased in a motorcycle boot of sorts but a gorgeous and expensive one, not like the kind you get on 8th Street near NYU for fifty bucks. It was a large foot, which caused me and the pastry chef to giggle from our hiding spot behind the dumpsters. We were sitting there so we could observe the whole visual experience. We were also stoned out of our minds, hence the giggles. Resting on the shoe was the cuff of a leather pant leg, which you could tell was hand-stitched and most definitely Italian, and as the man who wore them showed himself in full, you just couldn't help but notice how well they hugged his crotch and cradled his perfect ass. He was a vision. He looked like a perfectly ripened movie star, his eyes were clear and glassy, all at once, like a glass that just came out of a hot dishwasher, mainly because of the smoking, but they looked right through you like Superman could, and his hair was just perfect the way it rested along his thick hairline, and even the stray pieces sang to you as they tickled his eyebrows. He was fucking gorgeous and mean and sexy looking and, unbeknownst to me, he was the king of the gay wolves. I wanted to be exactly like him. I also hated and feared him all at once, knowing that he was the one to beat in my career, the pinnacle that was looking like an impossible goal to achieve.

I watched people scurry around like cockroaches in the light every time he walked into a room. He was revered and respected, and everyone wanted to be their best when he appeared. I sat back and continued to watch him transform the space with his team, who stood by him with pride in the same fashion as he held himself. Though they were not as shiny and bright as he was, they commanded the room and wore gorgeous clothes, too. They were his army of impeccable soldiers, the most sought-after event producers in the world, and they knew it. Much like the country club ladies used to clamor for my attention, this guy had people like presidents, princesses, rock-stars, and movie stars in the palm of his hand, and they were all waiting for a simple sign of when he would be ready to share his magnificence with them. He wasn't moody per se but more aloof, as if he was existing on a much higher plane than all of us mere mortals, or was just really stoned or both. He completely ignored me, even though he was technically crashing my house. He looked past me, not even through me, which would have at least engaged our sensibilities together, but it was a no go. From what I could tell, he was already bored with the event he was producing and was most likely thinking about the next one or what he was going to wear tomorrow. Either way, I learned a tremendous amount just by watching him work. The designs themselves didn't really blow my mind on an artistic level but the way he impressed his clients with whatever he did grabbed my respect. I learned that selling a design and having confidence in it was probably more important than the design itself and that it was all just a game, you just needed to be desirable enough to pull it off. The persona of a designer rather than being a designer is probably more important than anything on most occasions, especially, where he was concerned. I watched him delegate absolutely everything, down to having someone walk his dog after they had worked for 23 hours in a row. He didn't lift a finger except to use it in conversation as a hand gesture to bring a more flamboyant and convincing flair to the table. I was blown away by this option, as I stared down at my cracked fingernails and sole worn shoes. It had occurred to me right there and then that, even though I could never become a gay wolf, it was time for me to become a butterfly that would fly above the wolves and land on their backs from time to time.

I ran down the long hall of mirrors in the lobby, watching my reflection morph into something that was about to take flight. As I landed back in my shitty little office, I collected my sparse but extremely important rolodex, handed my clippers to my chubby assistant, and he cried in my arms one last time before I left through the service entrance, past the mounds of garbage piled amongst the dumpsters. I stepped in some horse shit as I closed the service gate behind me, and I threw my shoes away in the nearest garbage can and rode barefoot in the back of a taxi all the way home.

Part Two

Chapter One

"I am the greatest. I said that even before I knew I was."
-Muhammad Ali

My Smith Corona typewriter was on the fritz again, but that didn't matter much, since I was about to upgrade to a fancier model that was electronic, had a display window, and a self-correction feature. I had really hit the big time. My beeper had a sticky substance on it that I couldn't identify, but I think it had something to do with it being next to me on a table that I was having sex on the night before. Something was boiling in the kitchen. I had no idea what the fuck it was, so I figured it would just boil itself into an evaporated state at some point, as if it never happened. The beeper was going off and I needed to get my ass to a pay phone fast, so none of my new clients would be privy to my home number.

I had upgraded to a slightly more impressive apartment, which had a separate bedroom and a kitchen with a full-sized refrigerator, which I technically didn't need but it was good to know that I had one. I was working hard out of this apartment and playing even harder out of it. It was in a more central part of Brooklyn Heights, closer to the subway and to the local restaurants and bars, which I frequented so often that I would pretty much walk behind the bar and fix myself whatever I wanted or go into the kitchen and hang out with the chefs, as they turned over their dining rooms again and again. It was still a habit for me to hang out in the back of house areas. I supposed this habit would always be singed upon my psyche like a tattoo that looked bad but was too sentimental to get rid of.

Suzi basically snorted laughter at all of this retro information; she had no idea what a typewriter was. During this part of my tale, we were sitting on the floor behind the massive stage of the Victoria's Secret Fall Fashion Show. We had seen enough tiny titties, angel wings, and waxed genitalia for a lifetime. Sting would be hosting the after-party and we were taking a short break before heading over to the super chic West Village brownstone we were about to ruin with the evenings' festivities, along with the owner's good relationships with her neighbors. We had already bribed the local precinct with admission to the event; no man would ever turn down an invite to a VS after-party. All of our straight guy friends offered to work garbage detail that night even, only to be disappointed by the models were in real life, learning that they actually talked and felt exhaustion. They were more attracted to the model's publicists most of the time; pretty girls who, in their minds, were at least obtainable? Whatever, I had my own problems such as going way over legal capacity at this party.

It had been six months since I had left my job at the Jewel of Central Park. My mother had, once again, hopped into action on my behalf by printing announcements that I had left my job and was available for hire to make all the potential clients listed in my rolodex's lives a bit more fabulous, and luckily, my pager was beeping itself off the nightstand. I will never know if it was because people truly wanted my talents or if they were just hungry for new meat on the design market in New York City. Also, I was still young enough that I was sure they figured they could get me for an insanely cheap price, and they could at that time. I worked to live and I lived to work, and I don't quite remember being as happy as I was back then ever again. I was free to do whatever and whomever I wanted, and I didn't need to wear pantsuits and report to anyone but myself and to the herd of demanding clients I was about to collect. People have often said, "You're so lucky you don't have a boss." I quickly correct them and inform them that everyone who hires me is my boss, and sometimes, there are several at a time, so buy me a drink, shut up, and think about that for a cool minute.

I also had no fucking clue as to what I was doing in terms of owning a real business in NYC, so I didn't even consider paying taxes until my third year in, simply because I wasn't aware that I needed to. The little accountant my mother had hired for me years ago was no longer around, and we felt it best to fly under the radar, while I was just starting out as a new entity. I think my mother wanted to make sure I was going to stick around for a while before getting too deep into things.

Strangely enough, my very first client, straight out of the park, pretty much had nothing to do with the venue. The connection came from an experience I had at a bar I was drinking at one very freezing, cold late night after a particularly frustrating day of work. I was loaded, I had already made out with someone random outside, while smoking a cigarette that I would've never smoked in 'real life,' and in walked these two really striking women who must have mistakenly chosen this hole in the wall Irish pub type thingy I was hanging out in, just to get out of the cold. They were probably five years older than I was, but clearly a lot more mature and put together. They both carried large purses that doubled as briefcases or tote bags, made out of fine leather and probably went for about 3k each, so they either had rich husbands or daddies who were still chipping in for their lifestyles. Their cheeks were flushed with the cold and you could tell that their faces didn't need make-up, just some good eyebrow wrangling once in a while, an effective lip gloss, and a high-end self-bronzer.

I leaned over the bar and asked the big handsome and meaty Irish bartender if he knew them. He said, "Oh, yes, love, that's Katie and Annette, PR girls who live as roommates around the corner." PR girls stand for Public Relations girls. They usually start out as interns for companies that represent brands they like in fashion, beauty, and celebrity representation. The veneer of this career is so attractive and shiny it is almost impossible for a young girl to pass up, but the reality of their experiences probably resembles their worst nightmares coming true on a daily basis. Once hired, their salaries are probably even worse than working for free, since they would now pay taxes on their income. But they stay put because they are basically paid heavily in swag from the brands they represent, hence, the three-thousand-dollar bags they were carrying.

These girls were of the upmost interest to me, as I watched how they carried themselves in the atmosphere of this shit-hole of a bar, which quickly became a lot more glamorous, simply because they had walked into it.

Some observations about PR girls in general; their hair always looks flawless, they can walk incredibly well in heels for hours even days at a time, they always smell good, they usually have at least one pair of fake glasses, which make them look sexy and smart all at once and finally, they are *always* looking for husband material. Reminiscent of a Dr. Seuss book, whether it be in a train or a plane, or on the sea and while taking a pee, these bitches have an eye on the male species 24/7. Even in their sleep, these girls can calculate what time a desirable man will be going to the gym, including the exact moment to grab the treadmill beside him during the gym's busiest hours. She can also tell you within seconds how much he makes a year, what school he went to, where his 'people' are from, and of course, how big his dick is. I instantly sent two white wine spritzers over to Katie and Annette. I was going to need these bitches in my life. The other glorious detail about PR girls is that they need you for *everything* once you have gained their trust. They will call you to kill a spider and you can charge handsomely for it.

Suzi knew about PR girls all too well since she was closer in age to most of our PR girl clientele and she was able to form a supportive kinship with them. I never thought the day would come when clients would call the office for Suzi and not for me, but a large majority of this PR girl species rarely had any interaction with me, aside from me delivering the big money shot moment or the 'sell' of a huge concept we would ultimately produce for them. It was important that Suzi could play alongside these young ladies, so we got her fitted with a few pantsuits that could have fit my dog they were so small, yet they were Armani and these girls could admire them a mile away. It was impossible to get Suzi to apply make-up to her child like face, so we invested in eye lash extensions and a semi-permanent eyeliner application. She was well equipped to hang with these girls but not intimidate them with an overpowering beauty. She was beautifully 'Beige' and she gracefully permeated this crowd like a well-blended face foundation. She was also becoming outspoken like me. I could hear her quote sayings of mine such as, "We don't only wish to evoke a stunningly visual response to your events, but more importantly, a memorable emotional one as well that lives on long after the event itself." Or "It's not just about the wedding, it's truly about the marriage... but for Heaven's Sake, spend a lot on the wedding, just in case!" She delivered these scrumptious pieces of information as if it were being served on a silver platter atop with full Pink Champagne flutes topped with Cotton Candy garnish and the girls just drank it all up as they looked to her for the next informative course. This little girl from Queens, who lived in a house with aluminum siding, was becoming the Grace Kelly of the event world or shall I say, Taylor Swift, in order to be age appropriate.

I was like a mama bird who would regurgitate information directly into Suzi's mouth. Some of it she would feast off of and the other parts, she would spew into magazine articles and the open ears of our clients. My wise words coming out of a young face and body, was probably the most valuable weapon one could own.

Little did she know that not only was she becoming my legacy, she could very well be our meal ticket, too, as my passion for our current endeavors were starting to fade. The re-invention of the wheel had gone around so many times for me already in my career, while she was just pulling her electric car out of the garage for the very first time. My job was to stay relevant enough, while her baby seeds grew into a Garden of Earthly Delights.

The rest of that night with my new PR chick friends, was blur, infused with girl power and encapsulated in a cloud of glittery haze as we laughed until daylight in their apartment situated in a five-story walk up. They had landed a gorgeously renovated tiny place in a pre-war building and had turned the living room by day into one of their bedrooms at night with the simple addition of a shabby, chic sofa couch. A noticeable difference between me and these ladies was that they took painful measures to pull out that couch every night, after they had washed and done mask treatments on their faces and brushed their hair, no matter how loaded they were. Whereas if that couch had been in my home, it would have been slept on and never pulled out, complete with mascara smudges all over its throw pillows from my unwashed face. Believe it or not, these tiny acts of 'follow through' were what made me want to be a better woman and to grow up a bit.

Katie and Annette had created jobs for themselves within an up and coming fashion house. It was led by a talented and daring American fashion designer who had just gotten backed to the hilt by some deep-pocketed partners. He was about to open his showrooms, and he was taking the fashion world by storm, one preppy outfit at a time. The timing was impeccable. I will never understand how these girls made this connection but the benefits for me, just from knowing them, were tremendous. Before the designer even had any retail stores, he had three buildings in NYC's fashion district, ranging from 11 to 17 floors, and all showcasing his brand and collections. One floor would be menswear, then another would be boys, then girls, women, shoes, makeup, handbags, and finally, underwear, swimsuits, and intimates.

Each glorious state of the art chrome, glass, and 'everything white' floor was complete with fabulous reception desks, kitchens, conference areas, private offices, and of course, the showrooms themselves.

The final masterpieces were his private offices, flanked by his CFO, CEO, lawyers, accountants, massage therapist, mistress, chef/chef's kitchen, custom humidor, and walk-in wine fridge, located on the top floor of one of his buildings. This was his oasis, and he needed fresh flowers in every one of these rooms, along with every showroom and reception desk. Every day, I was going to need an assistant and/or a village.

There are so many amazing things about being present on the ground floor of something, before it belongs to the rest of the world. There is a new buzz about it all. Kind of like a deflowered virgin walking down her once drab school halls. She suddenly feels like a super-model on the catwalk after she lets the captain of the football team have his way with her.

I was amidst a constant state of excitement and I would linger on newly learned terms, such as pendant lamps, polished concrete floors, the word 'fabulous,' sushi, sconces, sisal, faux this and that. I was learning another dialect of luxury and, looking back on it, so much of it was completely ridiculous, yet so fucking desirable. Just knowing that there were Viking range ovens on every showroom floor started to elevate me to a whole other level of what my services could potentially offer. The breadth of what I needed to supply for this fashion house was somewhat overwhelming and I needed to gather some troops.

I had always walked over the Brooklyn Bridge to and from my tiny apartment whenever the weather allowed such an excursion. I was already someone who kept extremely odd hours, often getting to the flower market at 4 a.m., and then back home for a quick nap.

Then I would hit the local neighborhood gym, go back home to shower, and finally, I would start my day along with the rest of the world. This is where New York was truly an amazing city. No matter what your hours are, there are thousands of other people that are up with you, whether they are just getting home from bartending jobs, or still out partying or simply just awake and out. Garbage men have always been like family to me. They would creep down the streets, alongside of me, while I was walking alone, much like loyal lions watching over royalty.

As I approached the Lower East Side to get to the bridge one day, I walked past a fun-looking shop, which intrigued me by its neutral and mysterious appearance. The windows were filled in, so there was no sight line to its interior, and at first, I just figured it was a lube and peep show place. But it had a clean elegance to it that was simply too stylish to only be that, so I walked in. The place was completely buzzing. I felt like I was in a very fashionable sex lab with Swedish workers in lab coats and chunky framed glasses. The blonde wood-floors were spotless, and the shelving units were much like the fashion house displays; all white, chrome, and flawless. Upon the shelves were every kind of sex toy you could imagine, and they were all beautiful, artistic sculptures lined up in perfect formation. There was a leather section, whips, handcuffs, masks, etc., and every color and size cock and butt plug one could imagine, shining brightly underneath art gallery level lighting.

There seemed to be a class going on in the back of the shop, and its students were couples of all kinds; men and men, women and women, women and men, older couples, younger couples, and singles, all listening intently to a young woman lecturing them on the art of pleasuring one another mentally and physically and, of course, using some of the many products she offered in the store. I was mesmerized by this woman to say the least. She was very heavy-set, had crazy messy spiky hair that was a color wheel all its own, and her clothes were just sloppy and unique. She resembled a spectacular Muppet that I just couldn't take my eyes or ears away from. She spoke in such an intelligent and manic manner, waving her hands, as if they were doing the thinking as her mouth was doing the talking. It was like watching a magnificent carousel going around and at every angle there was a new color or shape to discover as she dipped in and out of her conversation. She was helping people bring joy and pleasure to their lives, much like I tried to do with my work. I waited until she finished speaking to all her followers, and I came to find out that her girlfriend owned the store. She just worked part time, was looking for other gigs, and was particularly interested in working with plants. Bam! I had found my assistant.

Her name was (or shall I say she answered to) Supreme Stephanopoulis. So, not a Jewish girl. She was physically lazy, which wasn't a great for my business, but there was something grounding and slow about her, which, somehow, complemented my insanely erratic and energetic state. She dressed atrociously, often wearing filthy clothing held together by patches and a huge marijuana leaf belt buckle, yet she was so compelling that everyone wanted to be around her. Straight, beautiful women found themselves leaving their financially stable husbands just for one night of finger play with her, and dogs and children crossed busy avenues without looking, simply to be in her company. I, too, was entranced by her presence, not to mention that I was set for life in the sex toy department. Looking back, I realize that Supreme was so incredibly important to me, not because she blew my mind in any major way, but more so that she was my first real employee, to be followed by a gazillion others. Nobody employs people thinking that they are going to leave you one day or that they could potentially disappoint you daily, as they determine what they will or won't do in terms of the job, all the while draining your bank account. I used to lead with my heart, instead of my head, and the two have never really seen eye to eye. I have continuously made the same mistake over again of being drawn to the magnificent misfits of society and trying to evolve them into something shiny for the rest of the world to see. I have finally come to learn so many years later that I really should avoid making the same mistake twice.

I knew that I would lose Suzi one day, too. She always declared that she didn't want children or get married, but that's hard to believe when coming from such a young person who changes her mind every three months, concerning major life decisions. One day, she came into work a little late, which certainly isn't like her and I was fully engrossed with a few of the other team members, but she twirled around our opulent waiting area, right in front of a team full of brides and their mothers who resembled waiting in a locker room like an estrogen sponsored women's soccer team. She had happy tears in her eyes and she loudly declared that she had met the man she was going to marry last night on a date her friends had randomly set up for her. The girls around me rolled their eyes, since I think that they had heard her say this before. Deep in my heart, I knew it was true. Visions of her childhood, Irish Catholic Church filled with people with last names starting with Mc something or other, huge bridal parties on both sides, Bachelorette parties, wedding showers, shopping, planning, cake tasting, beer, you name it, were flashing within my brain.

Our office would be a flurry of imbalance juggling our current clients, while celebrating her impending nuptials and I felt fucking dizzy. I needed to be happy for her; I needed to promote the fact that she would fully feel something that I never could in the form of love and commitment. It would be the one thing I couldn't teach her, along with cooking and doing most of the common tasks that she actually performed for me. Her man would become her sun, moon, and stars, and I would be the milky-way or a shooting star that only came around once in a while. There would be special moments with her mother, ones I wouldn't be a part of, unless I actually moved in with them in Queens. On the weekends we weren't working, she would have a busy schedule consisting of registering at Crate and Barrell, taking dance lessons, and talking to the Monsignor about what her ceremony would be like and bending the rules about the intense amounts of flowers I would be allowed to bring into his humble church. The church organist would fight back and take offense to me wanting Michael Bublé to sing, while she walked down the aisle and not him. My anxiety was at its peak, and they weren't event engaged yet, that would be a whole other ball of wax; the proposal process. Her man would send her ugly flowers that I would have to allow her to keep on her desk, but most definitely on the side that wasn't visible to clients, and overall, she would have another life that was outside of the one that she and I shared. I needed to accept this and condone her happiness. I would need to up my therapy sessions for sure and she would need to schedule them, no matter what. Then, there came the narcissistic fear of what would happen to me and my business. I hadn't really concentrated on deciding who else could take my place and keep the glamour motor running into eternity. I couldn't really sell, since there was no business without me or at least, someone who could act as me, which no on truly could, but Suzi was a close second. I started to panic a bit and for the first time ever, I experienced some real depression. My form of depression wasn't the 'can't get out of bed' type. It was a more manic display of actually getting my shit together. I, somehow, decided that if I became a clean individual, almost Holy, everything would fall into place. I realized that I should only focus on what I could control such as my body, eating habits, fornicating with strangers, drug intake, and spending money on what other people deemed as useless investments. I was going to become a focused, clean, consistently productive person who would lure the universe into taking care of me and helping me determine what the fuck I was going to do without Suzi.

My premier employee, Supreme, and I became a major force in the fashion showroom world. She would walk behind me yet protectively onto the job sites, quietly sweep up as I made my floral messes in those million-dollar kitchens, and she knew when to disappear when one of the higher-ups would come into the kitchen extra early, just to dry-hump me against the refrigerator before the building officially opened. He was a lot older than me. A real silver fox, he smelled of leather mixed with a hint of the humidor room. It never occurred to me not to accept the humping; it just seemed to fit into the existing rhythms of my work flow.

Supreme was discreet and she was just the rock I needed, until she up and quit one day, stating that she was ready to 'move on,' never to be heard from again. The heartbreak caused by an employee leaving of their own volition is probably the most painful thing one can encounter, simply because there is never any understandable resolution as to why they are leaving, because you are paying them to be there. You face insecurities, wondering what you did wrong. You find yourself asking, "Why would they want to leave me? Why don't they want to worship, adore, and try to be like me anymore?" The truth is that it rarely has anything to do with you at all. Usually, it's that they are either bored, found something that they think is better and for more money, have a wealthy significant other that allows for them to be unemployed, they want to go back to school after seeing how shitty real life is, or that they are simply just ready to move on with no real plan in site. Lord knows I certainly broke a gazillion hopeful hearts along the way by changing horses in the middle of the stream when I was working for other people those few times.

I will continue to have loads of employees come in and out of my life, breaking my heart and me, breaking theirs. It just comes with the territory I suppose, and I have grown hardened to it for sure. When it truly comes down to it, it's me or them, and that's a no brainer.

Throughout my career thus far, I have had people steal from me, fuck prostitutes in the back of my leased truck during a load in, do lines of coke on my office desk, steal cash out of the safe somehow, set fire to the inventory by mistake, pee on the inventory (by mistake as well), cut off fingers with flower clippers by being stupid and trying to start their own companies with my clients (*big mistake*), then they would have the audacity to ask for their jobs back. Can you fucking imagine? Being an employer has always been the toughest part of what I do, so much so that it has scared me out of any desire to become a parent for good, unless I could adopt a child old enough to work for me and at least help out.

The rest of my team, today, aside from Suzi, who is her own category, is a vagina force not to be reckoned with. All fifty women are smart, young, ambitious as hell, speak several languages, they are always clean, gorgeous, fashionable, and most of all, protective of their mama lioness—me. Not a single phone call or a piece of paper resembling a letter, or a bill is even allowed close to my orbit without them scouring and scrutinizing every detail of the matter at hand. I have an exterior team that handles all legal, financial, and business development issues. They perform like a justice league type of force, solving one finance puzzle at a time, including all my divorces, and any instances that have 'gotten out of hand,' simply because I am the one causing them. My taxes and financial profiles appear squeaky clean and are 'audit ready.' My investments are as close to perfect as they can be, including some of my side projects, which I don't care to discuss.

The production portion of my business, such as the warehouse, shipping, and where the 'building stuff' happens is all run by male animals, but not just any male animals. They are all spectacular, virile, strong, and smart, speak several languages and want to fiercely protect and be loyal to me, their lioness queen, much like my girls, except they have muscles.

In return, I am fiercely loyal to my team. I passively and aggressively over-pay them and spoil them as often as I possibly can. I make sure that my boys have gorgeous uniforms to wear that show off their muscular physiques, leaving other vendors to wonder whether I am sleeping with many of them in our off hours. You always want people to think that you have an insanely active sex life.

The love affair with providing my services for the fashion world didn't last forever. I learned a very hard lesson that went a little something like this; large corporations use everybody's money to make money. They spend whatever they have in the bank, even if it's owed to someone else, to support their own business habit. Thus, they usually pay vendors on a ninety-day cycle, which is an eternity for a small business like mine, that was often living hand-to-mouth. Most small businesses need to be paid before even completing the job, so they can live off a portion of it, pay their overhead, and afford the materials needed for the job. In this case, working for the fashion house, I would go to my mailbox regularly, only to find it *sans* payment for services rendered. This went on for months at a time. My invoices, typed so meticulously on my Smith Corona and threatening late fees, couldn't seem to demand the payment terms I needed to keep this relationship going. Soon, my little business was owed over $300,000, at least, half of which I owed to other people. Fuck! I was in a conundrum. My accounts were beginning to shut down on the flower market, and I couldn't afford to pay other people to assist me, so I was basically hustling for free, caught like a gerbil on one of those squeaky wheels that I just couldn't get off. Not only was I ashamed that my rock-star status was beginning to tarnish, I was facing an emotion I did not know how to deal with; fear. My rent was behind, there were yellow slips of paper in my life now, and yellow is bad. I started to feel ill and it was affecting my performance as a human being. I was sleeping late, and my muscles started to ache from the inside out. Soon, I felt paralyzed and I found myself visualizing cinematic scenarios of my life on the ceiling of my tiny apartment, much like a castaway does on a cave wall. I even considered ending it all, which, looking back, is overly dramatic, but I was still young and overly sensitive. My body and mind were aching for some type of resolution. I was never one for settling into a puddle of shit for very long, so I decided to become as physical as possible and hit the gym hard. After all, my membership was paid in full at the small gym in the neighborhood, so it was time to go and sweat some of my anxiety out and to deny my present situation the best I could.

I started out by running on the treadmill, which would have been boring, but the treadmills were situated around a basketball court where the local talent (young men) played rigorously. I relished in their laughter and teasing, but mostly in how the sweat ran down all the different types of male bodies. I was in a hypnotic state; watching how the sweat would vary from black skin to white, from hairy chests to smooth. I was caught in a deliciously exotic rhythm, and before I knew it, I was running six to ten miles every day. I loved watching how the players' feet intertwined in a fluid dance of sportsmanship. When a fight broke out, it was the highlight of my day, especially when the fight ended in a slap on the back, some smiles and a post-game beer. In ways, it taught me that even though a situation can get heated, it can also cool down and move on, without any defined resolution aside from acceptance. I learned a lot from watching them, and that not everything was so Black or White.

I have noticed that young people, today, still see things as Black or White with no gradients of Grays or Whites in between, and this included Suzi. We would often come out of a meeting and she would either say the job was going to happen or not, while I was already figuring out a way to sway the situation somewhere in the middle that was beneficial to me, no matter what. It's almost as if the alphabet only had the letters *A* and *Z* and none in between. It's such a freedom to think of the world as a place filled with options and not just some jail-cell with no parole or redemption in sight. I guess when you can Google something, and it's been proven that the first answer to something pops up as the most popular or as being 'right,' why look any further, I guess. There is such a finality to this that I wonder if there is any such thing as hope, any more in terms of options that we allow ourselves to dream of. My whole world has been built upon these options, so many and of such variety I can't even keep track or inventory of them. It's the options that keep me up at night in a delicious way, like deciding what to watch on TV or to read or what to masturbate to, once you have succumbed to the fact that you won't be falling back to sleep, at peace, knowing that you will or may not catch up tomorrow on this segmented sleep. These tomorrows are what I cling to like a sloth on a swaying tree; too lazy to jump off but just digging the ride so fucking much. There is stress involved not knowing or resolving certain things, of course, if this was all easy, we would be sleeping like the dead and that just leads to drool covered pillow cases and not your fantasies coming true via flowers, music, food, and looking overly pretty for at least six hours. The preparation of life's options is just as titillating. Once they are laid out for you like an outfit on your bed ready for the day, you decide how to best sport them in the most beneficial way, such as attracting someone, feeling powerful and beautiful, or getting rich. I wanted Suzi to feel the richness and depth of what we did, but I am not sure someone of her generation ever could. They can reap from certain benefits of it all, such as being successful, making a fine living, and being 'known' in the industry or even the world as being an expert, but could their souls expand and morph at the thought of making dreams come true for themselves or someone else? This made me sad. Why get up in the morning? For me, it was never to send someone off to school to have dinner with my in-laws or to watch someone graduate or plunk through a torturous piano recital. I didn't celebrate the 'normal' like everyone else did, but 'normal' suited Suzi just fine and she was my tie to the regular world, while she skipped in and out of both scenarios, just to keep us all in the know.

I could start to picture her with a baby, joining an all-girl's gym and even wearing compression pants while she dropped the baby weight and my mind just shut down. There was a part of me that just didn't want to accept her as being normal. I wanted her to come to my dark side and stay there. It wasn't that misery loved company at all; it was more like I just wanted more members of my magnificent team like vampires, biting people and infecting them forever, so they always had their favorite people around them, no matter what.

In the gym I joined, I started to play around with the weight room as well, and I formed some cool friendships that I wouldn't have made otherwise, simply through needing 'assists' while lifting heavy weights. The assists led to a tight friendship with a brilliant young lawyer in the making named Jay. I think that seven out of ten lawyers are named Jay, so he had a great head start. I finally came clean about my money woes, and he gave me some of the greatest advice ever by suggesting I ask the higher-ups at the fashion house for the money in person. It was such a simple request, but I had overlooked it in my overly dramatic state, thinking that the solution would be life changing somehow. Yet, it's the simplest things that often are.

I decided to proceed in a professional manner and to continue my design installations by using my very last penny, as I tried to figure out how to communicate my dilemma to the right person who could get me paid.

At 4:00 one morning, I was at work and feeling perversely at peace as I always did, while cleaning the pure white roses they insisted upon having on every desk by opening. Then I felt the silver fox's hands grab my breasts from behind. As he started to knead my nipples, I quietly started to weep. I whispered that I was in a horrible position, about to lose my business, and in a crazy amount of debt because of their lazy payment schedule. I felt his erection grow with power, knowing that I was a damsel in distress who needed his help; men love that shit. He never looked me in the eyes as he grabbed my hand, led me down the hall, sat me down at the chair at his desk, and wrote me a check for all the monies owed to me, along with a hefty late fee. This would be the easiest business battle I would ever experience, and there would be plenty more to come that an army would fight for me as I watched from a spectator box. I would learn, as my career aged, that I would never be able to collect on a late fee again, no matter how ironclad my contacts were. Late fees were just annoying flies that my clients would swat away, until they would deplete our collection energy. Wealthy people feel that if they finally pay what they owe you, that should be good enough, and I suppose that that way of thinking seemed to work out just fine enough for me to continue to do business with them. Everything was a trap. Money, commissions, vaginas, cocks, feelings, talents, schedules, you name it. I started to look at business as if I had a permanent ball and chain attached to me. I knew that when I was about to approach a new business relationship, I would have to go in with my wallet, mind and legs open. I would continue to shower Katie and Annette with gifts for many years to come, even after my relationship with the fashion house ended, just because they made the introduction. Even now, it's a regular occurrence to see where clients are dining from their posts on Instagram and send a bottle of expensive champagne to their table or a round of desserts that they would never order for themselves. This saved me an enormous amount of time from running around town, looking for people I needed to charm. When you think about it, people are so incredibly easy to please in certain ways. They want to know that they are attractive and they want free shit.

I kept my working relationship with the fashion house for many years to come, and I stayed in close contact with Katie and Annette, whose weddings I did, along with everyone else's in their families. Client relationships will be the only successful relationships I will ever have, aside from my pets, and that's only because I don't live with the clients, the pets don't talk and they never grow up, they stay our babies forever.

Having this one fashion house on my resume would open the doors to thousands of fashion houses, massive lingerie companies, supermodels' weddings, weekly flowers in pretty people's homes, fashion show custom build outs, such-as cat walks constructed out of plexi glass lit from within and suspended from unsuspecting warehouse ceilings. The mouths and ears of New York City's finest were so close together that even a whisper of my name was heard by thousands all at once.

I was feeling quite large and in-charge, and I often celebrated by frequenting my neighborhood bars and restaurants, but I was constantly getting rudely interrupted by my beeper going off. I was so young and selfish that I was more annoyed by it than thrilled. I would be making out with nameless boys and, as their hands gripped my ass, it would vibrate with that constant reminder that I had work to do and someone to answer to.

My desire to delegate to someone else was there, but I couldn't see a clear path as to how to do it. Everyone wanted me, and that would always be the tragic flaw in the shiny veneer of my career. In the meantime, there was no reason why I couldn't form a team to, at least, take over the fucking beeper.

Suzi currently has emails coming to her from seven different email accounts, voice messages left on ten different phone lines, and countless DMs on all of my social media accounts that she personally checks twelve times daily, not allowing anyone else on our team to do so. She answers as me at times eradicating offers of all kinds, including social engagements. She knows very well what I would want or not want to do before I can even engage in the pros and cons of attending an outing or even taking a call. She is, by no means, obsessed with me, but she has a consistent urge to control the rhythm of my life and to keep herself on the front lines at all times. I truly wonder how long she can keep it up, especially if she begins to collect her own life.

Chapter Two

"Reality is wrong. Dreams are for real."

-Tupac

The only way I can ever figure out how to do something is to close my eyes and visualize it. It goes far beyond daydreaming. I deliberately put obstacles in my way, such as mentally measuring a doorway to a possible new studio space and its ability to open wide, enough for my equipment to fit through. In my dream tour of my new office/studio, I would be able to place my employees at their desks, which fit perfectly not only in a Feng Shui way but also in terms of egress and natural flow of the space, especially in relation to where I am situated. I go into painful detail inside of my head, down to how many pens are held in a cup on each desk and the number of staples that are in each stapler. You've heard the phrase, 'If you build it, they will come.' Well, if I can visualize it, it will happen. I apply this tactic to all the parties that I produce.

I had a vision in my head of an office in a centrally located area of Manhattan; close to the flower market, with a large production space adjacent to it making the entire floor my own. Within the office, there were four women, a boy, some pets, and me. One woman was a receptionist type who would do absolutely anything for me, no matter how ridiculous. She would be very attractive but not sexy. Another lady was older than all of us and could be the 'mommy' of the group. She could handle the particularly grown-up situations with clients, and she would be angry at the world because she wasn't attractive or sexy. Next was the 'bulldog' of the group, a fiercely intense lady close to my age but who seemed older and was a lot smarter. Her looks simply wouldn't matter. She would oversee the rest of the group, mainly, me, and deal with money, so technically she was the most important person there. There would be a 'floater,' an artistic and asexual type who could morph into whatever we needed her to be at any time on any given day. Then, there was a handsome gay front man, who would be me if I couldn't be around. He would sell designs with such conviction and arrogance that clients may as well have opened their vaults, walked out of the room, and let him have at it. Everyone accepted a handsome gay man, no matter what the situation was, and they wouldn't make him fight to get paid either. He was my secret weapon.

I visualized every one of these people and it all came true.

The production space would require a whole other cast of characters. It's incredible how different the two teams were. I mainly related to the people 'in the back,' which were a group that were very reminiscent of my old back-room flower-shop friends, except that New York served up a much more varied palette of potential employees than a small town did. First and foremost, there was an insanely beautiful Nigerian man who literally followed me around the flower market any time I was there to finally declare that he wanted to work for me and to protect me with his life. I would later find out that he was an Oxford scholar who had moved to New York only to find himself in a homeless situation. He mainly slept on the subway and took showers in random gyms until he started working for me. We had the Dominican manly man who drove our truck, which I bought at an auction uptown for a few hundred bucks. He took such pride in that thing, which was actually an ambulance in its previous life. He would use the siren, saving the city one party at a time, getting our shit loaded into ballrooms faster than a speeding bullet. He also got more speeding and parking tickets in a year than economically possible. Then, there was the dude who handled everything in the studio; the flower orders, deliveries, and the conditioning of the flowers, cooler maintenance, building shit, fire codes, plunging toilets, you name it. He hardly spoke a word of English and frankly, he didn't need to. He was all about action, and words were a waste of time for him. He also managed the slew of freelance designers we would use for different jobs. This crowd was insanely diverse, ranging from transgender to lesbian, all the way to a random fabulous shy and preppy boy from Kansas who could design rings around everyone. All of them were strong and in high demand, and we found ourselves competing for them with other designers in the city, so we sometimes booked them a year ahead of time. The boys in the back would fight a lot, the amount of testosterone in the production space made my knees quiver, as I walked down the hall to check in on them. They all vied for my attention and were fiercely protective of me for the most part, but they would have stabbed each other in the backs in a New York minute. I was playing the role of a boss, kind of like some people play the stock market, but, much like when rainy weather ruins an outdoor wedding day, some things were just out of my control.

Items would go missing or the truck would be gone for several hours longer than it should've been and so on, but during events, the team would work so hard that you simply had to let things slide. Let's face it, if I were running it like a true corporation, the overtime hours alone would have put me out of business long ago.

The most challenging part was always the communication gap between the staff in the front and the back of the house. The folks up front would be selling these fabulous fantasies, and then the guys in the back would have to somehow figure out how to execute them and they most likely would only have half of the information they needed to do so. Then the fighting would break out, because in the end, no one wanted to disappoint me or the client. We would have production meetings between the two departments, and they would sit across the table leering at each other, most likely not retaining any important information whatsoever. The best part of the meeting was the snacks I would provide for them, just to insure their attendance.

I was still a little girl playing in a boss woman's role that far exceeded my years of knowledge and experience. I was winging it, and I had no choice but to trust in the people around me. I still don't have a choice in that matter. The job started to stray from the part that I loved most about it; the design. Instead, I was wrapped up in a tornado of taxes, signatures, other people's sick kids, tidal waves of emotional scenarios, and simply, just other people aside from myself. This wasn't my natural habitat and it was not my beautiful life.

These days I don't even know if something goes wrong in one of our studios or on the job. I will, sometimes, find out months later, if Suzi is a few drinks in, and she lets it slip that half of our team didn't show up for a job or that we'd been robbed at one of our warehouses. She would quietly take care of these situations at ungodly hours and report to work just a few hours later as if nothing had happened. After a hearty breakfast of her favorite Avocado Toast concoction (I could always tell when she had a rough night when there were two orders on her desk) and after picking off the brown layer, since she'd forgotten to eat them fast enough, I could see her little face wilting like her three-day old dry-bar hair-do. The stress one endures in our industry is indescribable, and the stress of not having this stress or a purpose of such multitude is even worse. Thus, I tend to continue to fuck up my life enough to keep me in a stress filled zone. It's like asking someone to quit smoking after they'd put away three packs a day for the past fifty years. The act of quitting, what was so bad for them in the first place, would be what could potentially kill them. It was a no-win situation and I had accepted it so very long ago. I was thrillingly saddened that Suzi had caught the same disease and knowing that there was no cure. I was fascinated to see how she would metabolize the disease in a more productive format than I ever did.

As a fully functioning team, we mainly had a large public relations firm that kept us very busy doing projects locally and in other cities, such as Miami,

Los Angeles, Chicago, and my most happy places aside from New York; London and Paris. I would often travel with the 'mommy' of my team, since she was always desperate to get away from her husband, children, and her New Jersey way of life, and frankly, I didn't blame her. I remember on our first jobs away we would be oh so accepting, flying coach, staying in shit-holes, often having to bunk together. Not like now, where all I do is fly private and stay in the 'Queen Bee' suites in all the swankiest hotels and resorts this planet offers. There was something so charming about those first times out of the gate into the rest of the world. You automatically demand respect when you are coming from New York to another place. People already know that your taste is going to be better and that you are going to expect great things from them, and they act like puppies, looking to please their owners when you meet them. The banquet managers show us around their properties with nervous pride, acting robot-like, as they open the doors to an unsuspecting ballroom that has just undergone a thirty million-dollar renovation and still has carpeting that one could simultaneously puke and shit on and it would probably improve the design. Why these properties never hire people like me, someone who knows exactly what the world wants a ballroom to look-like before spending that kind of money on a re-design, will always baffle me.

Then there is the blissful part when the representatives for these venues want to show you the 'best of the best' that they can offer, including but not limited to, food, drink, service, spa, and anything they can show off gratis. This is so we'll rave about it when we get back home and bring them those once-in-a-lifetime clients who can elevate their portfolios to a whole new level. Nowadays, if I Tweet or post on Instagram about a property, I can pretty much name a time or a date I would wish to stay there with ten of my best friends for free, even if they are booked solid. Yes, life is grand, most of the time.

Suzi never has the desire to go on these windfall trips; she would rather be home in Queens. If there is work involved, she is good to go, but otherwise, she just gets antsy in a resort fit for royalty. The private plunge pool, a tub fit for ten and faucets of champagne pouring out of bathrooms larger than my apartment holds no interest for her. I suppose, at this point, for me as well, it's just another place to watch Netflix but in a nicer robe and with a phenomenal view.

As you start to hit the road with jobs, there really is no hand-book for it, so you make a ton of mistakes. You find out that your trucks aren't allowed on certain roads at certain hours or over a certain weight limit, long after you've already gotten a huge fine for being caught on the wrong roads at the wrong times. Trucks themselves will always cause some of my biggest headaches, along with the drivers that jockey them to and from our events. Throughout my entire career, I will be faced with flat tires, nowhere to park, huge parking meter bills, parking garages that don't usually take large vehicles and need to be bribed, and so on. The drivers will be combating disenchantment with the job, hemorrhoids, and a slew of broken relationships, while stuck under a low wage ceiling that makes them exist in a constant state of disappointment and anger. I always said that if I ever had to drive for a living, I would just be stoned all day long, and my guys probably were.

My clients have no idea what we go through from the inside out, particularly when we are on the road. We get paid the same fees, but we need to educate ourselves for free. This part is usually a bit of a thrill within itself, but it's still time and money.

The issue of having to trust vendors that we have never used before is gut-wrenching. The work ethic found in workers in other cities simply does not match up to New York's standards, and I found myself dragging my entire crew along with me on away jobs just to ensure that the job would get done the way I had sold it.

The mommy and I went on countless site visits in different cities, learning the lay of the land, while taking food, spa, and pool breaks. It was like being on a constant middle-aged honeymoon for us, and the mommy was usually quite depressed whenever she got home to her real life. I, on the other hand, couldn't wait to get home, aching for my severe reality and planting myself deep into my world and seeing my dogs. The lush trips almost seemed too distracting for me; fleeting moments of joy and happiness were just 'blips' on a screen that kept me from my ultimate homepage. These trips stopped my visualization flow. I was out of my element, and my fantasies would get muddled, so I could only pay attention to the here and now and not the future. This was troubling to me and quite boring. People, all around me, are constantly stating that they need a vacation. For someone like me, it's the last thing I need. I am either a workaholic or a slacker, nothing in between. I simply need constant stimulation and I can get it from a butterfly floating overhead, I don't need to travel to find it. The only times this wasn't true was when we were called to go to faraway places where I had no foothold. I didn't know the language, the traditions or the rules, and the food usually sucked, so it would always pose a challenge for me. That was enough to keep my attention level active.

A few weeks after landing home from one of our banal excursions, we were called away to do a last-minute wedding for a pop-star, location yet to be disclosed.

I was told simple specifics via fax from the house man, such as the size of the bridal party and the number of tables that needed centerpieces and linens.

That was all I had to go on to gather the right people for my away-game team. It was specified that the mother of the groom knew a lot about flowers and *décor*, so she wasn't thrilled that we were called in to help out. That's always a great way to start out, going to a faraway land where everybody hates you before you even get there. I had a motley crew with me, but they were all very eager to be on this project, even though they knew little about it, so the enthusiasm made up for some of their quirkiness. In my industry, most people want to get away from home. No matter how happy you may be with your significant other or your children, home may be where the heart is, but the rest of your body wants to get the fuck away sometimes. The team of freelancers included a middle-aged gay man who I adored, but who had just had knee replacement surgery, so he would need a place to sit while designing. There was a gorgeous transwoman with magical tits and an amazing talent for climbing ladders for hours on end. The team was rounded out by a jovial heavier gay guy who was as strong as an ox, a lesbian couple who only worked together and were also as strong as oxen, and several clean-up guys who held brooms and garbage bags in their hands and followed us around all day while we made pretty messes. Finally, I brought out my core crew from the office and production space. I left my number two behind since she handled the money. She always needed to be stationed at home-base.

The pop-star's people sent a big black van with tinted windows to collect us and they had told us to pack for wet weather. They ushered us quickly though the airport to a special runway where fancy privately owned planes took off. The flight was long, but we spent most of the ride mapping out what we were going to do, even though we didn't know where we were going. There were no smartphones back then, so we just went by looking out the window at the stars and taking an occasional glance down onto the dark terrain we were flying over. Trips like this usually happened at night, so that even though we had all signed NDAs, we still wouldn't be told or be able to see where we were going. Truthfully, it was very exciting, not like today, when we know where we are going down to specific longitude and latitude measurements that we can view on our phones.

We had the desired color palette for the *décor*, and my main production guy was carefully tracking the flower order every hour via the private plane's telephone. The flowers were coming from Holland, but we needed to tell the supplier which airport they were flying to. We brought our most basic tools. Most florists are very picky about their knives and often hold them in close by hiding spots to where we would be designing or on their person if they can. Often a knife or a pair of clippers accidentally ends up in a trash bag during large messy installations, and it's as if the fucking moon melted. Everyone stops working to look for a tiny knife that has been 'broken in' exactly to a designer's specifications.

Alas, we landed in Glasgow, the largest city in Scotland and the third largest in the United Kingdom. Yay!

The initial excitement of landing in a foreign land almost makes you forget the reason you are there in the first place. The stimulation overload of different surroundings, the dialect, mental calculation of new currency, and deciding what you can buy to bring back to loved ones tends to send you into a tailspin that can knock you off course. I have often witnessed the vibe of depression falling across my team's overall mood once it really sets in that we are there to work, and that we will probably be isolated to some cold and dark room somewhere to produce in. Then we would be ushered back onto the plane for the long journey home, before we even got settled. We certainly weren't expecting to go on a hunt for the Loch Ness monster or anything, but we were all secretly hoping we could take a few fateful bites of haggis and don a kilt for a few stolen moments before heading back. I think I could speak for everyone on my team in saying that we weren't against experiencing some uncut cock along the way either.

In this case, however, once we survived the endless car ride to the property, we were greeted with the open arms of the elders who owned the property. They welcomed us with such vigor that I almost felt as though we were to never be heard from again. You could tell that these people didn't get out much and, after all, we did just stupidly put our lives in someone else's hands without even asking where we were going. There was no bread crumb trail to us, either.

The wedding was to take place in a real Scottish castle, complete with spires, thick stone walls, and everything that would keep out an enemy. If the wedding were to be attacked, we would be fine, no doubt in my mind. The castle rested upon a massive amount of land where the 'indigenous to Scotland' wildlife, such as red deer and mountain hares ran free. Meanwhile, the sheep, cows, and anything else cute and furry lived in fear of being next up for the slaughter to become the ingredients of the Black Pudding dish that Scotland was so famous for. They didn't just eat meat; they dipped their soda bread or brown bread into the blood as well. They cooked with the hearts, lungs, and livers of the animals and minced it with God knows what and stuck it all together with oatmeal. You could build the foundation of a mighty fine house with their meals.

We were shown to our guest cottage, which mainly served as servant's quarters, but the small house was lovely. There was a roaring fireplace and enough bedrooms for all of us, complete with bottles of malt whisky and a snack plate of Tattie Scones on each bedside table. There were no minibars in the rooms, but those items would certainly suffice. We were exhausted and misplaced, and right when we were going to turn in for the night, another old but friendly couple knocked on the door. They were the owners of the property and the parents of the groom. They wanted to tell us the history of whom they were and where their people hailed from all the way down the line from Charles Edward Stuart, 'Bonnie Prince Charlie' himself. They went on to tell us about all the fabulous things that came out of Scotland, such as bagpipes, Olympic medal winners, poets, J.M. Barrie, the author of Peter Pan, and finally, about Sir Arthur Conan Doyle, the author of the Sherlock Holmes novels. I am fabulous at listening to useless information, while doing a million other things in my head. I'm able to engage with anyone and interject intelligent commentary when needed. It's one of my finer talents. My team, however, who were made up of all the colors of the minority rainbow, gay and transgender, were looking at these chubby white people with rosy cheeks like they were about to rob the place. Or they might not have been able to understand a fucking word they were saying with their brogues and all.

My conversational talents are probably what annoy Suzi the most about me. Being a millennial, a lengthy conversation rather than a text is simply overwhelming and a horrible waste of time to her. I can feel her squirming beside me while I converse, and I can see her little thumb enact an involuntary movement, as if she is hitting the hang up button on an imaginary iPhone. Sometimes, I keep the conversation going, just to fuck with her and she knows it. Coincidentally, we were sitting outside of the SiriusXM studio, where I was about to go on an endless talk about shit that Suzi had heard a gazillion times. It was cracking me up that I was holding her hostage here, as the show was running at least an hour behind. I could tell that my Scottish tale intrigued her though. She always felt at home when I talked about pale white people who drank a lot.

The Scottish mother of the castle wanted to show me her extensive gardens in another part of the property, and we would need to either travel by horseback or golf cart to get there. I chose the latter. It was pitch black out, I didn't even know what time it was, and even though this place was in the middle of nowhere, there were servants awake and ready to cater to any need around every corner. Men rode ahead of us with large lanterns that gave off an impossible amount of light, and I was thrilled to be young and pretty at the time. I took my main studio guy with me, since he would be able to participate in 'oohing and aahing' over her gardens in the right manner. We traveled on an impossibly bumpy road, and he looked like he was about to vomit. Meanwhile, I was wondering if they were hauling us off to some land run by old world witches to be tied to trees and never to be heard from again. After what felt like an eternity, we hit a clearing, and for fuck's sake, it was magnificent. When someone wants to show you their garden in the middle of the night, it means that they have spent enough hours obsessing and working on it that they finally feel ready to show it off to the world, particularly to people who are being flown in and sought after for their floral magnificence. Gardening is an extremely lonely sport, and even though I am sure the mother had gaggles of people helping her with the more laborious parts, the art of the garden was mostly likely all her. It was in that very moment, when I gasped in delight at the sight of her gardens, that I formed a kinship with the lady of the house. The bride and groom didn't really matter at that point. It was she who I needed to seal the deal with. Come to think of it, I usually needed to bond with the mother of whomever we were producing the party for.

After all, everyone needs to get past the Mother to move forward in life. We spent hours that I didn't even know had gone by. We were practically doing the Highland Dance through the soft edged rows of her romance flowers. The buds that exist in this category are exactly how they sound, they are romantic. To name just a few that I could see in the dark were Peonies, Hydrangea, Garden Roses, Lily of the Valley, Delphinium that was taller than me, and Calla Lilies displayed in magnificent colors, some, of which, I'd never seen before. I was marveling at the logistics of her operation. Technically, many of these flowers weren't really 'Scottish soil friendly' and they were not in season either, yet they were thriving and flawless, like they were on the set of a Baz Luhrmann movie, so vibrant and looking as if they were ready to shimmy out of the dirt and into a table centerpiece.

I looked over at my guy knowing that he and I were thinking the exact same thing. Why the fuck did we need to order and fly in thousands of dollars of flowers from Holland?

We slalomed in and out of the rows of flowers to make sure that we had everything we needed. We hit every category; greens, filler flowers, berries, and flowering branches, you name it. She even had a few hothouses with orchids from exotic lands and lilac trees growing beyond their normal capacities. This would be her swan song, and we might as well have been using the crown jewels to decorate her son's wedding.

We put her to work. It was a pretty awesome sight, watching this extremely waspy woman, who was usually quite uptight outside of the flower arena, getting bossed around by my motley crew. If we had been allowed to photograph it, the photos would have been priceless. We put her in our company t-shirts, which read, 'Work Hard, Party Harder' or 'Keep Calm and Party Like A Rock Star.' Her doughy scone like boobs hadn't been that happy in the longest time, as they were resting inside of one of my company shirts.

We worked for three days solid, partly in the cold mudroom of the guest house to keep the flowers fresh and partly outside, next to a bunch of sheep that were blinking their long eyelashes at us in a Morse code fashion, begging us to free them before the slaughter or birthing more material for sweaters. Every morning, we were awakened with a proper full breakfast consisting of gallons of Lyons tea, eggs, bacon, sausage, buttered toast, and baked beans. If my crew is consistently well fed, I could make them work in mud all day and they would be happy. We ate and farted a lot. It was great.

We never really spent much time with the bride or the groom, since he was always hunting, and she was probably not on the property yet. She would most likely step onto the aisle just in time to be married, or at the earliest at the rehearsal dinner, you never know. Folks think that we are hanging out with famous people all the time, but it's their peripheral people you really want to connect with, since they tend to make most of the decisions and bring in the specialists like us. Back in the day, it was rude to try and infringe on a famous person's privacy. There wasn't such a difference between you and them, they just knew a lot more people and had a lot more money. You didn't try to get a picture or advertise your acquaintance with them on social media for the entire world to see. Back then, relationships were much more organic. I specifically remember a time when I was simply exhausted on a job site, and I had put my head down on the table and I felt strong soothing hands on my shoulders. The strong hands belonged to someone who was barefoot on the filthy venue floor, and that's all I could see of him with my head down through the site line between my thighs. I wouldn't know until later, when a member of my crew informed me, that Sean Connery had just given me a massage.

I like that Suzi couldn't care less about the people we, sometimes, worked for. She knows to lower her eyes if someone famous is parading around their dressing room naked in front of us or to never accept anything from them, not even a glass of water. She is a sparkling servant who cannot wait to get home to Queens and drink a box of low-grade wine on the train ride there.

The rehearsal dinner for the fabulous pair was probably my favorite part of the wedding. Rehearsal dinners are more of a relaxed animal in comparison to the main event. Families are often meeting for the first time, and getting to know each other, so they are on their friendliest behavior. The atmosphere is purposefully jovial, and it's entertaining to watch how the women look each other up and down, assessing their fashion sense, and the overall finished product of a person. The men become ultimately male, and they bond in the most primal and simplest of ways. A single good-quality cigar or a sports-based conversation can sew an everlasting friendship between fellas within seconds. I fucking adore men. In this scenario, the famous bride was American, and not particularly classy nor educated. The juxtaposition of her 'less than middle class' family and this magnificent clan of people and their castle-life was almost absurd. She sat there with her black lipstick, but at least, her hair was done up in a classy manner. Thank God tattoos weren't in style back then. She would have been covered in them. It was clear that her stylist had a productive moment of clarity and made sure that she was ready for this environment.

The groom was all cock and balls. Every time we caught a glimpse of him, he either had hunting boots on, a cigar hanging out of his mouth, a rifle under his arm, or all the above at once. Frankly, I was surprised he didn't come to the table in a suit of armor. Instead, he had this kilt on that mesmerized me to the point where I was standing inside of the massive fire-place that graced the great hall, hoping to catch a 'back-end' glimpse of him. Even funnier, as I shook myself out of my fluster, I smacked into a few of my crew who were doing the same thing. We all just blushed and went about our business.

As they were enjoying their rehearsal evening, we started setting up for the main event the next day. I had stepped in so much horse shit by this time that I was realizing that these away jobs were potentially a waste of my time, but I supposed it's always good to experience a change of scenery. Back then, when famous people got married, they weren't worried about drones flying overhead taking unwanted pictures or press waiting at the gates of their property. They just simply got married, right out in front of everyone. When they get divorced, usually a few months later, it's in front of everyone, too. If I had to choose, I always said that I would much rather be rich than famous.

The wedding went off without a hitch. It was quite boring, considering who it was for, but the flowers were fucking spectacular and the mother of the groom was beaming with pride. We hung out in our guest cottage, eating gross shit, waiting to break down. As the crowd was dancing and drinking, we made little cash and carry bouquets with the flowers from the centerpieces, so that the guests could take home an item from the party, aside from acid indigestion and shit-filled shoes. We broke the party down and were on a plane home that night. We never even said goodbye.

We would continue to travel all over the world. We girls covered our heads and faces in Abu Dhabi before it was popular for white girls to do so, we journeyed to Australia, Morocco, Spain, Paris, England, Italy, and even Greece, which I really don't remember due to excessive partying. Our passports began to resemble comic books and many of our personal relationships were going to shit. We had more free miles than humanly possible. We were gone all the time and when we were home, we were still gone; jetlagged and pissed off that no one was bringing us our breakfast in the mornings. After attempting to have some boyfriends, I finally gave up and went dormant for several years, aside from taking a cater waiter home from time to time.

We were making crazy money and we were spending it, too. I even bought a special sidecar for my motor cycle, so my dogs could ride along with me in an enclosed contraption, complete with custom pet seat belts in case I lost control or got over-excited. I bought a house upstate which I never went to, and the pipes froze over my first winter there, so I sold it at a loss. I would buy out popular restaurants to treat my crew to elaborate holiday dinners. I exposed them to Caviar and other fine foods, along with the best women for my guys that money could buy. My girls often got jewelry and even a down payment on a house for my top people. They all got cash, no matter what. My crew was growing. I didn't even know the names of them all, but I smiled at whoever crossed my path in the office.

We started turning away work, coming up with ridiculous reasons as to why we didn't 'feel right for the job.'

We had an arrogance about us, but a strength that people found attractive, and they were lining up to overpay us.

Truth was I was getting bored. But then, one day, I was handing out cash on the flower market, when a fierce gay wolf caught my eye. I had heard of him. We were technically competitors, but if you were as fabulous as I was at that moment, it wouldn't have phased you either. I didn't need a boyfriend. I needed a partner in crime and someone to play with.

Chapter Three

"I'm selfish, impatient, and a little insecure. I make mistakes, I am out of control, and at times, hard to handle. But if you can't handle me at my worst, then you sure as hell don't deserve me at my best."

-Marilyn Monroe

We became inseparable. He taught me things I will never forget. He lived in a total shit-hole in Chelsea, where his neighbors hung their laundry in the hallways and left their doors open while they cooked dinner for impossibly large families living in ridiculously small spaces. But his apartment functioned more as a sex house in a centrally located place, where his friends could do drugs, suck cocks, and do laundry at the same time. He even took out his stove, so he could get a small stackable washer/dryer set installed in his tiny kitchen. He was the cleanest dirtiest boy I will ever know. His shantytown bedroom was strange. He slept on a thin mattress on the floor that was literally a large rectangle of foam that I think he cut himself with a hand-held saw. The mattress was covered with some exotic-looking tapestry that you would see on a stoner's wall in a college dorm. A leather swing gently swayed back and forth, situated directly above the bed, the screw holes packed with some sort of asbestos-looking material that somehow secured it into the ceiling. God knows he tested it out enough to know that it would hold steady. The walls were painted in ridiculous colors, but miraculously, they existed in harmony to the naked eye. One wall was painted a deep gold hue, while the adjacent wall was covered in some suede-textured Ralph Lauren paint that wasn't completely applied correctly, so it looked like stucco gone very badly. It all came together, though, and several of us found ourselves spending most of our time there, even though our apartments were much more desirable. He had no T.V., only a small boom box that always played music I wish I had discovered. He was always one step ahead of me in some ways, and I was like a happy little puppy that gladly followed him down a K hole.

He was from the deep-south and he had an even deeper southern accent, even though he had lived in the city for over twenty years. He only dated massive black men and he did more drugs than anyone I had ever met. He had a very successful company that specialized in creating magical environments on rich people's terraces. Terraces in NYC are a rare find, but he had the monopoly on every *pied-à-terre* outdoor space belonging to the wealthiest people in the city, mainly located on the Upper East Side. If only half of these people could see how this boy lived when he didn't have his thumbs in their dirt. He didn't take shit from anyone. He would go to meetings in ripped jeans, most likely stoned out of his mind, and he would act openly belligerent to the client, if they dared to challenge his prices, shaming them into paying him even more than he had asked for in the first place. He got away with everything I wanted to get away with, and he simply did not give a fuck about anything but his own personal comfort, sexual appetite, and whatever his personal needs were at any given time. He was like a werewolf who didn't need a full moon to come out, he was out full time. He scared and intrigued me at the same time, and I was on the fence as to whether I should be more like him. I can say this; I respected the shit out of him, which was rare for me.

He was fiercely protective of our friendship and he was probably the most hospitable to me out of anyone. I was like his very glamorous younger sister that he never knew about growing up. He loved wearing my clothes, and he would always give me the first hit off whatever pipe we were smoking before all other mouths got to it. He didn't believe in stress or second guessing himself, which is basically what our business is made up of. I would talk to him about being upset about a client, and he would reply in a syrupy southern drawl, "Girl, who gives a shit, let it go." And suddenly, I did, in fact, let it go. I didn't realize until many years later that living in denial isn't necessarily a great thing, but it certainly worked for us for the time being, and he made a successful career out of doing so.

We went to Fire Island in the summers, where I was truly at my peak of gay saturation, aside from hopping over to Provincetown sometimes. We did drugs that took us into other dimensions that we snapped ourselves out of by eating spoons full of sugar, just so we could ingest another kind of drug right away to experience a different kind of high. Mary Poppins really knew her shit.

We had the same kind of dogs, which really confirmed our closeness, and the dogs would often wander around the island, while their fucked-up parents gasped for breath after realizing that they were under the water in the pool and not above. The dogs made lots of friends on the island and were well-fed most of the time. They went on colorful excursions that mirrored those movies where the animals formed charming unions and spoke amongst themselves, only to prove that they were much smarter than their owners. In this case, they most definitely were, and they found their way home in just enough time for us to board the ferry, head back to reality, and go to work.

There came a time when I would quietly wish for a client to call with an urgent need, just to beg out of hanging out with my gay wolf, now and again. I just couldn't keep up with him, and I feared that I was going to either overdose or, even worse, have a bad skin breakout or possibly gain weight.

To this day, Suzi basically hates every single one of my friends. She feels I give them all the benefit of the doubt, even when they don't deserve it, but isn't that what true friends do? I tended to collect people form everywhere. Depending upon my mood, I would become enamored with the world's strangest misfits. I was not the type to go out with a group of girls, do a happy hour or go shopping. I needed to be with people that took me on a constant adventure, whether it be good or bad. I needed to observe perversity and diversity; otherwise, everything went stale or moldy for me. Sometimes, my best friends would easily become strangers over-night and vice versa. The friendships that have truly and consistently lasted for me are with dogs and currently, Suzi.

When one of our largest clients called one Monday after another beast of burden weekend to hire me to consult on the opening of their new showrooms in Los Angeles, I jumped at the chance to go and detox for a bit. Believe it or not, I had been all over the world but never to L.A. I was always interested in the sunshine part of it, not really the Hollywood stuff, but I was looking forward to driving a car and getting the fuck out of Dodge for the next six months, which they had contracted me for.

I had recently taken Suzi to L.A. for the first time for a small gig we did for some influencer celebrity type and she hated it. Her pale body that had never driven a car just didn't belong there. Everyone took too long to get back to us about general things, and the food was simply too clean for her. Though this was, in fact, where she fell in love with Avocado Toast, so she did come back with something. Growing up, my mom never fed us anything green, and an Avocado meant Guacamole to us. Now, it's its own food group and an international delicacy.

I took Suzi hiking, which, to me, was the only reason to enjoy L.A. and she did try to like it but only for fifteen minutes or so. As we climbed higher up the canyon, I could see she was getting scared and she walked as far away from the edge as possible, completely missing the view. I could see her whole body deflate with relief when I told her we could head back down. Suzi is capable of many things, but she will never drive a car or much less sit in one for long, so obviously, L.A. just simply is not for her. 'My L.A.' consisted of a full-time driver, so this was acceptable to her but the sitting in traffic part overshadowed this acceptance quite quickly.

When I first informed my NYC-based clients that I would be living a bicoastal lifestyle for a bit, they all looked at me like I was out of my mind or as if they smelled something horrible. The only reasonable advice I got from anyone before I left was that I should never ever compare L.A. to NY or NY to L.A. and I should be fine.

I packed up the pups. I had two at the time and they were die-hard in putting up with me. I stored their cashmere sweaters and winter outfits, got them certified to ride on the plane with me, and we started our adventure.

I have always been adaptable up to a point. You can drop me in the middle of a forest, and I will enjoy it for quite some time, but only if I know, for a fact, that I am, at some point, getting out of there and going home. This was quite a departure for me, going to a land unknown, without my crew and starting anew on a wing, a prayer, and a hefty paycheck. The client had made a reservation for me to live in a hotel until I could find lodging and get myself settled. It wasn't as easy back then. You literally had to buy a newspaper and look in the classified ads to see if there were rentals available, and there was usually a phone number listed that nobody ever answered when you called.

The hotel I was perching at was a dream, and frankly, if I could have just stayed there, I may have lived on the beach forever, but at a thousand bucks a night, it was not a reality. I adore hotel living. I kind of live that way now, and I think I always will. The property was glorious, situated in Santa Monica, smack dab on the beach, decorated to the hilt with charming and elegant nautical-themed tchotchkes, roaring fireplaces, and pretty people everywhere. The pups and I were in heaven. We walked on the beach in the morning until we got a ticket for doing so, but I quickly figured out the safe places to go in the early morning, so they could get their exercise. I also got several tickets for jaywalking, which blew my mind. The client would send a car for me and I would sit in it for fucking hours. When I finally got to meetings in L.A., I would have a horrible tooth-grinding problem. As I spent more time there, I learned that no matter how many miles you were going or what time of day it was, you needed to leave an hour ahead of time, and if you got to your destination early, you should just go for a coffee or something and celebrate that you made it ahead of time or that you didn't turn around and go the fuck home. The traffic was a non-starter for me. At least, in NY, when you are stuck in traffic, you are going somewhere great. In L.A., you are just going toward more traffic. Apparently, the not comparing L.A. to NY and vice versa advice wasn't working for me either. When I finally did make friends out there, we would all constantly cancel if we didn't live near each other, simply because of the traffic and the fact that accessible driver apps hadn't been born yet and none of us could afford any more DUIs. It was a lonely place for me, and the work was bland. I figured out that L.A. was more about celebrity than style, and that doing the same all white furniture party was completely acceptable to them. All that mattered was that there was an impressive step and repeat area for photos, then the event would be a success. Most of the time, the celebrity would just show up to take the crucial photo and not even go to the party. To me, L.A. was just a very watered-down version of NY style-wise. So, even though the show-room I was working on was a lot bigger than the NY property, because the one thing L.A. did have was land to build upon, it just wasn't as fabulous, and it was lacking a certain organic sexiness. So much so that I felt hindered by the environment and was having performance issues. My creative process usually fed off the interaction and observation of people. In L.A., you went from your house to your car, to your job, back to your car, then back into your house, only to cancel the plans you had for that evening. My gay wolf buddy came out to visit me a few times, but he felt let down as well and was not happy with the choice of cocks that were situated nearby, so he left. I felt like if I was to succeed at blending in, I needed to move into an apartment complex and eventually buy a car, so I could at least converse in 'L.A. language.' I would also have to get tan, get fit, and eat shit I didn't like.

I hadn't attempted to buy a car yet, so I rented a bike from one of the beach kiosks and quickly told them that I wasn't a tourist and to go easy on the pricing. I wanted to rent the bike for a few months, thinking that it would be a nice thing to have around and so I could get drunk at a restaurant and get home. The guys looked at me like I was crazy. I threw them way off course, they didn't understand how to charge for it, and I rocked their worlds in my NY way. We made the deal, I got on the bike, and I started to roam around the beach neighborhoods in search of an apartment.

Without knowing any better, I gravitated to the wrong side of town, which, to me, still looked quite nice, once again in comparison to most NYC hoods that are deemed sketchy. I had crossed over an avenue into a supposed bad place, but I rode past the most charming house that had a 'for rent' sign on it, and I was intrigued. There was a yard where the dogs could play, parking spaces, and a few apartments in the rear of the house with a shared courtyard in the form of what they call a triplex.

There was a cool-looking lady outside, sitting on the main house stoop, along with a young couple who seemed to have been looking at the available apartments, too. I stopped the bike and walked over to them and immediately it felt right, even though I think I heard some gunshots going off nearby. It was unfortunate that the couple had just rented the apartment, but the lady gave me her number and told me to call her later anyway, in case their financials didn't go through.

Within thirty minutes, the woman drove up next to me, as I was riding along Lincoln Avenue. Just so happens she was gay, and she had gotten rid of the other tenants and freed up the apartment for me to have, since she thought I was 'wicked hot.' I had fallen out of my NY cave filled with gay wolves and had landed into the land of powerful pussies.

The L.A. Lesbian is a magnificent and powerful beast.

Suzi grew up living in her family's houses. She never went out looking for apartments or roommates, except for maybe in college. Currently, she lives in her Grandmother's house in Queens, which has four bedrooms, two bathrooms, a fenced in backyard, and a two-car garage. The boy that she recently met, whom she says she is going to marry, is moving in with her and they will be real estate 'set for life' at the age of twenty-five. They will be able to put away one of their salaries completely, while the other covers their very minimal overhead. They will never stress about money, which, to me, will be the potential key to their relationship success. Money is basically round since it seems to roll in and roll out constantly, but these kids have everything mapped out, including their future kid's college funds and though it boggles my mind, I respect the hell out of it, and maybe envy it a tiny bit.

Living my new California life, I had fallen into my landlady's circle of friends, and they were an intriguing group of women. They took care of me like I was their long lost, white, pretty woman/baby who ignited their maternal instincts and sex drives, all at once. One of them was a famous chef, another was an exclusive home delivery drug specialist (celebrity drug dealer), and there was a fitness guru, a photographer, and a very high-powered lawyer. I found that the difference between the gay male wolves and these women was that these chicks took me in with such fierce loyalty, it was almost shocking. They happily put my needs first and it made them genuinely satisfied. Boys just don't roll that way, gay or not.

After I got immersed into my circle of friends, I found myself going out at night to these all girl clubs in West Hollywood, where the more mature pretty lesbians would hold court in the back rooms, while younger girls would wait in line to basically kiss their rings. These women were spectacular, like modern day Greek goddesses but in the form of living breathing women. Their bodies were sculpted beautifully, their nails, hair, and fashion were flawless, and most importantly, their bank accounts were bursting at the seams. They were the perfect husbands my PR girlfriends all wanted, with the exception that they were women.

After a while, I felt like I was living in a bouncy house filled with tits, hormones, and tramp stamps, and I was craving some boy attention. One great thing I will declare about L.A. is that there is a population of straight men to play with. I cannot speak to the quality of the group, but at this point, if they were breathing and heterosexual, I would make it work.

The girls had been taking me hiking every morning when I was in town. There wasn't an inch of a canyon I hadn't seen or sweated on. I loved our early morning hikes. They made sitting in traffic, later in the day, a bit more bearable. There was a gym on every corner in L.A., so I decided to join one and work on fine-tuning my physique to its best potential. Also, I figured it would be a great place to meet uncomplicated boys. I can say that L.A. is where I really found my 'fitness self,' since it was what most people seemed to be doing all day long.

I chose a gym that was within walking distance of my apartment. As soon as I walked in, I saw a thick pair of legs that my loins said yes to. We were married eight months later, and I am not certain if we are legally divorced yet, even though I married several times since then. I do know, however, that he is still on my payroll.

I feel no need to get into my marriages because if they were exciting or even had any impact on who I am today, then I would be speaking of them a lot more. To me, marriage is like going for a hike on a familiar path in the woods and taking a different route from time to time. I still come out at the same place in the end, even though the view may vary.

I guess I felt I should've tried marriage from time to time, simply because everyone else was doing it. Let's face it, I saw my clients do it every week end and it was easy to get caught up in the gooey bits, even though I was often watching it from the inside out, which is never as pretty. There is and always has been a small part of me that wonders if I should care more about fitting in. In those insecure moments I join the band wagon and getting married is certainly a popular human custom. When Suzi finally informed me that she was getting married, I was thrilled at celebrating her 'normalcy,' while accepting, once again, that I would forever be a lone star, no matter how many times I walked down the aisle. Two minutes after she said yes to her school teacher, she picked up the phone, and planned her own nuptials within several hours. I, however, took several months, almost up to the day of her summer wedding to design it. I had never been so inconclusive. I would design it one way, show it her, she would love it, and then I would go home and delete it over and over again. Finally, I just asked if we could shelve it until it truly became the last hour in time for me to actually purchase the items to make the *décor* happen. For some reason, she agreed to do this, and she only checked in on me a few times, though I know the suspense was burning a hole in her little belly. I suppose that, subconsciously, I knew that if I finished the design, she would really float down that aisle in the opposite direction from me.

During that time, which seems so long ago, I was living like a bipolar rock star, going back and forth between coasts, living in a huge house on the beach on one coast and in a small apartment on the other. Funnily enough, I always preferred the small apartment. The big house had too many areas to decorate, and I simply couldn't relax around that many options, the creative excitement was too much to bear.

I had an interesting array of clients in L.A., mainly old school celebrities, many, of whom, a millennial wouldn't recognize, even though they may have discovered Motown or the Internet. I have fond memories of meeting such powerful types that often reeked of garlic due to an enormous consumption of a vegan diet adopted shortly after a 'scare' or, in layman's terms, a heart attack.

When I wasn't at work, my routine consisted of walking the dogs first, then hiking, and biking for hours. By the time 3 p.m. rolled around, I was wishing for the sun to go down. The sun was everywhere. It would flood into our bedroom, spill down the stairs, then it would whisper along the sidewalk, pausing to lick an orange tree or two and finally, it would situate itself into the front seat of my car, singeing my ass like a cigarette ash would. Its presence was so strong I could feel the cells in my skin sizzle like a fatty piece of bacon. I was scared that if I farted, my hair would catch fire, along with the rest of the landscape. The sun was both intoxicating and paralyzing. I was suffering from visual migraines at least two to three times a day, because the glare from the sun was permeating my nervous system. I felt like I was constantly running from something I couldn't get away from that was much larger than me. I was good at running away from myself, but I was no match for the California sun.

To a normal person, my life was enviable. I was part of two amazing worlds. I had a hubby who talked about having a child, but only when we were shit-faced, thank God, and only to be forgotten about the next morning. The only child I could even perceive of having was one I could get or buy, and it would definitely be a boy and one that looked nothing like either of us, so I could have something exciting to look at all of the time. This was also a fleeting desire and I felt it best not to act on something else I could never get out of.

I was in earthquake terms at a level five of boredom, even with my Bi-Coastal fabulous status.

I drove out to Palm Springs to produce an event that saved me from the minutia for a few hours. As I passed the gigantic steel windmills, they waved at me joyfully, as if they were looking forward to seeing me lie naked in the pool again. It was so fucking hot there that neither my dogs nor my hubby would tag along, so I was on my own this time, which I was obviously thrilled about.

The event consisted of only sixteen guests, two, of whom, were celebrating their fifty years of friendship and business relationship. One guy was the record label mogul who had discovered the other guy, and they sang to each other all night long, sitting at the dining table that I had produced for them out of solid planks of gold. Their heavily bosomed and fleshy lipped wives sat in hypnotic states, occasionally sipping on their gold-flecked champagne cocktails and licking caviar served in tight piles on gold spoons, of course. It was a lovely evening and if I had to list a favorite event of mine, this would have to be it. The flow of the event was so natural. The two men sang their hit songs to one another a Capella, as the palm trees above them swayed to their rhythm. The desert was so quiet, aside from the occasional coyote who tried to join in the tempo. The dysfunctional families from both sides sat in peace and respect, and it was one of the healthier moments I had witnessed amongst humans in L.A.

I knew then that this was as good as it was going to get for me out there.

Aside from producing an eight million dollar same-sex wedding (the first of its kind in Cali) in Malibu, I felt like my career had hit a Stop sign. Nothing was making me happy or inspiring me. The bigger and more glamorous the jobs got, the more I felt introverted. I had officially become the extroverted introvert, staying publicly alive, long enough to get the job, cash the checks, and go back to bed. This would be me forever.

I started hanging out more and more with my 'lady circle' again, particularly, the drug specialist. She and I were thick as thieves. We were both Scorpios and able to handle a recreational load fit for a drug lord. I have a philosophy about drug addicts. They are not worse than the rest of us, just more bored. She and I would trip through the desert or a random canyon every day. I was blowing so much coke and whatever else up my nose, I had eradicated any need for plastic surgery on my face ever. I didn't need Botox. My muscles were comfortably numb, as was my heart. Something happened to me during this time. I became paranoid. While others looked out at the ocean with pure joy, I was convinced the dolphins were mocking me and doing that cute talky thing they do behind my back. The sun got even hotter, and the grass was simply too green to enjoy. The once aromatic smells from the jasmine vine growing in my yard were making me nauseated, and I would throw up in my mouth just a little bit as I passed by them to enter my house. L.A. was making me sick for some reason, and I will never know why, aside from it just not being NY. I didn't even like my dogs as much in this environment. They had taken on such 'A plus B = C' personas, acting like typical dogs in a perfect environment, and they were lacking a certain amount of character and dimension. They were happy, I suppose, and to me, that was just beige. I was existing in the middle of a very boring color spectrum.

I started to resent my clients, and even more so, I dreaded getting into my car to go and see them. I felt super-imposed onto any environment I was in, and I was unable to permeate and solidify my surroundings. I thought I had outgrown my restless-ness, but it was just getting worse.

I found myself going back to NY a lot more often. I had picked up where I left off with my old friends. I was staying with them, even though I had an apartment of my own. My main gay wolf and I were up to our old shenanigans, trolling the town and sabotaging anything good that came our way. I was playing a vicious tennis match with myself. I would get a great inquiry for an event and not only would I not answer it, I would violently volley it away into an abyss of anger and disappointment that would ensure the client would never ever contact me again.

I began to wonder what happened to me. Where did the joy of watching a father walk his daughter down the aisle go? I used to cry so hard during these ceremonies, I couldn't even watch them. Or relishing in the sheer joy of a surprise party going off without a hitch, or a product launch that was so successful it would be on the cover of every newspaper just hours after it ended. My 'happy moments' bank was so full, I never even checked the balance on my other accounts, which were quickly surpassing the good times.

I sat by the Hudson River, which can already be kind of depressing and I played a montage of the shit I had witnessed over the years in my head. The joyous parts went by in fast motion. Then came the barrage of images that I must have internalized into a poisonous cauldron deep inside my being. I started to sweat as I recalled giving CPR to a father of a bride who had a heart attack right before the father-daughter dance. He died in my arms. The bride was having such a great time and was so drunk that I decided not to tell her until the wedding was over. There were visions of huge floral centerpieces falling over as guests crashed into dining tables because of drunken behavior. The large glass vases crashing onto the mirrored tabletops, shattering all the drinking glasses, as red wine spewed to the farthest corners of the room and onto pale-colored and most expensive dresses.

At a recent wedding, I had walked into the private back of the house bathroom to come upon the newly married bride giving a blow job to the best man. I saw so many unthinkable things in the private offices of event venues; they must have automatically been cataloged in a library of disasters inside my psyche. unbeknownst to me. I blamed my resistance to humanity solely on humanity itself. The naïve part of me had been so disappointed by being disappointed that I think I finally cracked. My so-called heroes or people that

I would long to produce parties for always ended up being people I didn't like, or worse yet, they didn't really like me. It never failed to shock me to be treated like the help, even though I was the help. We would work on million-dollar events, only to be told not to go inside the main house or ordered to drink water out of a garden hose on a sweltering day. I suppose it was hard to swallow being paid millions. while simultaneously being treated poorly. I think we all like to be kissed while being fucked.

The little girl in the back room of the flower shop was gone. I either had to beat them or join them, so becoming a walking disaster seemed like the right thing to do.

To this day, I am very cautious about spreading this kind of dread across my team, especially Suzi. When a leader becomes stifled or lost, it will ultimately cause a domino effect, leading to mass destruction. I used to be able to 'text' (lie/text) Suzi and say that I had a skin appointment or a meeting with our finance team for the day, when I was feeling less than happy and creative, now, she is on to me and knows that I am just stuck and can't engage. Most of the time it passes, and I come out shiny and fabulous again, like a car exiting a gregarious car wash, but I know it scares her when my spurts are prolonged.

Chapter Four

"Special people lead difficult lives."

-My mother

I was reaching out to everything like an insect caught on its back. I even tried my hand at appearing on television as an expert on a variety of news and design shows. Television was even more frustrating for me, since it seemed as if most of the production people were frustrated 'wanna be' actors and they were always waiting for lunch or designing the next tattoo they were going to get. I hated how that once I allowed myself to be put into other people's hands, they would, somehow, end up misrepresenting me, though it wasn't really their fault, since I was having a hard time figuring out who I was myself. The morning shows were stressful, mainly because I would often have to be on set at an ungodly early morning hour, and once I stepped onto set, I could never get a word in amongst the show host banter. Overall, I felt that television 'lessened' how unique a person I was, even if I wasn't a very good one. I even wrote a book that started out like a shining deacon of inspiration for me, but once handed over to the publisher, it became an item I banished to the highest point on my book shelf, never to proudly grace the center of my coffee table for all to admire.

I felt gagged. I would speak, and it would be what people wanted to hear, and never what I truly wanted to say. I was so good at the game but even when I was winning, I was losing. I had stopped calling my parents. They knew that if they didn't hear some drunken funny message eating up their message space at least once a week, something was terribly wrong. I wasn't depressed, I was just floating without any gravity supply.

I needed to do as the Australians do and go on a walkabout. Coincidentally enough, I mapped out my journey in a flower pattern on a world map I had pinned to the wall behind my desk; the edges of the petals touching upon continents and magical cities. My dogs followed my pinning motions with their huge ears and eyes, somehow, aware of my impending departure. Boston Terriers resemble *animé* creatures, especially mine, since theirs were a rare fawn color, rather than the usual black and white. Their eyes would easily bare into my soul, and they reached into a part of me that I didn't know existed. Essentially, I feel like they taught me how to love. In turn, they were the loves of my life.

I would make this a productive and inspiring trip, only stopping to check in on my team and to have an affair with another traveler in the form of a prize-winning photo-journalist. Our sex life would resemble the happy highlights of a massive scavenger hunt. We would come up with riddles for each other to decipher, if we would be in the same cities at the same time, etc. This never actually happened. I had just hoped it would to convince myself further to take the trip. Don't get me wrong, I fucked my way through the world in eighty days easily, but I don't recall a lot of it, meaning that part just wasn't memorable.

I was incredibly intrigued by Japan and they were quite fascinated with me as well. I was intensely tall and beautiful there, and they, somehow, knew who I was when I landed, and I was treated like a star, right off the tarmac. Technology and the production value of the city had me mesmerized. The video mapping, the LED lighting, and paneling, the Karaoke madness and the ludicrous elements that the population was addicted to such as Hello Kitty, robots, and eclectic fashion blew my mind. It was so fucking crowded, and there wasn't one dude I wanted to hook up with there, so I needed to move on, and I figured I could probably go to Vegas and get the same vibe there, if I ever needed a fix.

The poorer parts of any of the countries I went to were real downers for me and I immediately avoided that genre of exposure. After all, I was in a luxury business and I was doing this tough work to better my services and gain inspiration.

Parts of India and Africa were simply devastating and then, I would, somehow, go from riding through piles of garbage and seeing starving children to being seated in a palace for dinner or in a million-dollar tent flanked by men in tuxedos in a safari setting.

I went to places like Russia where I couldn't even grasp the language, nor did I want to, and in Brazil, I couldn't quite pick up on certain dialects either. There were times I felt nervous about not knowing where I was and by simply being a young woman. I was convinced that if I smoked Hashish in Turkey, my head would be cut off and sent back to my mother in Poughkeepsie with no return address. I was so very young, and I forgot to use that as an excuse for feeling lost, but it was valid, when I look back on it. For me, excuses needed to be few and far between and that taking the blame for everything was a much faster way for me to continue moving forward.

I felt very comfortable, mostly in London, because to me, it was New York with a different accent, and it was just as expensive. What I mainly learned about traveling is that what we all have in common, no matter where we live, is that we all wish to eat, drink, fuck, and feel attractive. These same rules apply to producing a perfect party, no need to travel all over the world to figure that out, but it was worth seeing the world's color palettes change as I moved between countries.

The bright Oranges of India's Marigolds, the Grays and Blues of the English Skies shocked out of their dullness by the bright red telephone booths lining the London streets, the intense Green of an Irish hillside, the clear turquoise ocean in New Zealand bordered by chocolate brown mountains, and the ethereal white hue cast over Iceland expressed through snow and ice gave my eyes some new wonderment material and I knew that I was getting ready to regurgitate some brilliant designs onto the party community back home. No matter where I travelled, I simply couldn't run away from myself. I was like an agitated boomerang that was running out of patience with my persistence to stay away from its starting point.

I had obviously been in touch with my team while I was gone. I woke up one morning in Portugal, looked at my pocket calendar, and I realized I had been gone for over three months. I mainly missed my dogs, but I also noticed that my team had scattered, much like children left alone for way too long of a time. Their morale was down, and the inspiration that I had once provided for them was gone and they were pissed at me because of it. A couple members of the team decided to go out on their own, taking a few of my clients with them, but for some reason, I just didn't care. Perhaps, they were doing me a favor.

For the first time, the business wasn't doing well, and it was losing money. This was not an equation I had even thought about, so I hadn't counted on ways to solve it, except to make my way back home again.

When I landed, my first mode of business was to see my dogs. They had been staying with one of the gay wolves, who was living in my apartment. The reports were fine, but I knew that if they were missing me as much as I was missing them, they would be in a fragile state. They were the only living things in my life that would never grow up and I suppose we had that in common. I was responsible for their happiness and they were easier to please than I was. They kept my blood pressure down and gave me the structure I needed to function as a part-time acceptable person.

I felt as if something was off as soon as I walked into my building. The once, jovial doormen, that would greet me with smiles and 'welcome homes,' gave me shady eyes and bowed heads. As I walked down the hall towards my apartment, I noticed a stale stench that was coming from my place. I opened the door to my former utopia and every piece of my furniture was gone, which was fucking terrifying. I instantly checked my safe where the designer jewelry originals, cash, and drugs were to make sure that was intact and thankfully, it was. Anyone stupid enough to steal my furniture would not be mentally astute enough to get into my safe. I had cameras all over the joint, so I needed to check the footage ASAP. The knowledge that I came away with after watching the footage was this. My gay wolf was consistently phenomenally attentive to my pups, which is all that mattered, but he was also the one that seemed to have sold my furniture. From what I could make out, watching the grainy footage, was that two huge men entered my apartment, there was an exchange with my wolf and then twenty minutes later, there were five huge men in the apartment taking away my furniture, and I swear it looked like one guy might have taken a shit on my bed, hence the bad smell, but I suppose that's all in the past. The building staff was so used to my strange lifestyle. I assume they thought it was all part of my landscape.

Apparently, my wolf got into some money trouble. People in NYC tend to live beyond their means. This is not a negative statement, it's just true.

From there, my life resembled one of those automatic toilets that got stuck and would continue to flush and flush and flush. The shit had really hit the fan and it simply wouldn't go down the drain when I attempted to clean it up.

For the first time ever, my money was seriously running out and the people around me, who I thought were loyal to my 'cause,' simply weren't anymore. My clients seemed to have scattered and to top it all off, an act of terrorism rocked the city of New York to its knees. Everything went dark, the phone went dead, and I was scrambling to keep up with my lifestyle, let alone pay the bills that were piling up everywhere. My entire staff had scattered, except for the main lady who never left the office, let alone her desk. I knew that I needed to hold onto her, everybody needed a side-kick and someone that would just be devoted to them blindly and unconditionally. We had to move out of my office in the middle of the night and transfer the entire operation into my apartment, which was looking haggard and empty without the furniture and the funds to replenish. It was a morbid ambiance and we all know how well I do with those. The phone would ring once every three days and it would be for jobs that were for a fraction of the price I was used to working for.

I think that I was in shock and I found myself just getting through the days. I had stopped showering and eating, but I was working out harder than ever. It didn't cost me anything, so I decided that my idle hands should hit the pavement in the form of running, biking, and just challenging myself physically any way that I could, simply because it was the only thing I could control at the moment. This way of life was not acceptable to me, I knew it would pass but I needed a bridge to lead me back to fabulous. I knew that I needed to keep up appearances within my industry to look as though I was just fine, as the rest of the world was in turmoil. I was untouchable and even an act of God or terrorism couldn't get me down; I was bigger than that. Even though I only had the one employee left, she still cost me over a half a million a year and the business and my 'savings' just wasn't supporting her, along with my 'I've far exceeded the Joneses lifestyle' debts.

I quickly sold off some of my 'toys'; the motorcycle, second car, my investment apartment, my 'out of the city but close by train house' and clothes and art. The problem was that I basically sold everything at a loss, since it was not politically correct for people to spend money on pretty things in the humid economic climate, money just wasn't circulating anymore.

There was a little bar that I used to go to when I was living upstate many years ago that was always hopping with a local 'trying to be trendy' crowd. This group wasn't wealthy enough to hire someone like me for jobs, but they were good enough to take a middle stream income from and they had no idea who I really was. Secretly, I approached the owner and asked to bartend there a few times a week. After all, this girl knew her cocktails and there is no better time to bartend than when the world is falling apart.

I was, of course, the reason people started coming back to the place, as with everything I did, and held a consistent interest in, I became the best at it. I was hoping that word didn't travel down south on the Hudson River to my clients, who were on a temporary partying hiatus, but I was bringing home nice wads of cash on a regular basis. It just wasn't enough to make a dent in my financial crisis. I wish to clarify that I was never ashamed that I had to take a job to survive. I have always done whatever it is I needed to do to keep moving in any direction, especially if it was forward. I have also always been either a workaholic or a slacker, nothing in between. I knew that my idle hands would only result in mass destruction, so taking a job was the responsible thing to do and I felt proud of that. There was a small part of me that felt deflated, of course. Every rock star feels a low after an electric performance; it's hard to keep going up from that. I was okay with my life taking dips and turns, if it didn't, I would get bored.

I never want Suzi to see me less than ecstatic about everything. For me, it's important to be honest with her, when I am frustrated or exasperated, but up to a point. I often catch her giggling as I struggle with something electronic and I sigh audibly. She really gets a kick out of it, but beyond that, she cannot know the really dark places my psyche visits from time to time and a bit more often as I get older. I never thought that I would be one of those people that takes inventory of what I have and haven't achieved in my life, but for me, still, it's never enough and that's a grimy cycle to be caught within. I have never described myself as a success because to this day, I still don't know that it is. Am I great at what I do? Fuck, yes, but am I horrible at life's obvious tasks, such as being in love, going to the post office, and overall consistency? Fuck, yes, too. I want Suzi to walk around my beautiful life and marvel at it like a trip to Willy Wonka's Chocolate Factory and never be able to look behind the scenes at the less than perfect mechanics of it all, but when you spend so much time with someone, it's hard not to look into those dirty windows and the simple truth is; I just don't want to depress her. Therefore, I need to pick and choose which pieces of my dirty laundry she is allowed to help fold. Some of my 'story' I choose to keep to myself, as I lull her to sleep with my tale, while flying across the land to ignite different parts of the world with parties.

One night, a charismatic man walked into the bar I was shamelessly working at. I panicked because he looked 'city' to me, but I could tell he didn't know who I was. It turned out that he was what they call a 'garmento,' meaning he was in the fashion industry, working as a liaison for major fashion brands and acting as the resource that got their products made. He was the behind the scenes guy for when someone like Ralph Lauren wanted to make shower curtains or underwear. He would make the deal with larger less-known companies to make the products at a low cost and produce them under the designer's name. It was fascinating stuff and for some reason, he said business was going very well for him. He was charming, Israeli, married, along with having a mistress, and the father of several children. I assumed that he wanted to add me to his brood, but when I looked at him, I simply saw an answer to many of my financial problems. I was going to approach him about becoming an investor in my company. I had never taken a partner or any real economic help from anyone, but it was time to do so.

When you truly cannot express to someone else what you do for a living, especially an externally glamourous one, you should never ever expect for them to fully understand the inner workings of a service industry. Particularly, if they are cut and dry business people, there is no way for them to relate to ambiguity of the hours you keep and how to properly charge for them and for your creative ideas. It's still currently one of the hardest things to define about my business. Sure, I can put a price tag on decorative items or staffing and trucking, but how do you negotiate pricing for a vision or a dream you've been having for over a year and then turning it into a reality that all can share? This turned out to be a business marriage, where two people's moral codes had nothing in common.

I warned Suzi to never ever take a partner; it was bad enough that she would be taking a husband one day soon. I would continue to make mistakes every day in my life, but this was one mistake I wouldn't make twice.

Me and the 'garmento' met at a kosher restaurant in midtown during an off hour, so I felt like it was a safe choice. I realized that he had no idea as to why I asked to meet him, so for the first time, since I was very young and I was feeling extremely nervous, I was clearly off my game, I felt ashamed and dusty, like I was coming home from a night filled with irreversible disgusting decisions that could potentially haunt me every time my guard was down. Asking for help was more demeaning to me than being a bartender.

Luckily, he beat me to the punch and before even ordering a drink, he said that he found my profession exciting and he wanted to be a part of it, *Mazel Tov* to me!

Oh, how, I wish I had Suzi's young girl distrust of the world at that very moment to have reeled me in, but I was a very different young girl than she ever was. Back then, meeting someone organically and without an introduction or connection from someone else was still considered justified. You couldn't do a google search on them and find out if they had any prior arrests or misdemeanors, you just had to decide whether you like the person or not and go on my, then, undeveloped internal instinct. Suzi started out distrusting everybody, so they would have to win her trust over, in order for her to invest her time or mine. There were associates of mine that I had known and trusted for years, yet Suzi would make me aware of a side to them that I had been blind to in the past. Thus, I turned off the trust faucet and potentially avoided a world of hurt and disappointment.

He wanted to throw a huge party to announce our partnership; it would be the party of the year, especially since the world had gone to shit. I was drinking his Kool-Aid every second, entranced by his '*joi de vivre*,' and his successful and shiny exterior. I had met the wife, the kids, the mistress, and his personal trainer, which he happily hired to keep my body to the next level; firm and in tip-top shape to become a success again. I would be the toast of the city, and we would live as one big happy, modern, and fucked up family. We were so codependent; both looking for shiny diamonds buried within the rubble of the city's disaster site, much like stubborn pirates looking for treasure in the most unforeseen places.

The party was fucking amazing. He gave me a cool million as a starting budget, and I resembled a hyena with that kind of money in my paws, grabbing and tasting everything in my path to include in the festivities. I flew in circus performers from France that would serve our guests champagne, bouncing from bungee cords rigged from the ceiling. The band would consist of Stevie

Wonder's studio musicians and the Rolling Stone's back-up singers, and while dinner was served, a small orchestra of electric violins and harps would lull us into food coma. After eating a fourteen-course tasting menu created by a five-star Michelin rated chef, complete with wine and champagne pairings offered by a fabulous sommelier, of course, we would need to get dancing again, so the hottest club DJ's would duel across the dance floor to get our asses shaking again. The room filled with huge bubbles, floating across misty light beams to make the dance floor look 'celebratory.' The bathrooms all refurbished with black lacquer counter-tops, perfect for doing lines of coke on, would have queues waiting around the corner waiting to get in. While guests were on line, servers made sure that no one wanted for anything by tray passing truffles, champers, chilled shots of vodka followed by caviar, just to solidify the luxury of it all. The *décor* was magnificent. Huge Italian leather sectional sofas spanned the entire perimeter of the thirty thousand square foot space, allowing guests to admire the view of the Manhattan and Jersey skylines, even the parts that were now sadly missing. The linens were hand sewn, of course, by an academy award winning costume designer created out of the finest Dupioni silks that I had imported from my connections I had made while traveling in India. The flowers, Oh, the flowers… Well, I did a large portion of them myself, along with a team of twenty designers this time. It was my new-born baby swan song and I was back in my true element. I chose to go full on Dutch Flemish Style to express the true voluptuous vibe of the evening. Peonies spilled out all over the tables traveling down onto the floors, climbing up some of the dining chairs, landing back onto the table again, smack dab next gigantic Baccarat cut glass candelabras shimmering with gold and black taper candles. The china, serving, and glassware was all perfectly and strategically mismatched and was as prominent as a Technicolor dream coat, creating a visual palette that permeated every brain in the room to create a party that no one would ever forget. We added a philanthropic element to the evening, just long enough to be politically correct, by having the mayor get up and speak a few words about rejuvenation of downtown and let people know where they could donate to the cause on their way out. I think we helped raise a significant amount of funds that evening, so the debauchery didn't seem too politically incorrect.

My partner and I got up and toasted the crowd hands held high in the air like a president and vice president on a campaign trail and the crowd went wild. Was it possible that I was back on top that quickly? Could it be that easy? Nothing is ever that easy.

I found myself always waiting for the axe to fall, things were going so well. The phone was ringing off the hook; my partner had moved us into new office digs with a killer view of Madison Square Park. I had a new team, along with my old and faithful right-hand lady, who, of course, hated everybody else who came in. She felt threatened that I would have to divide my time and attention amongst others. He had introduced us to the other fashion houses I hadn't worked for before and it was more business than I had ever seen at once. He even brought in a killer Israeli lady to negotiate our contracts with them and to get us paid on time. In hindsight, this is where I would've taken the needle off the record and question why I would allow a stranger to come in and take over my finances, but I didn't. I couldn't even pronounce her name, so I just called her 'The Lady.' She was mean, and she wouldn't engage with anyone else in the office, which caused a 'vaginal rift' amongst my girls. Her lunch food was odd, and she never got up to pee, even for hours at a time. I requested a meeting with my partner to discuss this barnacle that had invaded our existence. Strangely enough, he hadn't returned several of my calls. He did travel a lot and perhaps, one of his wives or girlfriends or whomever told him not to speak to me, but I was starting to think it was all just too easy. I tried to swat my feelings away like a fly, but at this point, it wasn't my first time at the rodeo, and I needed to learn to trust my instincts. I wasn't going to panic; instead, I decided that I was going to dissolve the partnership.

I called one of the lawyers named Jay that I had met awhile back and asked to discuss what my options were. He informed that if you ever want to get anyone out of your life, you would have to pay them to do so, and this has proven to be true many times in my life. Jay was right on target, I told 'the lady' that I wanted her to find my partner and tell him that I was ready to buy him out. She seemed incredibly animated about this and even became friendly towards me; she was getting out. Miraculously, she contacted him and got him the necessary papers to complete the deed. I never spoke to him or saw him during this time, or ever again, for that matter. The papers were signed, 'the lady' was gone, and the enormous payment was made to him and I felt like a free rock-star again. I was so thrilled and elated to be autonomous again. It was clearly my most natural state.

My new relationships held strong. It wasn't as if I didn't know what I was doing, so business was, once again, going great and I felt invincible again. I started to build my team up, and I even began considering office spaces in other cities such as Chicago, London, and believe or not, Ohio. Lots of shit was happening in Ohio. Many of the fashion houses I was currently working with had huge headquarters there. I never really asked why, I suppose it had to do with available real estate and its friendly price point. I just knew that when the mail came, and something had an Ohio return address on it, there was usually a big shiny check inside that cleared very quickly. My financial and legal teams were working very hard to keep an eye on the bouncing balls of my multi-faceted career and I was enjoying my kangaroo like existence, hopping from one thing to the next, while collecting money in my pouch and punching out obstacles as they got in my way.

One specific day became one of the most memorable of my career to date. I will never forget how the wind felt on my face, the minty taste inside of my mouth, and the sounds of the city around me, how the cloudless bright blue sky stung my eyes, and the way the cool grassy ground felt as I fainted upon it. It was a real spring day in New York, with an added layer of chill to it as if the environment had a fresh fan set on auto, so as soon as you got too hot or too cold, it clicked on and off as needed, just to keep the temperature absolutely perfect. I can still replay my slow fall to the grass while the blood and breath evaporated from my current self.

I had decided to walk through the park on the way back to the office and as I came out near Columbus Circle, there were a group of well-suited gentlemen waiting to speak to me. At first, I thought I was just going to go through a heavy audit or that one of my parents had gone bat-shit crazy in a mall or something. I had never bargained for what really happened. The men were from the FBI and they were looking for my newly former partner, who, without my knowledge, had cleaned out my bank account, along with several of my client's accounts as well. Mine was easy; I stupidly never took his name off our business joint-account after the partnership had been dissolved. He had full signing and withdrawal privileges, it was an abominable mistake on all our parts, but he would have gotten to it anyway, since, obviously, it was the plan all along. The others were the work of a mastermind hacker and I have a feeling that 'the lady' was his partner in crime. I never liked that bitch. The total loss was about thirty million or so. The banks did everything they could to support my situation, but the money was gone and so was he, never to be heard from again. The FBI is still currently looking for him, and it's been rumored that he was tortured to death in some back alley in Tel Aviv. One could only hope. The biggest issue of all was that I was fucking broke again, beyond comprehension. I didn't know how I was going to get out of this one, but I was not going to skip a beat this time. I was going to get revenge and I was going to get it by living well.

Chapter Five

"It is better to risk starving to death than surrender. If you give up on your dreams, what's left?"

–Jim Carrey

Along with living well, functioning in a full state of denial proved to be an incredibly useful tool found in my virtual survival kit. I got up early every day, I kept up with my gym workouts, got my hair colored, face pinched, nails polished, and every bit of my exterior was exfoliated until I shimmered like a newly painted G6. The sun would dance off my glimmering skin, yet my soul had become calloused and my spirit was hardened like the shell of a ninja turtle. I was, somehow, invigorated and feeling creatively ambitious and unstoppable, and my AMEX became my favorite husband. I was appropriately deranged.

At this point of my story, I saw Suzi grit her teeth and tears pinch out of from her little eyes. Thank God she didn't wear mascara, so she didn't make much of a scene, as we sipped away in a true Moroccan Tea house after a party well done. One thing Suzi knew was that the little bit of heart and sincerity I had, went fully into what I did for other people via designing and creating the perfect experience for them. To have it all taken away and put back and taken away again, was more than Suzi could bear imagining me going through. I waved it all away, because obviously, I had come out on top and she was sitting there with me. I envision myself as a King Kong type, who stands tall and is able to swat away hundreds of helicopters flying at me full speed.

In truth, I was devastated and stressed the fuck out during this very trying time of my life. My teeth grinding issue became one of massive proportions, and my neck muscles were so tight I couldn't turn my head to look at and speak to people. There were no CBD oils or Meditation Apps back then, just pills and self-medication, which was never a good route for me to take. I didn't want to tell anyone, much like the last time I had to secretly become a bartender. I was never able to admit to others that I was in a bad place; particularly, my gay wolf friends, I was too ashamed. I felt that if I admitted it publicly, then it would really be true, and I simply couldn't face it. My skin was breaking out,

I had night sweats, and my stomach was churning an acidic volcano every time I tried to eat. I walked down the street thinking I was the only one in the world that was having a hard time. It was my Vietnam, as crazy and disrespectful as that sounds. I had to make a choice here. It was either him or me. The anger started to develop within me and help me get moving again. There was no way I was going to let this guy ruin my dreams and my ability to make money. Once I made that decision, the clouds began to clear, and I started to focus on getting out of my shit-puddle. Most people have someone they completely confide in; a priest, a parent, best friend, or some random stranger that would listen. Again, I was too ashamed to share my tale with anyone. I just needed to state the facts that were necessary to move forward, there was always a way to move on.

It was time to go full OPPS on this disaster, and I called a meeting of the minds with my team. For the first time, I was completely transparent with them. I watched their faces go white with the fear of losing their jobs, bonuses, lifestyles, and overall stability; welcome to my fucking life and putting my name on the door. By the end of several hours of meeting, I, somehow, turned a negative into a positive and we had our plan set into place. We also ordered pizza, so we were good to go. If you ever need to motivate young women, buy them pizza and a cute clutch. They'll throw the pizza up later, hopefully, not in the clutch.

We set the office up like a telemarketing stable, pushing our desks near each other, including mine, and we even hung a huge dry erase board in the middle of the room resembling a 'how to track a murder' display. This was not something I would have tolerated in my previous life, since I abhorred the look of a dry erase board, but desperate times called for desperate measures. I decided that it was time to make my travels worth something and I pulled out my contacts from everywhere I had traveled to in the past couple of years and put them up onto the board. The plan was to have my team and I call my contacts from all over the map; the people that I had partied hard with and offer to do the types events they had never seen before for at cost. We would bring NYC style all over the planet for a digestible amount of money, while clearing our overhead and spreading our name across the world, just like a perfect schmear on a bagel. The words 'at cost' caused a flurry of commotion, and suddenly, doors were opening everywhere, and I was paying back my massive debts little by little. The entire human population around the world wanted to party like a NY'er. Even NY'er's themselves were always raising the bar and inventing ways to celebrate, so it was something to strive for all the time, and it was a goal that could never be truly met. It's the love affair that would last forever for me, even long after I am gone. This affair for New York goes so deep because of this; it's the bar that's been set for all of us to strive to keep up with. Everyone needs a goal, and New York regurgitates goals in a New York second. It supplies the structure and the dangling carrot or shall I say, apple, that is in range, just enough for me to graze my fingertips on it, while wanting to obtain the full grasp.

I called my friends in India first and told them that we would do their next huge wedding event for cost and create a *Mandap* that would blow people away and literally take their guests breaths away, only to blow it all back into them in the form of pure joy and inspiration. We would create a new kind of look for entertaining in India, while incorporating traditional elements and color palettes. We would mix white lacquer contemporary tables topped with their indigenous Dupioni Silk runners and tip their Marigolds with Rose Gold paint accents and recreate huge Marigolds in the form of paper lanterns that would be lit and sent off into the universe late in the evening. We offered the same types of advanced styling in Africa, Italy, France, Brazil, Portugal, Germany, and even in New Jersey. We were going to splatter my style across the continents in a gorgeous, messy, and fast way, just like Jackson Pollock did on his canvases.

The girls were incredibly excited. We divvied up the projects by country and within days, my team became autonomous international event producers, all under my name, of course. I wouldn't be able to be everywhere at once with them, so they got on track very quickly with their language and currency lessons. They left their tiny apartments with fresh passports, asked their roommates to feed whatever plants they had taken home from our events, and packed their bags following the TSA guidelines, knowing that if they missed any of their flights, I would send them packing back home permanently with no job to go to.

They would leave as little girls but would come back as fierce women, and the envy of their friends. On the flipside, they would have no lives to come home to. The 'iffy' boyfriends would be long gone, even the roommates would start to advertise that there was a vacancy. I felt a little sad for them in a way, I was adding to a demographic of women that would never have a lifestyle that could contribute to a fruitful, home life. They wouldn't have husbands and if they did, the men wouldn't stick around long, and my girls would be replaced by other young women that would be there for them on a consistent basis. They would open their legs and have babies, thus, creating the missing fruitful, home life. They would get their waxes on time, stay thin, and own all the best denim. On yet, another side, the husbands who wanted this fruitful, home life could potentially tire of that existence and then turn his focus back onto the young career woman who doesn't give a fuck as to whether he was around or not. Or better yet, he could just start fucking the nanny and everyone collects a paycheck just for creating that so-called fruitful, home life. In conclusion, it was every girl for herself. Instead of feeling guilty about providing the poisonous fruit that these young people could potentially get addicted to, I simply had to realize that no one guided me out of that flower room as a young girl to warn me of the potential danger my lifestyle would be in by following my creative path to destruction. I made every choice, mistake, and success by myself, and these kids needed to do the same. It was like watching young beautiful people jump into a volcano, which stirred a delicious anticipation inside of me, as to whether they would be spit out into pure glory or swallowed up into the fiery abyss. It was best for me to sit back and let things fall where they may. I had my own fucking problems.

I truly believe that Suzi would be the pioneer, as the one person of my team to achieve normal and lunacy, all at once. I saw in her the perfect stoner snack; someone who was salty and sweet, anxious and calm, beautiful and plain, all at once. She was the rare gem of a person whom you meet once in a lifetime. She would put Queens on the map for something, other than broken down transit and Irish Pubs.

With my new plan in place, the team and I would divide and conquer, and I would come and see each one of them on site at every location, kiss the rings of the clients, and then hop back onto the plane to get to the next event. My financial team convinced the banks to front me some private jet money and they were strategically keeping me financially alive, enough to keep up my rock-star persona. They knew I was going to find my way back; they would bet their lives on it and lend me the money to do so. I was raging with power and *chutzpah*; nothing was going to fucking stop me, nothing. My girls and I were focused and living day to day with blinders on to everything else, aside from the tasks at hand. They were calling upon their parents as reinforcements and soon, there was a small army of retired parental soldiers picking up our dry cleaning, firming up flights, buying groceries, walking and feeding cats/dogs and watering plants. They had taken over our office and answering our phones, while dealing with our local clients. We set their electronic devices to large font settings, gave them a crash-course in how to check the phone messages, and how to communicate with us while we were travelling. We even installed a wall of clocks that told them what time it was in every country, so they could keep track of when to call us. We were a fine league of people steadily falling back into the rhythm of success. It was better than sex.

I had decided long ago that if I was to ever fall or fail again, I would spring up and forward, before fully hitting the ground. I would continue to only blame myself for these situations not others, it was just quickly resolved that way. It was my duty to propel my employees along with me and to act as the hot-air

141

balloon of innovation that would raise them high off the ground and make them glide gracefully over others, only to land long enough to collect money and adoration from them. Each moment of adoration acted as fuel to raise us higher and further each time, there was no looking back but fuck, it was exhausting. I had been to thirty countries in twenty days. I wasn't even wearing underwear anymore or eating and sleeping. The party people of the world were sucking off my teat of inspiration, which was thrilling and depleting, all at once. It was like I was breast feeding a large portion of the world at times and pumping and dumping in my off hours. There was a perverse sense of accomplishment to all of this, also a severe feeling of alienation from the rest of the world coupled with a little resentment towards being stuck inside of my own life, which must have looked fucking phenomenal to the rest of the world. I was finally realizing that anything that came easy simply wasn't worth anything at all. If I had an easy day, I was always looking out for the truck that could potentially hit me and end it all within moments.

My industry was starting to populate with others as well. I knew that I needed to stay in my own lane, but I also wanted to be relevant amongst my peers. I started attending event summits where there were endless parades of fabulous egos on two legs that also languished in the luxury of making other people happy. I always felt like I was in my own category, my associates regarded me with caution and fascination, much like they were approaching me as a person who was on pink glittery fire. They didn't know whether to put me out or just watch me burn bright. I was and always have been a category all my own and one that is impossible to put a label on.

One morning, I woke up in Russia, and it was cold beyond expression, so my love for animals had to be put on hold temporarily, while I insulated myself in furs. I had flown in from Dubai to arrive in time to produce a wedding for a gorgeous young princess type. Everyone is a princess in Russia. She was perfect; tall, slender, blue eyes, blonde hair, the works. From the first moment I glanced at her, I knew that she hadn't always been a woman, but it seems like I was the only one that noticed. Was this type of stuff acceptable in her world? I would assume not, but when I met her father in person, I started to see how she got away with it. His kindness rolled off him like a custom aroma formulated from scratch. He ignited smiles from everyone he met. It sounds so corny, but he was a ray of sunshine in this monotone country, and more so, in this morose environment. His daughter was not happy to be getting married and I had the distinct feeling that she may have owed a favor to someone. Her fiancé was dumb as shit. He was loud, boring, he spat a lot when he talked, and his eyes were always out of focus. In fact, he seemed a bit touched and blurry around the edges, like he was punch drunk or something. I came to find out that he was, in fact, punch drunk, after all. He was a retired heavyweight champion boxer, and he didn't even know where he lived, even though he resided in the largest home in Moscow, amongst several other homes spread across Europe. The supposed princess was a rounds girl. She was obviously the black sheep of the family and rebelled against her previously planned upbringing, but it was clear that her father loved her very much, regardless. I never met her mother nor was she ever mentioned. She paraded around in the boxing ring, practically naked between rounds holding the numbers up high while her breasts reached out to the crowd, hypnotizing them into a joyous oblivion. It was an obvious match, the boxer and the rounds girl. It was either him or the mafia guys that watched her from the front row, patiently putting up with the sweat and blood flying off the athlete's bodies while staining their custom-made suits. They sat there just to stare and her and to try and mentally will her to fall in love with them. She ignored it all, glued herself to her boxer, knowing that he would be quite simple to live with and he was rich as fuck.

They started dating and the tabloids went ape shit. It was like royalty had gone rogue in such a delicious way. At the end of the day, he was a bad boy and every girl wants one of those, even so-called princesses. The tabloids, however, were focusing on another kind of story, one that zeroed in on who the princess really was and where had she been all our lives? The young princess, newly named 'Bogdana' meaning 'God's gift' and who always takes the right decisions thanks to her intuition, was really born as Boris; the name meaning Fighter and born to famous bearers and this baby had a penis.

Just when you think your world has gone to shit and you are envying those who seem to lead such a shiny existence, you gain a peek into what their lives are really like and your perception of them goes haywire. I cannot imagine what this little boy must have gone through to get him to where he is now; a beautiful, wealthy supposed princess of something, that was marrying a man with even more money than her and who had a huge cock. The steps between A and Z of how she got to where she was currently, was baffling to me. How did she overcome his/her fear to become someone totally different? How did he/she know what she truly wanted to be? And mostly, how the fuck did he/she tell her parents? Oh, and did the boxer know? I was mystified by her and I felt an emotional kinship. Our situations were similar in a way. I had parents that loved me for who I was, no matter what, but would they ever truly know how much emotional turmoil I was in most of the time. Did they know that I lied to myself and to the rest of the world daily? And did they know that deep down, I was the good person they believed in, but that I was turning rotten very quickly, like an Avocado left on a counter top?

My head was spinning and these people were depressing me. I only wanted to deal with folks that were shiny, inside and out. I didn't want to be privy to character flaws or emotions, I just wanted to do their fucking parties and go home. I was vacillating between getting to know her more and just not engaging with her at all. I already knew what she and her father wanted in terms of her wedding; typical over the top 'fuck you' money kind of shit, so it would have been easy to cut and run, since this was the type of event I could have done in my sleep at this point in my career. The thing is that Russia was not my natural habitat and I was stuck there for some time, while we got this event underway. I decided to take the plunge and take my internal focus off myself and onto getting to know her. I had always been attracted to people that have faced adversity and he/she certainly fit into that category.

Suzi was used to 'colorful' people, whereas my first run in with diverse people, such as folks that were in transition in terms of gender, was very new and quite exciting, since 'normal' people were so bland to me. I was thrilled that there was another species out there for me to get to know and genuinely relate to as a sister in arms type of way; all of us swimming upstream in search of something we didn't already have. The difference was that I had a choice and they simply didn't, though a common thread was that our happiness, both, seemed to depend upon discovering something new about ourselves and the world. I liked that even though Suzi came from small surroundings, her acceptance of everything, unlike her, was vast and genuine.

I did a 'drop by; at Bogdana's family estate where she and her father resided. She wouldn't be living with the boxer until after they were married. Her father opened the door and I instantly regained my understanding of how handsome he was. There was something so regal about him, even though I knew he really wasn't royalty of any kind. He was well respected and he was rich, which can certainly make someone quite attractive. He seemed happy to see me, relieved, even. He quickly looked behind me to see if I was the only one rude enough to drop by unannounced and then quickly ushered me in. I didn't think of having my driver wait for me, I was just going to visit a client, which seemed innocent enough. I had no preconceived notions of what their house would be like, but amongst the incredibly chic and contemporary *décor* were piles of cash, guns, and drugs. Their great room resembled a land fill with endless piles of the stuff and instead of getting scared, I realized I was wet 'down there.'

Just because I was jaded, didn't mean that I wasn't still a bit naïve, but I caught on soon enough and damn I wish I could be adopted by these people. I soon realized that the leader to the men, watching the beautiful numbers girl at the boxing matches, was Bogdana's father. He was king of the 'Russkaya

144

Mafia' and the men were protecting his most valued possession; his only child. My very first thought was if he would be willing to find my ghosted thief of a partner and kill him even more, even if he was already dead, just so I could get the last word in, and some sort of resolution to my nightmare. Then, I automatically couldn't help but to take a mental monetary inventory of what was all around me. Let's just say that I couldn't count that high. Finally, I started to wonder what came next. While their housekeeper was offering me tea, they were pushing away some of the 'items,' so I could be seated. The father told me that he was quite happy that I stopped by; they needed to speak to me about something. I mean what could we possibly have to talk about? I had a synapse fire of fear that almost hit my bowels, but before it could, his cool blue eyes soothed and lulled me into a plush chair by the massive fireplace, which was the only area in the room that wasn't consumed by contraband. Bogdana's eyes never left my face. She really was exquisite. Everything about her, the way she moved and the way she stared into your soul like a cat that really wanted food. It was just so endearing. I felt calm finally, drinking the tea that could have easily been laced with something, but my intuitive self was telling me that these people meant no harm to me. After all, I was broke.

They had a plan that they wanted to run by me. The tabloids had ruined Bogdana's image in Russia. The bullying that she endured as a young boy, before her transition, was all coming back and she couldn't bear it. She didn't love the boxer really, he simply wasn't her type. In fact, she preferred women and that was not going to happen in her current environment. What I loved about all of this is that her father knew everything, and he supported it a hundred percent. She would speak in broken English as he watched every syllable that came out of her mouth. You could see him trying to finish the sentences for her mouthing the words that weren't coming easily to her. They wanted me to take her back to the States with me, and they wanted me to help make her 'disappear' on her wedding day and get her settled in the states. I could name my price and I did. It was time to get out of my financial mess and breathe easy, even if it meant doing something quite unconventional.

Out of all of the crazy shit I was reporting to Suzi about my past, this was the one time where I felt she truly thought I was a true idiot. Suzi was a much more logical thinker than me, therefore, she made about ninety percent less mistakes than I have. We shared an attraction to the dark side, but she knew when to divert and take the high road, where I simply did not. I chalk it up to the fact that she was raised with GPS and I wasn't.

Bogdana's father would take care of her new identity and paperwork, while I would continue to plan her lavish day and figure out how to get mountains of cash home, without any raised eyebrows and then disburse it to my awaiting debt collectors. I immediately got in touch with my financial team, who reacted with pure joy, since it was confirmed they would get paid back and then some. Now, it was time for them to figure it all out, and I knew they would. I had done some questionable shit in my day, but I was now becoming legitimately corrupt. I couldn't wait to start my new and improved fucked-up existence.

During the next few weeks, I saw the stress literally depart from Bogdana's being, like in a science fiction movie. It was as if I could see it seep off her body and fly up into a vortex, hopefully, never to return. She was glowing with happiness and she looked like a woman who was thrilled to be getting married, even though I knew what she was really thrilled about. She was getting out.

I, however, found myself falling for her father. I, too, felt stress-free, knowing that my money situation was going to work out, but I was questioning the type of man I was falling for. He thrilled me. He did everything I was too scared to do. He took things when he wanted them, created chaos, where there was calm, and vice versa, he was fiercely loyal to those he loved, yet devastatingly dismissive if he didn't like you. There may not even be a reason for him to dislike you, he just felt it and acted upon it or even worse, he didn't acknowledge you. If you felt invisible to him, it was the worst feeling in the world, and he had a natural capacity to make people want to please him. He even killed people or had them killed and that was way beyond my pay-grade, as high as it was. That day, in his home, where he approached me with their plan, I realized that I would have done even more for him if he had asked me to. It was like doing something hugely deceitful and illegal wasn't enough of an expression of my awe of him, I was constantly searching for ways to get his nod in my direction, and I realized, for sure, that I was in love with him. It may have been the first and only time I would ever be in love. I had never been nervous about a man returning my affection, knowing that if I wanted them badly enough, they would come around at some point. He shared my feelings and he felt guilty about pulling me into his web, but like in the movies, our passion was so great our love plan conquered all. I even considered staying in Russia. After all, my money problems were over, but it would mean leaving my business and my entire identity again, which never worked out well. Also, it would mean I would become a mafia wife, which is something I had always aspired to be in certain fantasies I had, but I never even considered they would become a reality. I would have to get fake tits for sure...

In the weeks preparing for the wedding, we lived as a happy ambiguous family. I was part step-mother and part wedding planner for Bogdana. Her father gave her and the boxer anything they wanted. The boxer wanted white tigers as his groomsmen and we would make it happen, in cages, of course. It was one of the happiest times of my life. I made them move most of the questionable items out of the main rooms of the house, just for comfort level purposes. I had never been at ease with guns, so those got put away in a room that I didn't have access to. The house was more massive than I thought. There were secret stairwells, panic rooms, safes as big as bedrooms, and closets as large as my NYC apartment.

The wedding was about to happen. We held a large and lavish rehearsal dinner at the Boxer's gym that he owned. We made the place look amazing and put the Boxer and Bogdana right in the fighting ring at a table set for two, so they were the center of attention. I dressed Bogdana in a chic sparkling pinstripe custom pant suit with leopard skin boots. She looked spectacular in absolutely everything and the clothes enjoyed being on her body, just as much as everyone loved looking at them on her. She was an unsuspecting super-star, which is my favorite kind. We painted the place, carpeted the floor, replaced the hanging punching bags with cascades of flowers and used the locker rooms as coat check and specialty cocktail bars. The Boxer dozed off at the table halfway through the festivities, so we called it a night and got ready for the big day.

The plan was all set, but it would take a village. We decided that for me only to escort Bogdana out of her world wouldn't be very safe and that I would be too exposed, so I called in some reinforcements. I figured that hair and make-up artists always seemed innocent enough. Their lives were always naturally dramatic, so I didn't think there would be any shock value to our situation, and I was right. They couldn't wait to get involved and they were already picking out their getaway outfits. They also traveled in packs, like wolf spiders moving across the desert, so they were a strong unit. I felt that Bogdana could easily morph into one of their groups. The plan was that we would start her hair and make-up late morning, as we usually do before large affairs, so there is ample photography time for all parties involved. We would keep her bridesmaids separate from her in another part of the house, so they had their own beauty crew to themselves. The boxer, his family, his guy friends, and his fucking tigers would also be in another area of the mansion, so my team and I could volley back and forth between everyone we needed to deal with.

The pictures went off without a hitch. The 'first look' between the boxer and Bogdana was so breathtaking, I saw her father lose it a little and he started to cry freely. No one knew that he was about to say goodbye to his daughter, possibly forever. I was quite sad as well, knowing that I was taking her home with me and not her father, it was an emotionally charged afternoon. He and I kept stealing away to one of his secret rooms to play a little Russian Roulette with his penis and my vagina, it really made the day go by quickly and kept our minds off what was to come. We would go through with most of the wedding, it would be too risky not to. As the ceremony time grew near, there were nerves on top of nerves and Bogdana looked a bit faint, but she rallied.

She was a masterpiece of a bride and Russian Vogue would have a field day with this one, she was total cover material. Because of her tabloid issues, we had moved the affair from a massive venue back to their house and the guest list was cut down from seven hundred to three hundred people, who all had to enter through a secret area to avoid any possible media. We took all the announcements out of the papers and bought the air space above the estate, so no media helicopters could catch a glimpse of anything from above. There was only one aircraft near the place, and it was there to take us away. As dumb as I thought he was, I felt as if the boxer knew that something was wrong. After all, he really did love Bogdana and seemed genuinely happy to be getting married to her. His family was nice enough; they seemed a little shell shocked having come from modest means and all. They resembled Russian 'dead heads,' like if they were born in America, they would have lived in Woodstock or something, it was calm and perverse, all at once. They didn't seem to notice if their son seemed anxious or not.

I really had to give it to my hair and make-up people who played everything off like pros. They just popped their gum and made everyone look beautiful, without a blink of an extended eyelash. After being in the biz long enough, nothing truly shocks you, I suppose.

We used the huge central staircase for her to descend. Her veil and train were so long that it was still on the top step, even after she reached the bottom. Reem Acra was our wedding dress designer, of choice. The beading on the bodice alone made the dress weigh over 35 pounds, but the princess held her back straight with her tits out like a real champ. She made the walk herself, just for the drama of it all and her father waited for her underneath the wedding archway that was so chock full of flowers I thought it was going to bruise the marble floor. The boxer wanted to come in on his own as well. He really wanted to ride a tiger in, but thankfully, we talked him out of it and just put a spotlight on him instead, which he seemed to enjoy. I watched the ceremony from an archway, which kept me half hidden, so I could firm up the getaway details, along with making sure the candles were lit in the dining room. It would be a European style evening, they would enjoy toasts and dinner and then the guests would move into another area for dessert and dancing. All of this included a copious amount of drinking. Vodka and Caviar would be oozing out of people's pores within hours. The Russians seriously knew how to party.

There were several dress changes on the schedule for the evening, along with make-up and hair adjustments to go along with the styles. She went from a Reem Acra dress to a Pnina Tornai, then into a Herrera for dancing and finally, I picked out a fabulous Gucci departure outfit and packed her suitcase filled with everything Alexander McQueen. We had shoes lining the hallway for her, including some diamond crusted 'comfy shoes' for late night dancing. The good news is that most 'he's' that become 'she's' can really go the distance in a pair of heels, so we weren't anticipating a lot of discomfort. We also had her bags packed, already put into the chopper, along with several cases of cash for me. The evening was appropriately boring. Toasts were made, which the team and I could only understand bits of pieces of. Not everybody spoke English and the ones that did had such heavy accents we were perplexed. Mix in gallons of champagne and everyone became completely inaudible. My team needed to keep things running on time, so the evening didn't skip a beat and cause any kind of concern. We decided that it would be best if Bogdana and the boxer cut the cake, did their first dance, and then after she would go in for her final costume change, and we would cut loose and head to America, the Beautiful. I watched her father throughout the evening. I caught him staring into his glass and playing with his cuff links a lot. It was such a narcissistic thought, but I was hoping that some of that sadness was for me. Just as I was thinking it, his eyes met mine from across the room. They were glassy, and he nodded *yes* to me, I had my answer. The boxer was getting very drunk and sloppy, go figure. He was angry I could tell, I just didn't know what was making him that way. It made sense that I would be paranoid with everything that was about to go down, but I was trying to keep my cool. He was pacing a bit; waiting on his new bride anxious to continue with the evening. He started calling out to me, "Where the fuck is she, what have you done with her?" The whole crowd just stopped. I urged the band to keep playing, but the forcefulness of his voice shut them down. Even the tigers were scared. I looked over at the father, he gestured to me that it was time to bust a move; he would take care of the rest. I just turned and walked out of the main room; never looking back but the hair was standing up on the back of my neck. I quickly got the beauty crew together and gave them the signal that it was time to head up to the helipad and they instantly sprang into action. Bogdana took a moment and looked down below for her father but she couldn't catch a glimpse of him. He had promised that he would be visible, but we both knew we had to get moving. No one could ever say that I didn't do a lot of shit for my clients.

There was a loud commotion coming from below in the great hall. There were gun shots and my final glance caught a blurry vision of the boxer shooting my beloved, Bogdana's father in the chest. As the helicopter lifted off the roof, I looked down through the huge skylight onto my love, who was blowing a kiss to me as his blood seeped out all over the custom-made mercury glass dance floor.

Suzi was speechless. Her little mouth gasped open and she was even shaking a little bit. She had asked me often if I had ever been in love, and my answer to her was, "Maybe?"

Part Three

Chapter One

"Are you reelin in the years, stowing away the time?"

-Steely Dan

It seemed that at this point I would never have the little black baby boy that I sometimes wanted, but instead, I had a stunning Russian daughter who proved to be a wonderful addition to my life. My crew and I immersed her into our lives; we changed her look a bit in *lieu* of being cautious, and most importantly, we introduced her to people just like her. Aside from being a mafia princess, she had a lot in common with many members of my design team. They talked about the estrogen treatments they were on and compared surgical scars or beauty marks, as we would call them. She wasn't an anomaly anymore, in fact, she was popular.

She was also an incredibly quick study. She had a knack for my business, and I brought her on board fully. We mourned her father more often that I thought we would and she even had moments of missing her boxer husband, who, after killing the God Father of Russia, died a violent death shortly after our departure by the hands of his crew. I found out that she was twenty-three years old and that her mother left when she realized what she was, never to be heard from again. She could not accept her he/she son, it just wasn't fashionable yet. I asked her several times if she wanted to look for her, and Bogdana held steady to an adamant "No." I like to think that I was somewhat responsible for her feeling loved enough by a mother type of influence in her life.

I was consistently surprising myself and marveled at my ability to care about another human being almost as much as I did for myself. She was the first thing, aside from my job and my dogs, that I had such an intense attachment to, one that never seemed to wane. I never got bored being her go-to person. I would say that my relationship with her was amongst many of my phenomenal accomplishments. My gay wolves adored her because she was perfect to look at. They dressed her up and paraded her around, becoming territorial of her beauty and claiming her as the supermodel child they had always wanted. She went from one kind of jungle to another falling into a pit of people that selfishly fed off her perfections, hoping that she would permeate our flawed existence like human growth hormone injections. We loved her the only way that we could, which seemed good enough for her.

Something I didn't plan for was that she was not growing into a woman like me. Her tastes were simple, and I suppose, that for someone that overcame the hardships of transitioning into womanhood, it was normal for her to want to be a 'full on female.' I didn't quite understand her desire to become a wife and mother, and the thought of her wanting those things repelled me a little bit. Emotionally, I knew that my reaction was fucking ridiculous, but I was having a hard time getting it under control. I was a career narcissist; that was clear. The thought of losing her to becoming more of a 'pedestrian' and being part of a larger club that I didn't belong to, was too much for me to bear, so I joined her in the mediocrity zone and started to look for a husband. If you can't beat 'em, join 'em.

I think this is why I am able to accept Suzi wanting to get married and have a family, Bogdana paved the way and I got my 'hurt out,' long before Suzi came along.

Bogdana and I made it like a game; she and I, trolling for men on the Upper East Side, injecting conservative neighborhoods with our strong sex appeal and passionate influence. We were quite the team; a Lone Ranger and Tonto of sorts in matching town cars. I would scope places out, and then she would strategically join me as a good friend or daughter of a friend. I never felt competitive with her, but her beauty was a game changer most times. Most of the men we met seemed to know that after a short while with her, they would never be able to keep up, so I seemed like a wonderful second choice. It was like they were still getting an amazing woman, but at least, I was one that was okay with them watching the game, leaving me alone, and not having to support me financially. My autonomy was what I really had going for me in terms of meeting men that had already been taken to the cleaners, financially, by previous wives. They knew that if they were going to attempt to be with Bogdana, they would need to start from square one again.

She ended up falling head over heels with a 'regular guy,' which kind of killed me, but there was no stopping it. He was a mortgage broker, *ick*. I would be supporting them for the rest of my life, but she was so incredibly happy I couldn't help having gushy moments over them from time to time. It wouldn't be long before she would make me a 'Glam MA' by having some boring white babies I would feel guilty about, because I would never care about them much. She did have a boy that reminded me of her father, so he gained my affections. The other three, were just a blur to me. The straw that really broke that camel's back was that she moved to Jersey, that's just fucked up. I rarely got out there, even though I could practically see their loft across the river from my floor to ceiling window in my apartment. I wondered about the pain that 'real' parents endured from having their kids grow up and away in ways they didn't want them to, and it made me think about the amount of feces I threw onto my parent's plan for me. I made up for it by giving them enough bragging material for a lifetime, and I kept them out of the bad shit. As far as they were concerned, I was fucking perfect.

Coincidentally enough, Suzi's dream man had turned out be a regular dude as well; the teacher won the prize. These days, they get paid better, and I came to accept that being able to teach in general is an incredibly noble characteristic. I felt like I was re-living my love for Bogdana through my relationship with Suzi, and I realize that the cycle of my life would supply me with this type of evolutionary love, long after Suzi became a mother and potentially moved to Long Island.

With Bogdana out of the house, I got back to the love of my life; my career. The thrilling jolt it once gave me was now leaving me depleted and let down. My industry was changing, too. There were others catching on and giving me cause to have to sell myself and God forbid compete for business. These fucking new-comers with their flashy technology and completed educations had me on my tip-toes from time to time. They never had to practically sell themselves on a street corner to survive, they just had to write a strategic email or gain a shit ton of followers on Instagram, and they would gain clients left and right, whether or not they could keep them was another story that I don't think they cared much about. They would never have my rolodex, but they would know the young assistants and the employees of my clients and they would take them out and get them hand-crafted, mother-fucking cocktails with large ice cubes and my number would slip off everybody's speed dial just like that. Colleges even offered Degrees in my field now, which Suzi had, which was great, even though I felt it was ludicrous in some ways. The only way to really gain expertise in my business was through experience, and these kids were skipping the hardest steps. The only way to not experience the agony of defeat was simply not to be defeated. At the end of the day, the proof was in the pudding and I was simply the best at what I did, but for the first time, I had to explain why, how, what, and where. I didn't like it at all. I had plenty of money in banks I didn't even know the location of, and technically, I should have been thrilled with how my life was turning out for the time being. If you knew me by now, you would know that I was miserable. Suzi didn't love networking, so the both of us really preferred going home and watching Netflix, rather than trying to charm the current decision makers, and money does always run out.

I decided to ignore everyone else and act like a pro golfer and focus on improving my personal score. I started to teach at prominent art schools, I wrote 'how to' books, art directed sets for Broadway, did speaking engagements all over the world, and finally, I took another husband and got some more dogs. I could tolerate the husband only because I got the dogs at the exact same time. It was like buying an entire set of eye-shadows just to get the one pretty color you really wanted, but it wasn't sold on its own, for some reason.

Suzi robotically supported my marriage and tried to engage with my hubby, though they had absolutely nothing to talk about, except for having me in common. She even fussed over me as we got married in a very small very private ceremony in our living room officiated by one of my gay wolves. She knew that mine and her relationship was much more intimate and honest than the one I would have with him. She performed practical magic by planning the small luncheon we had in a secret room at the top of the Chrysler Building called the cloud room, since it was so high up, and no one else was allowed to use. The original Humidor room was still there, where back in the day as far back as the 30s, business gentlemen kept their cigar collections and played cards; no women allowed. She made sure I had everything I needed, knowing full well that none of it was what I wanted. She quickly learned that I loved things because I needed them, not needing them because I loved them; I wasn't capable, this was clear to her and she didn't judge it.

My husband wore tortoise shell glasses from Warby Parker and looked great in jeans and or a suit. He had a full head of hair but wasn't hairy everywhere else, so my sheets and sink stayed clean, which was a plus. He was almost as narcissistic as I was but not quite, so I was always the one doing the stinging. At some point, his defense mechanisms helped him sustain his dignity within the marriage, but we were both anxious to live autonomously and only reunite for public appearances. We looked wonderful together and that was important. He knew when to put his hand on the small of my back and when not to, and my gay wolves adored him because they all wanted to fuck him. If they only believed me when I told them that weren't missing anything, but none of them wanted to let the fantasy die. Suzi did try to adore him as well, feeling a bit of relief that I wouldn't be moving in with her during my lonely, golden years. The hubby and I gave up my place and formed a new environment into a charming Jack and Jill type of a situation. We got two apartments next to each other and created a connection between the two. We were organically mindful about barging into either space. Short of leaving a sock on the door, my husband was always cautious before entering mine and painfully aware that he may walk into something he couldn't come back from.

I, however, didn't give a shit and if I wanted to see him, I just did. My life was a fantasy, for the most part, which made reality so much more devastating than one could ever imagine. I could orchestrate fantasies at my jobs, and I was also able to bring many of those elements home with me, such as the food, wine, ambiance, and such but the joy was left out of it by the time I got home. Who the hell was I to complain? Sure, I had my ups and downs, but I was living an exquisite life when you tallied it all up. I always thought that rich and famous people were selfish when they would leave this planet voluntarily, thinking how could people that have it all take everything for granted and just off themselves? There were moments where I truly understood that it was just never enough. For me, I often realized how much I had but in ways, it was also just never enough. It wasn't about material things per se, but more like how could I be better, do better, feel batter, and look the fucking best? I was getting increasingly tough on myself and I was itching for something. I just couldn't pin-point it, which was becoming a front and center issue. I needed a night out with my wolves. I needed to feel gorgeous, sexy, and belligerent. It was like putting some much needed fabulous and magical glitter gas into my thirsty engine.

My boys always took me to the best places. The music was loud, the bathrooms were the place to be, and the champagne flowed like fucking Niagara.

I would observe everyone in the club, particularly the dark corners, where people felt the least inhibited and free to express themselves however and with whomever they wanted. I loved watching club culture. People would walk into a club all pristine and shiny and leave gritty, sexed up, and flawed in such a magnificent way. They went in as 'boring' and came out as wildly textured beasts that would go to work on Monday morning as more evolved and happier people with an acceptable hangover, simple because it was worth it. They would get through their work week patiently waiting to get back to the mecca that elevated them as human beings, it was that effective. The formula was simple; dark lighting, great music, beautiful people, drugs, liquor, lightning fast bartenders, and a great relationship with the cops. It was a lot like doing big parties, but it raised a lot more cash and it was an even more fucked-up environment, which was extremely attractive to me.

Fuck it, I was going to open a club, perhaps, a string of them.

Chapter Two

"Passion is energy. Feel the power that comes from focusing on what excites
you."

-Oprah Winfrey

Many smart people will tell you that when opening a new endeavor, you should
never invest your own money and that you should embark on your journey,
along with partners, and never go it alone. Due to my near economic death
experience with my last partner, I was adamant about going about opening my
clubs completely solo. By solo, I mean that I would have a team of lawyers,
bankers, managers, publicists, realtors, and thugs, but I would not have a pen
and paper partner.

   I felt it best to cross pollinate between the party and club industries the best
I could. I would use the same type of wait staff, security, chefs, DJ's, and
bands, lighting, AV and staging dudes, riggers, designers, and even the coat
check staff. This was because these 'party people' really knew how to serve a
crowd. They knew how to spot an almost empty glass from across the room
and get it filled before someone of importance even knew what was happening.
This all stems from years of catering to the family of a bride's needs or a
corporate big wig and working in environments that didn't allow for dress
rehearsals. There was no room for error with parties, because if you didn't get
it right the first time, there was no make-up game to earn back your points.
With clubs, it is more of a permanent existence and it's normal to make
mistakes constantly as you figure out what works the best. The crowd is always
changing as well. You may get some regulars, of course, but you never know
if an English Prince is in town and wants to go to the hottest club with fifty of
his besties, or if there is a Drag Queen parade happening and they want to party
somewhere wonderful after the festivities. Something that I would not do is to
use Suzi or any of my girls from my office to run these clubs or anyone I
remotely thought couldn't handle the pressure and the anti-climactic way of
life. If you think being an event producer is alienating, try managing a club. At
least with events, you go home eventually, while managing a club, you may as
well sleep on the floor in your grimy office and shower with the soda gun

behind the bar. Your best friend is the poor *schmuck* that cleans the place, and the sunlight becomes your enemy. The deadly cycle doesn't end there. Once you've been up all night and made sure that no one has crawled under a banquette to stay the night, counted the money, and paid everybody out, it's time for breakfast. Breakfast only consists of the worst coffee in the world and whatever sticky donut thingy that is being served at the street cart outside the club. After breakfast, the deliveries start. There are so many deliveries, only a manager can truly keep track of what could potentially be missing, and the stakes are too high to go without that bottle of Glenlevit some douche bag banker had to have. If you, God forbid, didn't provide it, that same douche bag would 'shit can' your reputation all over town and you could possibly lose a lot of douche bag business just like that. These 'FFs' (fickle fuckers) had the power to keep you running on the fast track and they knew it, so treating everybody like royalty was the only way to go and I certainly knew how to do that. The issue was that for a manager of this type of environment, there was no time to sleep, shit, eat, or fuck, beyond anything I had even seen in the event industry. He (they are always a *he*) would need some help to stay up and alert to the cause, which is why I was no stranger to visiting them in various rehab places regularly. I would get them cleaned up, so they could get back into the game again. Let's just say that these guys had an open reservation for any facility that was efficient in spitting them back out into debauchery as quickly as possible.

Daytime in a club is a strange animal. You see the flaws behind the magic and the remnants of what happened the night before; semen covered banquettes, chewed gum stuck everywhere you could imagine, dust settling on every surface, and confetti stuck into every crevice that even the cleaning crew can't get to. The daytime crew is just depressing. These guys are left over from the night time after they had just washed dishes, mopped up sticky spills, and were verbally abused by customers that weren't getting bottle service fast enough. This species of people existed at the bottom of the barrel, carrying the weight of everybody else's fuck-ups. If the bartenders weren't slinging drinks fast enough, or if the server's tits weren't big enough, these guys got blamed and perversely enough, they seemed just fine with it or their English was so bad they didn't understand the insults being thrown at them. They, too, were addicted to the rhythm of the night and to the 'prettier parts' of what clubbing seemed to offer, just like I was. When a club is hoppin,' there is nothing like it. Pure energy and sexuality flows through a room and touches everyone in it. It's like a pulsating indoor rainbow that sheds its magic on all who are lucky enough to get in and experience it, and the VIP lounge is the pot of gold at the end of that rainbow. Most of these clean-up guys were living in one room apartments in Queens or East Harlem, along with seven other members of their families, so coming to the club was like a dream for them. These fine people are what I called my 'loyals.' I knew that they would be true to me for the rest of my life, unlike everybody else I employed.

The managers were cartoons of themselves; they couldn't afford to be happy, not even for a split second for fear of stuff just falling apart. They didn't even know what could potentially fall apart, yet they were terrified about whatever it could be. I call it 'fear in advance' or just 'for the fear of it.' They never ate aside from 24-hour diner meals that had enough bad-shit in them that would sustain their active ulcer level for several days. Their teeth would rot out of their heads due to excessive smoking and coking. They could only get erections by watching porn and we're not talking regular boy-girl porn, more like twisted shit beyond your imagination, and if they had a notion of trying a real-life relationship, it would end in a level of disaster beyond belief and only after impregnating someone during that once a year five-second hump, they wouldn't even recall. They were night crawlers who had given up on ever infiltrating normal society and coming out into the light on a normal day. They were sad creatures, but they shined in a very niche role, which made them proud enough to avoid hanging from the rafters. They stole from me, too, but never enough for me to call them out on it. I needed them to run the show. They had to deal with the plethora of personalities that made up the club staffing pool and for that, they deserved to be knighted. Coat Check girls were taking pregnancy tests in our bathrooms, emerging from them, crying their eyes out, becoming useless for the evening, while figuring out how to dispose of their newly formed problem. There was always a problem and solving it and moving onto the next one was the only rhythm these people could relate to.

Suzi understood these people all too well and was on the cusp on becoming one of them before I plucked her out of that existence and placed her into mine, which, deep down, wasn't much better just a lot prettier. She, also, couldn't be high on our jobs for the most part. As an event was nearing the end and everything was running smoothly, she could potentially be just fine elevating herself synthetically, but she was usually so tired by then, she would skip getting high and indulge in her avocado toast instead. All in all, she was getting healthier that way working for me, but I wouldn't want to get a CAT scan of her brain patterns, thinking they would resemble an etch-a-sketch that had been rolling around in the trunk of a car that was doing donuts in some suburban parking lot.

My clubs were spectacular looking, duh. I spent a fucking fortune on every detail. I had opened the three types of clubs all at once; a supper club with live jazz, which doubled as an after-hours joint, an insanely joyous disco, and strangely enough, an underage 'tween' dance/arcade type of place, which resembled a Bar/Bat Mitzvah on steroids. A few years later, I opened an elegant and sophisticated Strip Club, modeled after the clubs I had held Bachelor parties at in Montreal for some of my 'baller boy' clients. Those *Canuks* really know their shit in terms of strippers. Every club was designed with eclectic elements, each boasting of traditional textures mixed with the most up-to-date and tech forward equipment for lighting, sound, and even the toilets were heated and flushed themselves with an amazing cleansing treatment that I could never quite place but was addicted to the smell all the same.

The Supper Club was created in a town-house on the upper east side of Manhattan. I bought the place out right against my financial manager's advice and gutted it internally, while paying off the wealthy elderly neighbors to lessen their annoyance at the noise I was causing. Strangely enough, I used the Italian crew I had used on that very first job I got no credit for so very many years ago. It was like I wanted to recreate pieces of what I had done, so I could finally get that moment of glory I got fucked out of many years ago. I installed a massive stairwell that resembled my original client's foyer and I used the same glass blowers from Italy to create the most talked about chandelier on the planet. People come from all over the world just to take photos underneath the magnificent concoction of glass opalescent orbs that seem to smile down at you while standing underneath them. Their reflective surfaces capture every angle of the grand space and of the people floating upon the massive stairwell. Without knowing, I had created one of the first most 'instagrammable' moments of this century. To me, this was one of the most spectacular focal points I had ever designed, and it wouldn't need to be torn down at the end of the night, since it wasn't being used for party purposes. The joy in starting to design for more permanent environments was feeding my soul a lot more than creating temporary ones for the time being. The huge main bar was crafted out of the most exquisite leather base, which acted as a foundation to a true alabaster counter top. The banquettes were hand sewn with double layered cashmere and accented with huge velvet cushions. Every chair had arm rests and oversized cushions, which was rare in New York, because everyone was always trying to squeeze as many people as possible into their establishments. Not me, I preferred quality over quantity and space and comfort over the turnover of clientele.

The parlor floor of the town house hosted the main bar that most people could come to without a reservation, but the upper floors were a bit more selective and used for private dining and intimate musical performances. When Wynton or Chick or other Jazz greats were in town, they would skip playing the usual jazz 'go to's' and come to my place to entertain a golden crowd. I kept the side rooms of the house private, in case anyone needed to stay there. I never had offices on site at any of my clubs. I didn't believe in it, it took the fun out of it all. We had small back of house areas where you could count money and the employees could have a cup of coffee and get changed but that was about it. The real business at hand was only handled off site. Once you went up the back private stairwell (which very few people knew about), you came out into a charming and homey atmosphere, which made you forget that a public establishment co-existed at the same property. There was a cook's kitchen which opened to a solarium and a landscaped roof top complete with a small greenhouse for my orchid collection. This place became a real oasis for me and when my husband couldn't find me, he usually looked for me here first, even though it was probable that a jazz man would be in my bed with me.

The disco was my 'evil girl' place because it was always filled with my worst and favorite influencers; my gay wolves. While the supper club hosted a bit more of a sedate yet celebratory crowd, the disco was just bat-shit crazy and the environment was always short of dangerous in the most delicious ways.

The look of the place was slammin'! I created a massive disco ball out of mirror pieces I had collected from France. Many of the segments were tarnished and they told a history through their somewhat filthy yet reflective surfaces, which were veiny from attempts at cleanliness and refurbishing. These practices made the entire piece exotic and beautiful beyond belief, and despite its imperfections, it captured every light and shadow within reach. It was like a bright, shiny, sexy ugly planet that nurtured the entire club's ambiance and all the entire place needed, aside from this mother-ship were people, drugs, alcohol, and music. This would be my only successful property out of the three and it often had to carry the financial weight of the others. I adored having these "vanity projects" so much so that I was still willing to produce huge parties, just to support this very costly habit.

I suppose I was subconsciously thinking that these properties were my legacies and proof of how fabulous and important I was on this planet. Since it was looking like I would never be a mother, and even though I could and would leave my world to Suzi, let's face it, I would be gone some day and my star would shine brightly from somewhere else that wouldn't really affect what was happening in the current world. It killed me to think that if I came back as a ghost or hopefully, as a puppy walking past my properties, that they might be vacant and run down or even worse; a Popeye's; the franchise that simply fucking won't go away.

Suzi loved having these miraculous places to ship clients off to, and honestly, she wasn't even seeing them in their heydays. Since I did pluck her out of the night club scene, she was thrilled she could still dabble in the 'pretty parts.' All she had to do was get them there, wait until they got settled and paired up with attractive people, then she could leave, and be home in time to heat up her portion of the subscription food plan she and her man had signed up for. Her teacher boyfriend, now fiancé, would cook the carefully measured meal they would receive in the mail weekly, pop it into some Tupperware, and leave her the 'warming up' instructions on the counter, as he joyfully lolled into a video game oblivion. According to my standards, this was an incredibly civilized practice, one, of which, I respected very highly and perhaps, even envied a bit.

The VIP area of the disco was my happy place. This was another space that the public didn't know about created in the penthouse of the old warehouse building in which the club existed. There was a separate entrance to it burrowed within the adjacent alleyway and if those walls could talk, there would be enough material to create a huge bible of gossip. I created an expansive sunken living room, kind of like one you would see in a Bond movie. The lounge was sexy and comfortable, and people never wanted to leave. The huge round sectional couches were built low to the ground, reminiscent of the earth-ship décor I had experienced in Taos so long ago, so they were purposefully hard to get out of once you nestled in, but there were built in retractable side tables that were conveniently on stand-by to hold your drink, drugs, and a call button that would make a server appear within fifteen seconds. We rehearsed the timing of this type of service every day to insure its consistency, much like the first-class cabin of a high-end airline. I am proud to say that only three overdoses occurred in this space, which was impressive considering how many drugs were floating around. Nobody died, but let's just say that those urgent ambulance calls could harsh on one's mellow. We did everything in there; talked, fucked, drugged, watched private movie premiers, and we even held a memorial service there for a loyal customer. He put it in his will that he wanted his funeral in the club, which we felt was too morbid, so we moved it to the private space and then 'saged' the shit out of it.

Believe it or not, we had to deal with some very grown up issues in the young adult club which I simply couldn't wait to close and turn into a full-time Bar/Bat Mitzvah venue. It was depressing enough that we were fucked up as people, but even more so that thirteen-year old kids were getting caught in the bathroom doing drugs, trying to get drunk off mouthwash, snorting their mother's pills, and blowing each other. It took all the glamour out of everything, it was too much to bear and too large of a liability. Even though I adored the idea of a funky urban setting for young people designed to the hilt by famous street artists and outfitted with all the coolest styles and newest video games, I knew that this was out of my wheel house and I quickly grew bored with its existence. It became my step-child of sorts and I basically ignored its presence, which was always my mature approach to things I didn't wish to deal with.

I was relishing in the grand entrance part of every night. I would, sometimes, come down in a glass elevator from the top floor of the disco as guests looked up to see the magnificent woman behind the dream-world they were partying in. It was becoming almost as addictive as pleasing party clients, except that this was all for me and that was never a good thing.

I was living as a second person traveling parallel beside my usual self, and I was becoming the essential ring leader to everyone's good time. I was losing track of who I needed to be. I would wake up every morning, work out, and check in with my events team and then head over to whichever club I felt like being in. I was evolving into a being who had no consistent place to rest my brain or my jittery body.

Cocaine had always had an adverse effect on me. While other people started to get amped up once that powdery ejaculation swam up their nasal canals and into the crevices of their brains, I was looking for a private place to shit and go into a deep slumber. The coke would lull me into a sleep that was so deep and filled with dreams. The problem was that it would only last for a few minutes, though it felt like hours, and I would jolt awake in a panic, afraid that I had missed everything important in my life. Then that would bring about an anxiety from trying to answer the question of what was important in my life. It was a vicious cycle, so I chose to ignore it and move forward. I would smoke joints like tiny little cigarettes, one after another, and they also had the adverse effect on me. I would get so hyper while smoking that all my bad habits would go into overdrive. I would spend more money, open more businesses, fuck more men, and get more depressed about not being satisfied. Suzi found me the perfect poison; CBD. It was like ninth wonder of the world for me. I could literally roll around in it and stay focused, productive, and happy all day long. Suzi, however, preferred hard cider and an eight ball, which I thought had gone out of style, but things came back around at Suzi's age, I suppose. Either way, none of it affected her performance on the job, but I had a sneaking suspicion that demons continuously developed within her little body like internal barnacles, but you would never know by looking from the outside.

The clubs were bad for me, let's face it. They didn't really make a lot of money and they served as other places for me to hide from anything that resembled reality. My financial team was at a loss. They had no reign on me anymore, and I was grabbing at anything that would ultimately lose everybody money. It was clear that I was sabotaging myself, which I had always done but this time I didn't have a plan B, aside from sabotaging myself even more.

The clubs were also a constant carousel of change in terms of their clientele, new music, and dance styles, but just like everything else I encountered, the behind the scenes situation was always the same. Employees were always looking for more and it seemed the more I gave them, the more they became dissatisfied with what I was offering. Money was still so round in my hands that it was rolling out a lot more than it was rolling back in. Nothing was ever enough.

Underneath it all, I was living in a world of 'have to's' not 'want to's,' when I wasn't doing drugs or having sex. No matter how glamorous and well-designed my surroundings were, there was always a virtual Brillo Pad scrubbing away the pretty parts to reveal all the ways I *should* be living my life. I started to look around outside of myself at other people my age. They had normalcy, kids, vacations, body aches, and wine of the month club memberships. I didn't have any of that. I had known true love once with the mob boss and become a semi mother to Bogdana up until she drifted into 'normal,' along with the rest of them.

At the end of every disaster was my career waiting for me, like an old buddy picking me up from my stay in jail. We would get into some big fabulous black car with suicide doors and gold rims on the tires and we would cruise back towards my career. I would have mixed emotions; some fears mixed with the excitement of cleaning up my act and getting back to work. It was the right thing to do.

I vowed to go home every night, eat something that came out of plastic with my husband, maybe even subscribe to one of those food thingys, and spoon with him for at least ten minutes at a time. I would detox a bit, I mean not fully, that was just too theatrical. We would drink wine with dinner and maybe lunch, but I wouldn't blow lines in the bathroom or pop pills for a few days at first, just to get my "good girl" training wheels in motion, with which the CBD stuff would certainly help. We would even go out to the Hampton's and try to socialize, but for me, it was just another place where I would bump into my clients and they would immediately ask me to go and assess their living rooms or help them entertain. I might as well have been walking on the Upper East Side rather than the beach. It just wasn't enjoyable for me. All I ever wanted to do was to get somewhere quiet and dark that smelled good. I was consistently the ultimate extroverted introvert. The one thing you could certainly count on with me.

I sat on some charitable boards and grew somewhat passionate about certain causes, mostly involving animals and their well-being. I would produce their non-profit galas; stemming from the creative crevices of my heart and it was good for me. I was starting to produce from the inside out. Because I was off the hard drugs for a while (it wouldn't last long), I was experiencing emotions and tearing up listening to testimonials at my more emotionally driven events. I found that I couldn't even watch the wedding ceremonies I produced for fear that I would burst into tears. I was becoming a bit soft and it scared me, but my event work had never been better. It seems that the more I became emotionally attached to my work, the better it was. It felt like my olden days, which wasn't necessarily a good thing. I was even visiting Bogdana more often in New Jersey, where she insisted on living permanently after I had hoped it was just a phase. As I predicted, she and hubby were about to become parents via an adorable surrogate whom I was paying for. It was really happening, I was about to become a 'Glam MA.' I had work to do; I needed to look as young as possible, so I wouldn't tire of people telling me that I could never pass for an elder. I would spend some time 'going away' and getting whatever work I needed done in some far away healing place and come back looking more like Bogdana's slightly older sister.

On top of it all, Suzi came into the office with an elegantly small diamond on her finger, which didn't surprise me at all. I was genuinely thrilled for her, but I felt a door closing within me, knowing that she was about to soar a bit higher in the sky than I could reach on a daily basis.

My driver would pass by one of my clubs, as we came out of the tunnel coming from Jersey, and the pull to go in was still as strong as it ever was. I would roll my window down slightly, just to catch a glimpse at the huge door men arriving at their posts and re-positioning their ear pieces. They would be standing on the red carpet, which would be speckled with a horrid amount of lint. Fuck that, it was the last straw, the carpet always had to be spotless, and everybody knew that. I got out of the car before it was fully stopped. Apparently, I wasn't thinking while I was overcome by the need to get back into my club scene and as I was envisioning another one of my grand entrances, when my clumsy and fast exit from the moving car left me with a few broken bones that I simply couldn't ignore. This was incredibly frustrating on every level my body was aware of. I hated being injured and even worse, I couldn't accept missing out on my world, but I was going to have to. I felt like a pendulum that had stopped swaying and got stuck in the middle. Luckily, I was a fast healer, and if I promised to stay still and let the shattered bones of my ankle re-form, the doctor vowed to keep me rich in a magnificent supply of my favorite pain meds. During this period, I felt like a drunk, happy cowboy, laid up in a whorehouse from a different place and time. My gay wolves visited me often, but my boys didn't like when things got 'un-pretty,' so they kept a bit of a distance, while they showered me with large amounts of lavish gifts to keep themselves in my good graces and to still gain VIP access to the clubs.

I started to think about who my real friends were, and did I have any? And did I truly want any real friends? The truth is that when the shit hits the fan, no one wants to stand close to it, which makes perfect sense to me, I get it. I knew that when I could put my mangled foot back into a Jimmy Choo, everyone would be right back at my side. My husband, however, was there the entire time, supportive, loving, and driving me out of my fucking mind. Poor Schmuck…

Suzi was there, too, though I think it scared her to see me in a less than powerful moment. It was best she didn't see me this way, and I often made excuses for her not to come around. I needed to maintain my super natural existence with her, like in the movies when the mother of a super hero, who is long dead, appears as an apparition when the hero has a problem she or he cannot fix.

Life is all about balance, right? Well, as I was aging gracefully, I truly felt that I could have it all at once. I could enjoy my clubs, do parties, and be a wife, an employer, a 'Glam MA,' and a bit of a misfit now and again. Just because I was trying to act grown up and consistent didn't mean I needed to completely lay down the sword to having a fucking blast. I made a schedule consisting of my deviant times. They would fall in between of the all the things I had to do, including my husband. In the 'off times' or as I liked to think of them as negative and positive spaces, I could do whatever and whomever the fuck I wanted, while maintaining a passing grade on my record. I saw it all like designing one of my parties. I needed to fill a space in the right areas; balancing the highs and the lows, the tastes the sounds, smells, and touches. I needed my overall existence to resemble an equalizer on a stereo, perfectly balanced so that everything was just right and that everything would come out A-Okay. Easier said than done, but the desire was there.

I started to dream of things that I wanted to do that I had never done before. Aside from a few skipped pages of the Kama Sutra, I was really reaching. I had travelled all over the world, met all kinds of people, 'been undressed by kings and seen some things,' and so on. My Strip Club was well on its, way which was something I was developing down under, no pun intended, but basically, nobody knew about it. I was buying up an existing club that was in a shitty neighborhood, but it was slowly coming around to being acceptable. I was gutting it and pouring immense amounts of cash into it to make it sparkle like I did with everything else. What I have always said about being a great designer is that you can design all the way from the Crack House to the White House for sure. I had proven that theory with this club. The existing place was

167

fucking disgusting, but it raked in mega bucks, even on the slow nights. The original owners were an odd pair. One guy was Greek and ornery but smart. The other was a young, doughy Irish boy with a gorgeous brogue but had an impossibly tiny dick; don't ask me how I knew this, I could just tell and knew it wasn't worth the effort. He was emotionally smart though, and he was impressive in the way that he kept the stables of girls in line, and obviously not with his dick. He had a way of talking to people or shall I say, demanding things of them. Before he finished a sentence, the person listening to him would get going on doing whatever it was he was requesting, even the Greek guy. He reminded me of my Russian love, and I kept them both on as co-owners at a smaller percentage, I mean where the fuck would they be able to go after where they'd been. I taught them a lot. They had no idea that when you light a naked woman from below, it will show every cellulite secret which her body could potentially tell. We're talking Eastern Block girls here, too, not too shabby, so it was important to make the new lighting system a priority. I hired an in-house live DJ, too. Not just a local guy, but a world-famous spin master, who would draw a crowd, whether they liked titties or not. I also created a high-end 'couple's night' one evening out of the month. They would get an off the hook prix-fix dinner, curated by one of my famous chef friends, free matching lap dances, and their take away was an incredible sex toy kit provided by my first assistant Supreme and her now wife who owned the largest chain of sex toy boutiques in the world. I felt like I was giving back to the world and pumping sex into many dry marriages.

I even tried my hand at creating some gorgeous coffee table books of my work. I will tell you this; don't ever think you will make a dime on a vanity project such as that, unless you are Richard Avedon or a Harry Potter collection of some sort. Books are simply a painful representation of how important photo shop is, and once the book leaves its coveted spot on a centrally located coffee table to move up to a high point on a book shelf somewhere, you may as well just deny you were ever involved in the project at all.

I continued to host radio shows, which soon became podcasts. I did guest appearances on all the morning news programs as well. I still had that 'get up and go' gene inside of me, and it was mainly diffused by powerful workout sessions. My sex drive was on over-drive, which was great since all my women friends weren't interested in sex anymore or maybe, just their husbands. I just did better 'ignoring' all that pedestrian-shit that happened to other people. The main thing was that I was staying away from the clubs. I would peek my head in for an allotted three times a week, but I only really blew it out once a week and only while hubby was away at our upstate home. I don't know how he convinced me of this, but we bought an 'old as fuck' house near Rhinebeck,

NY which was the apple of his eye and the anus of mine. We had to run the water for what seemed like a lifetime until it wasn't brown anymore, we had to shovel the fucking sidewalk, mow the massive lawn, and even kill spiders. I hated it, but it was a good place for him to be kept out of my business, so I supported it and the dogs loved it, too, so that was enough of a reason to hold onto it.

A big part of me wished he would meet a retired super model that had moved upstate, so she could still be the prettiest girl in a smaller and more achievable town as she grew older. By meaning older, she would be just under thirty and still able to give my man a family and a more realistic illusion of the relationship I felt he truly wanted. I would even finance it, but he was still stuck on me for some reason. The house became a gathering place for people I didn't know, so I hated it even more when I would pop up there and my living room would be filled with a book club or even worse, a meditation group. Once, I drove up unannounced and I walked in to find my hubby eating and laughing with my parents. It was so perverse.

For the first time, I felt like I had nowhere to live. I was hopping around a lot, but I was never able to stay in a place for more than a few nights. I had the clubs, the NY apartment, which would always be my go-to place, the house upstate, a small bungalow in Cali, and a chic little flat in London, which I kept forgetting about. Even when I travelled, I found myself changing hotels within a few days out of sheer boredom or some sort of angst discomfort. I was constantly redecorating, too. I wasn't really allowed to touch the house too often because hubby was always there, but there would be times that I knew if I looked at the same color a wall was painted for an extended period, I would go mad. My hubby would enter the house and he knew that something was different, but he just couldn't put his finger on it, even though I had completely re-arranged the furniture and changed the wall colors. If things stayed the same for too long, I would get depressed, if I got depressed, my production level went even higher, as if I was running away from myself and as if my ass was on fire. Depression was never a bad thing for me, I knew that I would land on a higher plane each time I exited my frame of mind and onto something successful somehow.

I had officially become middle-aged by definition, and that blew me away slightly. I decided to fight it with everything that I had in me, including my incredibly young and un-formed brain. I just didn't feel that way, but if I took a moment and visualized the inventory of my life, my age felt quadrupled in years. People were now creating vision boards of what they want to see happen in their lives, while I only wanted to shut down for a period of time, if possible. I needed to be cut-off. I had reached my visualization quota long ago. I jumped into my life mid-motion, never taking the time to plan or weigh out the pros and cons. This was something that I did, in fact, regret. I admired people that took the time to do research before buying a product or investing in a car while I just saw something and knew if I wanted it or not, within seconds, only to most likely regret my decision later. It does seem that no mistake is truly irreversible, but it would've been nice to not have made them in the first place or to keep making them at my age. I didn't seem to know how to make anything but mistakes, they made up ninety percent of my life, like water makes up a human body. I hated admitting that I was sweating in our office while Suzi and the rest of the girls were wrapped up in their pashmina's they kept in their desk drawers, because of my turbulent menopausal body temperature.

Suzi was always scrambling for ways to keep me occupied. She knew that in order to get what she needed out of me, she needed to join the movement of keeping me entertained and engrossed. She made me teach workshops that she would charge people insane amounts of money to attend or she would purposely choose ugly photos to put on my Instagram, so I would freak out and want to pick them out myself.

She even tried to get me involved in conversations about her wedding, graciously involving me in her family politics or her bachelorette party details. We both knew that there was nothing left to do concerning her wedding, but to just go with it and have fun. This was incredibly Black and White to the both of us, she fell in love and she would make it official, and then report to work the following Monday, until they took their Honeymoon several months later after our party season had ended. We would text a gazillion times while she was away, though I would attempt to study the time zone she was in, so I wouldn't wake her at least. I knew, however, that if I truly left her alone, she would hate it. Were we co-dependent? Yes, we were, but when did that become a bad thing? Isn't that the same as being good friends or in love?

I tried painting, sculpture, knitting, but *never* cooking. I just had no desire to even try it. I took on creating a landscaped garden at the upstate home, as if it was going to be my legacy. I conjured up images of the garden we marveled at in Scotland while producing the pop-star's wedding, and I tried to replicate a lot of it in my backyard. The soil was very different, and our yard was filled with creatures that were hosts to dangerous disease-carrying ticks, so my project was feeling less glamorous by the moment, but I wanted to accomplish my goal of making the most talked about installation created in a privately-owned environment. I got back in touch with my fashion designer friend, whom I had met up there so many years ago and who had since become one of the most famous designers in the world. He still had a home in the woods close by, and he was feeling the same way about his career/life, so he joyfully joined me on my crusade in making something magnificent in my back-yard. We kicked my hubby out of his happy place for a bit, promising that his euphoria would be even greater after we had created this final and missing piece to his mecca. The designer had a boyfriend who was twenty-five years younger than him who I happened to adore and since he was so young, he could help us with the heavy lifting. I was back in my element, just me and a couple of gorgeous gay men. I loved being surrounded by man-meat. I figured out that both guys were sick. This was happening a lot around me still to this day, and my gay wolves were dropping like flies while succumbing to most erosive illnesses I had ever seen. These beautiful men were wasting away, they were trapped in a situation that plucked out their glamorous feathers one by one, until they were left naked; their scarred and bruised skin became exposed as they danced with death. Their skeletal frames were so intricate, like a new type of architecture that hadn't been discovered. I was constantly trying to formulate how they were still able to move with such strength, grace, and dignity. Most of the guys joked and said that they hoped they would go quickly and leave a somewhat attractive corpse, but there was nothing fast about what they were going through. They were floating in a membrane, forcing them to tread in a cesspool of fear, humility, and disappointment; there was no ladder to help them climb out of there, this was a one-way swim.

The urgency of creating something beautiful for what seemed to be the last time for these two men was what drove us to work harder than ever before. Creating something with such an emotional foundation was slowly allowing them to die, while I was coming back alive. Life is so fucked-up that way, then again, so is death.

We needed more room. The design was bigger than all of us and the current yard, so I took out the back deck later to be elevated above our creation, so people could float within the design, while becoming inhabitants within the nucleus of this magnificent universe we were creating. I included elements from my past lives, such as sand and rock sculptures that reminded me of the Rio Grande in New Mexico. There were areas that represented New Orleans, such as massive walls constructed out of Magnolia Tree trunks that were sewn together by Spanish moss. My designer friend incorporated things that inspired his fashion style by building a natural Butterfly Habitat and a place where we kept Bees that worked their honeycomb magic. He was always inspired by flight, and the things in nature that could fly naturally and in the most mesmerizing patterns. Butterflies were one of his main inspirations and I truly believe that his spirit lives within the largest and most regal one that floats around my head while I sit and pretend to read in that part of the garden. I started to spend a lot more time there after he passed away and he was buried just a few feet away from where he knew I liked to spend time.

Chapter Three

"Life is not measured by the number of breaths we take, but by the moments that take our breath away."

-Maya Angelou

I had been through a lot. Most of it had been brought on by myself, and not all of it was bad, but losing a lot of my friends to an evil illness was a bit more than I could bear. It was also the only thing that could potentially catapult me again into going back to my original work and getting onto a straight and narrow path of some sort. I was so fucking sad that I wanted to go back to the simple things, like the back room of a flower shop even. There was never a way of fully going back to those days, but I very much wanted to enjoy the simplicity of them, though I didn't realize they were simple at the time; we never do. I wished to cut a flower, smoke a joint, pay my rent, fuck a boy, and repeat. Most of all, I wanted to become invisible again. I didn't want my name on the art department of a school or on a museum exhibit or a club. I just wanted to hold my breath, disappear, and then regenerate as something else or just go through becoming me all over again. Maybe, I would do it differently or perhaps, I wouldn't.

I still didn't enjoy being married, but I stayed put. My new 'self' was cautious about dragging another mate into my demented form of monogamy, so may as well keep the status quo.

As the 'club goers' demographic started to change from gay wolves to young hip pedestrians, I was losing interest in my properties as well and left them up to Suzi's friends to inhabit. I was still a success, despite of myself though, and my event business was seriously booming. Because of my colorful and explorative history, I gained an incredible amount of experience in all things concerning lifestyle, so I had a lot to offer. When I met with clients, I could basically solve any design or entertaining issue they had that went far beyond parties. If their kid was going off to college, not only would I re-design and re-purpose the room the kid had left empty, but I would also create the most fantastic dorm room for him/her, which, in turn, would make them an instantaneous and popular hit on campus. I was amazing at taking drab to fab, no matter what the circumstance was. I specialized in making people look and feel so spectacular they couldn't get enough of my mojo, and once again, I was in a full-time cycle of being the go-to gal. I had succumbed to this gift once and for all and decided to embrace what I was put on this earth to do. I also knew that I needed to nurture a species that would be just like me, so that I could leave this earth in a gaggle of capable and sparkly hands. I wanted my lunacy to live on.

I started to spend a lot more time with my employees and not only with Suzi. I made it a point to report to my offices every day for at least a few hours and I would tour my warehouses and production spaces weekly. I started to quiz myself on the names and back stories of everybody that worked for me; right down to the people that cleaned the loading docks and garbage areas of my production spaces. I went to lunch with my financial and business managers and looked interested in the pie charts and facts and figures they showed me. I tried to eat dinner with my husband again on a more consistent basis. In fact, I let him cook for me outside of the meal plan and I praised him for a job well-done. We washed the dishes together and retired to the same room, which was still really fucking annoying, but it was the right thing to do. I was in the here and now, I was present and involved. I was really growing up.

I felt diluted. Kind of like I had gone for a lobotomy and had given into that 'Step-ford' way of life, but I also felt lighter and less guilty about the times that I did give way to the temptations of drugs and men.

Speaking of drugs and men, there were all different and new types on the market. The men were getting younger because I was getting older and that seemed to be very much okay. It seemed the older I got, the less men my age looked at me and men that were young enough to be my much younger brother or even my son were all over me. Fellas my age date women half their age, too, so everyone was happy. The great news about my situation is that my boys could go all night, without having to take a little blue pill, but I had to pay for everything, they can't even afford a sandwich, and certainly not one that I would eat. Do they even make Champagne and Caviar sandwiches? They should...

I was leading a fluid life. I felt somewhat invigorated and replenished towards my original career. Basically, I had just taken a few different paths over the year, but let's face it, I always knew where home was and how to get back to it. The open arms of the party world have always welcomed me and nestled me against its bosom. Like a puppy, I sucked off a row of nipples that kept me fat and happy. I was comfortable being a caricature of myself and being super-imposed onto everybody else's life. I dove hard into my party world. In fact, I performed a perfect fucking cannonball. Suzi was a strong force beside me. Clients were calling the office asking for her and not me pretty much all of the time now, which made me proud as fuck.

I had succumbed to acting like an event producer. once and for all. It took me almost thirty years, but I was finally settling in. I fraternized with others in my field even. We went to lunch, and to other associates' milestone birthday parties. We traveled together while partaking in the buffet of endless pro-bono, promotional luxuries. I even joined a group where we could discuss the perils of being magnificent. It wasn't easy. I am proud to say that I still held onto a piece of myself. I purposely didn't introduce my husband to anyone or even admit that I had a husband. Nobody knew about my clubs either, that was my business. I dressed the way I wanted to, even when everybody else was wearing their 'going out' uniform, I strayed from the norm by being a bit more casual than everybody else, while successfully conveying the message of 'I don't give a fuck what you think of me.' It seemed to work in my favor no matter where I went. I felt more normal, even though I knew I wasn't. It felt good to know that I could immerse myself into whichever gradient of acceptable I chose. I was the king and queen of being a manipulative yet passive mother-fucker. I think that my serenity also doubled as a form of depression, which I wasn't aware of, but it seemed necessary in order to sustain my existence. While sparks of my myself were dying off into hot embers, my soul was trying to adapt to being calm; a state, of which, it has never known.

Suzi knew all of my secrets, except, maybe, about my true love for her since I just wasn't able to express it. She guarded my world with a fierce strength and respect, which I never asked for. She never judged my insanity, only regarded it as part of my genetic being that I had no control over. She knew when I was lying to a client or over exasperating about a situation as it rolled over her naturally like a calming gust of wind. I respected this woman/child to a point that pleasantly surprised me more often than not. Our relationship was like a shiny present within another present that never got fully opened. She simply wasn't in the same category as all of the other young people that were starting to infiltrate my world. I had tried to become a better woman for her, like I fleetingly did for Bogdana, and she ignored my dips in and out of drug abuse and any other habits that I fell back into.

For some strange reason, donuts, photo booths, and bullying had become popular while I wasn't looking. Was I out of touch? As I was still dallying in blowing lines of coke, the drug had somehow gone out of style and then back in again. Even a lot of my clothes were coming back into fashion and I slowed down on my consignment action. Other things happened, too, like young people in general. They were everywhere and they were running the show.

Many of our corporate parties were now focused on anti-bullying tactics. When I was a kid, you waited 'til the fucker came out of school, held him down, and farted on his face, no slogan or hashtag needed, thanks.

The young people were kind of lazy, unless they were doing something called spinning. They didn't seem very edgy or sexy and they were way too smart for my liking. They knew about so many more things than I did, therefore, they worried more, which is a bummer. This all led to popping designer pills; pills that could make them happy or sad, skinny, fat, or to help them concentrate better and then go to sleep at the drop of a dime after they were done concentrating. They were 'girl-scaping'; waxing their pussies, asses, and nipples. They were straightening their hair, which lasted over a year, wearing nail polish that not only lasted for months but had original art on them and jewels even. They were constantly downloading apps (Holy fuck, the apps) that enabled them to receive deliveries out the Ying Yang of God knows what at any given hour. They could fuck a stranger and take a pill the next day, in case they accidentally got knocked up, and they could get a vaccine that could keep the HPV monster away and a pill that kept the HIV away, too. Instantly, they could get a town car (a choice of a few different cars available to them) to transport them anywhere they wanted to go, while they booked travel for the week end during the ride. They could find their date for the evening, decide on monthly outfits to be delivered, order groceries, schedule a dog walker, download several novels, and even speak to a licensed therapist for a mere thirty dollars an hour compared to my four hundred dollar an hour psycho-analyst. They could pick out paint chips, have weekly flowers delivered, and choose food that will come to them within ten minutes or their money would be refunded. Some of my favorites Suzi told me about included money transfers within moments, beauty appointments that were home-based at a fraction of my beauty team's costs, and having my chart read by some of the finest astrologers in the world. This shit was available to me, so as soon as I had let Suzi take over my phone and she downloaded some apps I would certainly become addicted too.

The young people also wanted to make a lot more money, which really sucked. They never had cash. In fact, I don't think they knew what cash was or the art of pressing a tip into someone's anxious palm and experiencing the smile it caused. They used credit cards to buy tiny purchases, such as a pack of gum or a bonus round on a video game.

Overall, I felt it was a good idea to put the young people in-charge of the client appreciation party I decided to throw, since it seemed like we should, just to create some marketing hype. All my girls were consistently wearing contrived curls in their hair, like matching uniforms. I think they called it a

'Mai Tai' blow out or something like that. They would keep this hairstyle for days and when it got a bit oily around their scalps, they used something called dry shampoo to revive the hairstyle. What the fuck is dry shampoo? And how does it smell like cotton candy? My girls could find out whatever they wanted about a guy before they went out with him just by typing his name into a search engine on a computer, and at the same time, they could determine whether they liked him enough to go out with him at all. This was all a bit sad to me, but they didn't know anything else, so fuck it. As part of our client appreciation party, they wanted everyone to take a spin class during the day, then nap before attending the big event. Exercising in a group before a party? Are you fucking kidding me? The last time I saw that was a circle jerk amongst my gay wolves before going clubbing. I had been slapped up-side the head with all this change and I felt it best not to engage. Let them take care of this, while I perched upon my comfort zone.

Words such as 'retainer' were being thrown around in the office. Apparently, we were supposed to collect a fee before giving away our creative ideas. I had never heard of such a thing, and I thought it was a brilliant idea. I would be richer than ever! My young team was teaching me so much. I decided to go with the flow. I felt more and more like a hologram within my business. I was present but in a translucent way, as my team started to tackle me like football players to take the ball down the field the rest of the way. They had my business, my whole identity really, and I was left with contemplating re-inventing myself or just letting myself become a drifting vapor.

As my team was setting up for our grand affair, I decided to focus on one of the bigger weddings we were currently producing, which brings me back to where we started; The Plaza Hotel.

As I said in the beginning of this shit show, I was connected to my clients in such a nice way that evening. The world was spinning evenly around me; my team was doing their stuff, I was doing mine. The girls gave me my A-list favorites to support me on the job, along with Heath, the intern, and we were having a blast and enjoying every part of the evening. The day-time portion ran smoothly, the bride was dressed, primped, and ready to go right on time, along with her gang of bridesmaids who were getting along swimmingly. All the parents were being civil to one another and the groom and his guys were being well behaved by subtly pulling off their flasks and not blatantly sucking on beer bottles. I felt at peace, relaxed, and for once, content. I had already promised Heath that we would catch a buzz since the guy was working for free, but I could have gone without any drugs that night and I probably should have. I was also feeling a serene sense of loss, aware that Suzi was getting married soon. Would it break my heart? Would it be the end of 'us'? I wasn't sure, but it was there in my being, like the lint in my dryer filter, which I hated cleaning, but it needed to be done in order for the machine to keep working. I had learned that there were no answers to these questions and that I certainly couldn't stop my life by waiting for them. I had also come to peace with the fact that I needed to be open to life's options and to not only see things in diamonds and leather.

I remember heading out to the ballroom to do my rounds and I decided to embrace the love I felt most of the time for my job. It hit me like lightening, the raw animalistic joy I felt for what I do, much like a mother feels for her child after he/she enters the world during those first moments of his/her public life. I was filled with pride, look what I have done so far in this life of mine, not too fucking shabby. I teared-up a little as I caught a few moments of the father/daughter dance. I was so fucking emotional that night and it felt good though. I didn't know what to do with my emotions. I was intensely proud of Suzi, too, who I caught taking inventory of the room to see if she wanted to reproduce any of it for her own upcoming wedding. She was the lead on this event as she was on many others, but I realized how incredibly flawlessly it was executed; reinvented perfectly as my desired vision and experience.

I ended up on the floor while the room continued to live on without me. I remember thinking that the lighting guys fucked up the cue for the shooting star effect that was supposed to travel across the ceiling of the ballroom, as the rest of the wedding guests joined the bride and her father on the dance floor. Chaka Khan was singing 'through the fire' as I felt my chest tightening and my arm go numb. I was on fucking fire and I guess I was having a heart attack, though I always felt so invincible and didn't think it possible.

Luckily or not so luckily, this was all happening on one of the elevated balconies, where the cake was displayed, and no one could really see me there holding onto the sequined table linen for dear life. I looked at my apple watch, my heart rate app was flashing angrily, while simultaneously my meditation app was begging me to breathe. Did my life flash before my eyes? Not really, just lots of visuals of pretty color combinations, cocks, dogs, fields of flowers, and vats of champagne, which was what I normally envisioned anyway. I was quietly screaming for Suzi, where was she? Usually right by my side; she suddenly seemed completely erased from my world and I was wondering if she ever really existed at all. I felt a tear run down my face as I envisioned her walking down the aisle, knowing full well that I wouldn't have attended the Church ceremony no matter what, but I could still see her…then I envisioned her again, having her first dance with the teacher and later dancing with her father, whom, strangely, I have never met.

For a moment, my view of the ceiling was blocked, and I said to myself, "This is it, I am going to black out, and if I black out, it means I am dead." As

178

the lights shifted in the room, a man's face came into focus above me. It was a sexy ugly face I think, I knew it wasn't God 'cause she would never have chosen to look like that, and this was definitely a dude looking down at me. He was talking to me, not really asking if I was okay but more like he was introducing himself, as if me lying on the floor wasn't an oddity at all. Everything became so clear in that moment and it was as if the whole room went quiet and we were the only ones in it. I could hear his words and he had an English accent, "Hello there, my name is Richard Branson and I was told that you are the only event producer I should align myself with. I was hoping that I could share with you my personal information, so we could speak about you doing the very first Party on The Moon, once the whole flight situation gets sorted out and such."

I took a deep breath in and I felt no pain at all. As the projected stars were finally shooting across the ballroom ceiling and while Chaka was belting out her tunes and urging everyone to dance, I stood up, smoothed out my DVF skirt with pockets, and took Sir Richard Branson's hand as I followed him into the moonlight. I blew Suzi a kiss once I spotted her tiny pretty face in the crowd and she smiled and mouthed, "I got this," as her tiny thumbs gestured towards the sky.

9 781645 751021